LORD EDGINGTON

BOOK 10

BLOOD
ON THE
BANISTERS

A 1920s MYSTERY

BENEDICT BROWN

COPYRIGHT

For my father, Kevin,
I hope you would have liked this book an awful lot.

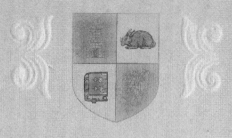

The Duke and Duchess of Hinwick

request the honour of your presence
at the marriage ceremony of their daughter

Lady Cassandra Unity Fairfax

To

Albert Doris Prentiss

at St Mary's Church, Hinwick
on Saturday, the sixteenth of July,
nineteen hundred and twenty-seven,
at twelve noon.

READER'S NOTE

I try to write the books in this series so that new readers can enjoy them without having read any of the previous ones. All you need to know is that Lord Edgington is a legendary former police officer who investigates murders with his slowly improving assistant, his grandson Christopher. In this book, Christopher's soppy brother Albert is about to get married.

At the back of the book, you'll find a character list, a glossary of unusual words from the period, and two whole chapters on my historical research and inspiration when writing this book. I hope you absolutely love it!

CHAPTER ONE

At the beginning of 1927, the winter seemed to last forever. It was almost June before the spring really made itself known to the world and, by that time, the arrangements for my brother's wedding were well underway. Albert's fiancée, Cassandra Fairfax, had chosen her dress. Whole fields of flowers had been ordered to decorate the church, and I was trying my hardest to understand what being a best man actually entailed. The most difficult task, however, had been delayed, put off and finally postponed until it could wait no longer.

"Cook, what I'm trying to say is…" My brother was sweating from the pressure. Although it might just have been the heat in the kitchen.

"Yes, what we mean is…" Cassie wasn't having much more luck.

The queen of cuisine at my grandfather's grand estate stared back dumbfounded. "I don't know why you're fretting. I'm more than happy to prepare the food for the wedding. We had bigger events than this back when Master Albert's grandmother was still alive, and I'm sure that we'll do a good job."

Albert looked at Cassie, who looked straight back at him and urged him to speak. "Yes, and we are very appreciative of the offer. It's simply that—"

"Ahh, good. You're all here." My lordly grandfather marched into the room to interrupt. "I think it's wonderful that Henrietta will be curating the menu for the wedding banquet. I genuinely believe that there is no finer chef in the British Isles."

The couple's faces turned yet paler. It was rare to see my future sister-in-law lost for words, but Grandfather had rather pushed his experimental cook upon the wedding and, try as they might, they had not succeeded in escaping his ever-so-generous unilateral decision.

I'd been standing to one side, enjoying the spectacle, but decided to step in to save them. "Henrietta," I began. I'd built up quite the confidence with our cook over the last couple of years, and I knew that she wouldn't be offended if I spoke diplomatically. "What Albert and Cassandra are trying to say is that they would like their wedding banquet to be a traditional affair."

This somehow only encouraged her. "Oh, yes, I can picture it now! There'll be white tablecloths and pretty floral centrepieces. We'll start with a broth of lamb's brains – you can't get more traditional than that. Then, for the main course, I keep changing my mind between veal liver and spit-roasted ortolans. Each course will be interspersed with some of my own appetisers. I was thinking that haddock and honey vol-au-vents, along with canapes of mustard-coated turnip, would be very suitable for a wedding."

"Absolutely!" Grandfather declared, and he rocked on his heels in pleasure at the thought of his favourite employee's culinary gambits.

"And, to finish, the piece de resistance."

"Cook, I'm sorry to interrupt," I tried once more. "As delicious as that all sounds, I'm afraid that the bride and groom have some ideas of their own."

"I don't see how you can improve on Henrietta's menu." Grandfather did not believe in keeping his thoughts to himself.

"I am always open to suggestions," Cook insisted. "What did you have in mind?"

Cassie looked at Albert. Albert looked at Cassie and, this time, she lost. "Well, to start the meal, Albert is very fond of duck. We wondered if you might make strips of duck breast in a fruit of the forest sauce."

Grandfather communicated his disapproval with a simple huff.

"And then between courses, we imagined something lighter, like tiny pastries with bites of brie or perhaps Parma ham."

Our skinny cook could make little sense of this. "I thought you wanted something traditional. None of that's traditional. I can't plan a menu if you're not clear."

My brother was fairly hopeless when it came to fighting his corner or, for that matter, any kind of confrontation. There was no turning back by this point, though. With a rebellious wave of the hand, he declared, "Profiteroles!"

Cassandra clearly understood what he wished to communicate with this strangely high-pitched statement and helped to bridge the gap between her fiancé's wishes and the dear domestic's understanding. "I think Albert is trying to say that he has a certain dessert in mind, and anything else would be a disappointment."

Things would surely have gone more smoothly if my grandfather hadn't been there to complicate the situation. "This is insanity. Every Frenchman has a choux dessert at his wedding. It's so uninspired. If you want a traditional wedding that stands out from every other Tom and Tib's, I have a wonderful book of recipes from the fourteenth century in my library. It is rumoured to be one of the very first cookery books in English and includes instructions to make a pickled vegetable aperitif. From there, you could move on to mushroom pasties, mutton stew and, for dessert, rose pudding, which I have always been curious to try."

I couldn't resist asking, "Grandfather, what's rose pudding?"

"It's exactly what it sounds like, boy." He looked at me as though I was quite the dunce. It had been some time since I'd endured such a reproach. I'd been in his good books since I'd helped him solve our last case, but that was all undone thanks to a thoughtless question about food. "It's a pudding made with the petals of a single white rose, mixed together with flour, milk and spices. It is often served with nuts and dates. However, I would recommend a delicious cherry potage."

This had done little to resolve the impasse, and the couple went back to exchanging nervous glances.

"Don't you worry, Master Albert," Henrietta said to comfort him. "I have been making your food here at Cranley since you were six months old. I promise that we'll create a menu together that will make everyone happy."

Grandfather's face at that moment said, *Don't give in to their foolish demands, Henrietta. Resist! Resist!* But the bride-to-be spoke before he could say anything.

"Thank you so much. We really are grateful for all the work you do." There was a warmth to Cassie that made it hard to do anything but smile in her presence. She was just that kind of person.

"Jolly good, miss. I will do my very best."

As we'd been speaking, several members of Grandfather's staff had arrived in the kitchen for their lunch. Instead of gathering around the immense wooden worktable where they tended to take meals, they had formed a semi-circle by the door. All the maids stood in height order from the smallest – dear little Irish Alice – to Dorie and her sister, who were bigger than I was. Our head footman, Halfpenny, was there, too, along with various gardeners and the newest addition to Cranley Hall, our fourteen-year-old page boy, Timothy. Inevitably, though, it was the recently promoted 'Head of Household' – my grandfather's sometime chauffeur, Todd – who would speak on their behalf.

"Master Albert and Lady Cassandra, the staff have asked me to say that we will do all we can to make your wedding a success. As there are only a few members of staff at Hinwick House, we will be there on the day to make sure everything goes as it should. And, may I say, it is a great honour to be included in your plans. We wouldn't miss it for the world."

I was worried for a moment that Albert would cry with the emotion of it all. He'd always been a wet leaf of lettuce, but since his girlfriend had agreed to become his fiancée, he'd positively wilted. He was forever singing, went everywhere with a poetry book in one hand, and the sight of a flower or a prettily shaped cloud provoked regular bouts of emotional incontinence. It was a sight to behold.

"Thank you so much." His lip was already trembling. "I couldn't ask for a better group of helpers. I really couldn't. In fact, Cook, we take it all back. You know what you're doing with the menu and don't need us interfering. I'm certain that whatever food you pick for our wedding will be just delicious."

As Albert did his very best to stifle the sobs, Henrietta and my grandfather shone like chandeliers. Cassandra, meanwhile, looked as though she might have to call off the engagement altogether. It was a truly lovely moment, at which I couldn't help smiling.

CHAPTER TWO

So, yes. I was to be the best man at my brother's wedding, with all of its unique food. I was still unsure of what I actually had to do, though, and chased after the soon-to-be-weds before they could escape in their car.

"Is it my job to organise some kind of send-off for Albert?" I asked, standing in front of my brother's Salmson AL3 to block their path.

They looked at me sympathetically, and I already knew the answer. "Sorry, old chap." Albert put one hand on my shoulder to break the bad news. "In Cassandra's family, the groom always spends the eve of the wedding at the bride's house and vice versa."

"I'm certain that my brothers will take good care of you," she added, sounding far less confident than she claimed.

"I also wondered whether I would have the responsibility of looking after the rings?" This was hopeful on my part.

"Now, Chrissy…" Albert searched for an excuse, but we both knew he'd never trust me with anything so valuable. "We don't want to overload you with responsibilities."

"So what *does* a best man have to do?"

Albert turned to his fiancée, who did her best to answer. "Well, you have to make a speech for one thing."

An idea popped into my head. "What about the bridesmaids? Do I get to dance with the prettiest one?"

This made the dear woman incredibly happy. She jumped from the shiny red vehicle to give me a hug (and carefully manoeuvre me out of the way of the car).

"There is nothing I would like more in the world!"

"Splendid." I think I might have blushed at the thought of it.

"My cousin Margaret is as pretty an eleven-year-old as you could hope to meet, and she will be over the moon to dance with you."

For some reason, dancing with a child did not appeal to me a great deal.

"It was lovely to see you," my brother said, already pulling away with Cassandra back in her seat. "There's not long to go now!"

They both waved as they sped off along the drive. Our dog

Delilah chased after them, and I felt rather left out. My parents were forever driving about the county making preparations, and I was at a real loose end. Normally, I would have spent my days working in Grandfather's library, studying old case files and perfecting my purl stitch – don't ask – in order to become the greatest living detective since... well, since my grandfather. But even my lessons had been uprooted by the hurricane wedding.

Grandfather – or, the famous Lord Edgington, scourge of Britain's criminals, Marquess of Edgington and former superintendent of the Metropolitan Police, to give him some of his titles – kept nipping out of the house to "check on a little project", the details of which he would not divulge. He still found time most days to lecture me on the art of detection, but there was little real instruction included. It didn't help that no one had reported any suspicious happenings, blood feuds or heinous crimes to us recently, and it had been months since we'd stumbled upon a body.

For the first time since he'd informed me that I was to be his student, I felt ready for the challenge that even the most dastardly criminals could present. And yet, instead of chasing after such devils, I spent my time wandering the gardens of my family's vast estate. Our dear golden retriever usually accompanied me and, perhaps I was pushing my emotions onto her, but Delilah looked just as encumbered with ennui as I was. Without her master's attention, there was little to entertain us.

It wasn't until a week before the wedding that I found out what the wily old chap had been doing. He swept into the library one morning looking like a dog who'd got into the larder. As it happens, I know exactly what a dog who has got into the larder looks like, as Delilah once found the kitchen deserted and sneaked inside. Suffice it to say, she ate well that morning.

"Christopher, we're going on a little trip." I believe that Grandfather licked his lips in anticipation.

I'd given up on a less-than-fascinating case file from his days on the police and was reading a mystery novel instead. "I have to finish this first. There's only one chapter left."

"What is it?" I'd piqued his curiosity, and he picked his way across the room.

"It's called 'The Layton Court Mystery' and whoever wrote it decided that he couldn't put his name to it."

"So you wouldn't recommend it, then?" He eyed the cover and did not find it to his liking.

"Not in the slightest. The detective is unbearable, his assistant a total swine, and the resolution is so predictable that I'm only still reading to confirm that it's as bad as I think it is."

He laughed without making a sound. "Yes, that is one drawback to the job we do; fiction can sometimes lose its charm."

"I won't be long." I didn't look up at him but continued reading the book.

He evidently didn't think I was serious, as he hung expectantly at my side. "Oh, come along, Christopher. This is ridiculous. I'm not going to stand here watching you read."

I said nothing but turned the page. I'd learnt not to be intimidated by his domineering ways, and he would have to wait. To my surprise, that's just what he did. He stood waiting until my three remaining pages were read.

"Was it as bad as you expected?" he asked once I'd slammed the book down on the table.

"Worse. Let's go."

He didn't even complain about my grammatical faux pas, but waggled his head in amusement and escorted me outside to his waiting car. Todd was there to drive us. Despite all his other duties, Lord Edgington's right-hand man still occasionally acted as our chauffeur and clearly knew all about the scheme Grandfather had hatched. I still couldn't understand why my perplexing forebear trusted me to be his assistant yet kept the details of his day-to-day existence a secret.

"Is everything prepared, Todd?" he asked as transparently as ever, as his man waited to usher us inside the shiny new Daimler.

"That's right, M'Lord." The smartly liveried young fellow did not tap his nose conspiratorially, but he might just as well have. "I have rung Master Albert, and he will be meeting us in Woking with his fiancée."

"Jolly good. Off we go then."

Grandfather climbed into the backseat, where our beloved dog had found a comfortable spot. I say she's our dog because I was the one who'd been spending the most time with her recently, even if she did, nominally, belong to my grandfather. I was also the only person in Cranley Hall who gave her biscuits, and I think she liked me best. She showed her affection by jumping onto my lap when I sat down in the capacious vehicle. With its black leather and walnut interior, it truly was a majestic machine, though I can't say I approved of my grandfather buying yet another vehicle.

"Don't look so disapproving," he scolded me as the car moved off along the drive. He was reading my mind again. I hated it when he did that. I tried to keep my face blank and not think of anything significant, but the words, *you'll run out of space in your barn-like garage,* could not be suppressed.

"If I run out of space, I'll just have to build another one." He laughed at my irritation.

"Don't read my thoughts!" was all I could summon by way of a response, and this made him laugh even more.

"You give too much away, Chrissy. You need to hide your emotions better."

I wouldn't let the issue go. "Come along, tell me how you did it. I know you're no magician, so tell me how you knew exactly what I was thinking."

He would need a few seconds for the hilarity to subside. "You're absolutely right. I am no magician. Were you to think of three objects off the top of your head, I would not be able to tell you what they were."

"Tennis racket, colander, bedpan!" I replied, for some silly reason.

"Precisely. Whereas I would have guessed fountain pen, sextant, shaving brush. That notwithstanding, when you entered the car, you smelt the new leather, looked awfully impressed, then shook your head and turned pensive. I know how you feel about me buying my twentieth car."

"You have twenty now?" He was right; I was no expert at hiding my emotions.

"The obvious extension of your concerns was where I would find the space to store the cars. My response was the one I would have given had you expressed all those thoughts out loud."

We pulled onto the country lane which skirted Cranley Woods, and I fell silent to consider his explanation. "But how did you know I wasn't thinking about food? I often am."

16

He put one hand out to pat Delilah's warm flank. "It is always a possibility, but I know you rather well. You have a certain face when thinking about food."

"I have a food face?" This was even harder to believe than the idea he was clairvoyant.

"Indeed. You look as though you've just relaxed into a salt bath. It's quite charming."

"I will make sure never to think of food around you again." I was perhaps a little sulky by now.

"I very much doubt that is true, but learning to control your thoughts, or rather, the way in which they manifest themselves physically, is a key skill for any detective."

I'd fallen into a bout of cogitation and required some time to consider what he'd said. Could I really master the control of every muscle in my body? I would have told him that I thought it impossible, but he presumably already knew what I was thinking.

We drove to the spot where Albert and Cassandra were waiting in his sporty French vehicle. It wasn't so much a car as two bicycles strapped to a box with an engine inside. Grandfather's immense, regal Daimler limousine made the so-called automobile look like a toy. We waved to them as we rolled past at a stately speed, and I felt just like a king.

From there, we drove north to a small village on the Surrey-Berkshire border where my dead uncle's family had originated. It had been some years since I'd visited, but it was one of the grandest estates in the family, and I knew it well. I'd heard that the place had been left to ruin when my wild-blooded cousin George had gone off travelling around the world. I couldn't think why we were going there now.

Left to ruin was clearly an overstatement, as the gold and black front gates sparkled in the sunlight, and the neatly sculpted hedgerows that led us towards the main house were as neat and sculpted as ever. Todd drove slowly, and I enjoyed the sound of crunching gravel beneath the thick tyres of Grandfather's car.

"What do you think of this?" The old lord made sure to disembark before anyone else and stood in front of the palatial property to hold his arms out like a... well, I would have compared him to a magician, but we'd recently established that he was not one.

"I think this is Trevelyan Place," Albert replied, clearly just as unaware of the reasons for our excursion as I was. "What I don't understand is what we're doing here."

There was a definite smell of fresh paint and varnish coming from the exquisite house, and I believe that I twigged what was happening a few seconds before my brother. Though it was not nearly as large or old as Cranley Hall, there was something indescribably grand about the home of my now-deceased aunt and uncle. The eastern façade was all Doric columns and wide windows, and the first floor had a stone terrace that spanned the breadth of the building. It was a century old or less, but the sparkling white property was quite majestic, and I wasn't the only one to notice.

"It's perfect," Cassie whispered to herself as her beloved finally understood why we'd driven there.

"You don't mean…" Albert had to repeat himself, as he couldn't believe his luck. "You don't mean you're letting us live here?"

Grandfather hid his emotion behind his snow-white moustache. "That is just what I mean, my boy. Your cousin telegrammed to say that he never wishes to see the place again, and I thought you might make good use of it. The staff have been retained since your aunt Belinda died. It is ready for you to occupy, just as soon as you are married."

Albert's jaw hadn't merely dropped. I believe it had dislocated entirely and was hanging loose. "But… How… If…" He'd never been a great speaker and gave up at this point to run inside the house.

Cassandra stayed behind for a moment to express her gratitude. "I can't tell you what this means…" Her voice cracked just a little, but she recovered her composure to plant a kiss on the old man's cheek. "It's the house I've always dreamed of having. I can't express how happy I'll be here." Her young, smooth hand found his not-so-young-and-smooth one for a moment before she turned and ran inside. "Albert, wait for me!"

Delilah rushed after her, but I stayed outside. I stood next to my grandfather, looking up at the house where our family had so often convened to celebrate special occasions over the years. "You know, Grandfather," I took my time over each word as though I were a jeweller assessing the value of a clutch of rare stones, "you really are a very kind man."

"That's nonsense. It wasn't my house to give them. I merely asked the right person if he'd mind a young couple turning it into a home again. It's been years since there was much life here, but I have no doubt that Albert and Cassie will make the estate their own." I could see that there was something he wasn't saying. A lightning bolt of sadness crossed his features, and I was certain that he was thinking of his daughter, who had lived at Trevelyan Place until her untimely death. "I just hope that they make the most of it."

It was at this moment that we heard a shout from within the house. "Cassie, come and see the sculpture gallery," Albert yelled, before his fiancée replied, "Where's the sculpture gallery?" We heard doors slamming and excited footsteps descending the mosaiced floors. "And for that matter, what's a sculpture gallery?"

"Shall we join them?" Grandfather was finally smiling.

"Of course, old friend. After you."

CHAPTER THREE

"I'm nervous, Chrissy," my brother told me as we prepared to head to Hinwick House on the day before the wedding. We were once more standing in front of our grandfather's country pile. The cars were all packed, but our grandfather was yet to appear.

"There's no need to worry," I told Albert. "I'm sure that everything will go off without a hitch when you get hitched." I thought this a rather witty play on words, but he didn't smile.

"It's not just that I'm getting married, it's the thought of joining a new family."

I'd been giving him regular talks to bolster his confidence, and I'd finally reached the conclusion that this was a best man's main job. He had never previously spoken of Cassandra's family as being any obstacle to his happiness, however, and the information surprised me.

"I thought you had a lovely Christmas together and everyone got on like a burning bush." It's more than possible that I'd mixed my metaphors here.

"We did. We absolutely did. They couldn't have been more welcoming at their winter house in Cornwall." He was plainly trying to convince himself of this. "Her mother was lovely – even if her father was a little sullen."

"So why are you worrying?"

This seemed a simple enough question, but he struggled to answer it. "Because…" I thought I might have to pull on his ear or elbow him in the ribs to get any more out of him, but more words eventually came. "Because I'm yet to meet her three brothers. They spent Christmas with their elderly grandmother, but they've organised this party for me tonight, and I'm terrified."

"The plot thickens!"

My mother had been giving Todd instructions on some matter related to the wedding and came over to see what had upset her firstborn. "I don't know why you're fussing, Albert. It's a tradition in Cassandra's family for the bride and groom to swap houses on the night before their nuptials. Your wonderful fiancée will be safe and sound here with us, and you'll have a grand time with the Fairfaxes. Your father is sorry he won't be there, but he is taking a whole day off work for the wedding tomorrow." There was a note of disapproval in her voice.

"Yes, Mother. Of course, Mother." He did not sound convinced, and I believe there was only one person on earth who could make him feel better at that moment.

"Oh, Albi," Cassandra said as her own sporty car pulled to a halt on the gravel drive, and she caught a glimpse of his worried expression. "You're not still worried about meeting my brothers, are you?"

"Why are you only meeting them now?" I asked, a little undiplomatically.

"It will be fine." She directed an angry glare in my direction as she spoke. "Charles, Eric and Stanislas may seem frightening at first, but they mean well. In fact, they're good friends with the last man who wanted to marry me." Cassandra had a forthright air about her and stated these facts as though they were of no concern.

Albert's eyes had expanded to fill his face. "Hold on just one second. Who tried to marry you before me?" Looking on the bright side, at least he wasn't worried about her brothers anymore.

She shook her head as if to imply, *Oh, Albert, you really are too silly*, before saying, "Oh, Albert, you really are too silly. It's all forgotten now. I was young and foolish and thought that I was in love. Luckily, my mother knew what was best for me and stopped me making a mistake. I'm much happier with you than I would have been with Lord Ruskin."

Albert had to sit down on the running board of the nearest Rolls. "Oh my goodness, he's a lord."

"My beloved Albert, please don't worry yourself." Despite wearing a rather pretty white dress with tiny yellow flowers on it, she crouched down to be at the same level. "I swear that I have no feelings for the man. It is you I'm marrying, and we didn't even invite Damian to the wedding."

"Well, that's something at least." Albert took a deep breath and, as I was his naughty little brother, it was very difficult for me not to want to tease him.

"Wonderful news. Your fiancée's ex-fiancé will not be at your wedding. Now can we please get in the car? It feels as though I've spent half of the last month hanging about in this driveway, waiting to go somewhere."

22

"Then I'm clearly just on time." Grandfather had sneaked up as we were talking. Though dressed in his usual dove-grey morning suit and top hat, he was a little more flamboyant than usual. He wore a sparkling diamond tie pin in his silk cravat, matching sparkly cufflinks and even a small stud on his lapel. I could only conclude that he was greatly anticipating the wedding.

On seeing her father, it was my mother's turn to worry. "You will look after my boys, won't you, Daddy?"

He looked a little insulted that she felt the need to ask such a question. "Of course I will." I believe he even emitted a brief huff. "I am escorting them to an intimate soiree at the home of one of the most distinguished families in the British Isles, not taking them up to Soho for a Bacchanalian carousal."

Even with this reassurance, Mother looked uncertain. The faint creases on her forehead folded together like a paper fan.

"I will miss you every moment we are apart," Albert said to his sweetheart (and, thankfully, not to our mother). His voice was terribly dreamy, and he pouted as he spoke. "Just think… the next time we meet will be at the altar of St Mary's church. This time tomorrow, we will be man and wife."

I grabbed his arm to pull him away, as there was only so much mushiness I could take. "All right, you two, enough of that. You'll have your lives to stare lovingly into one another's eyes. If we don't go now, we'll be late."

Grandfather had already taken his place in the back of the Rolls Royce Phantom, and I sat in the front passenger seat. On any normal occasion, he would have piloted one of his many lithe sports cars, but a wedding called for certain standards that even my modern-thinking grandfather could not ignore. Albert gave Cassandra his hand one last time before climbing into the back of the dark green tourer.

"Until tomorrow, Albi." Cassandra looked a little dewy-eyed by now and my mother put her arm around her shoulders.

He held out his hand to her through the window, and perhaps I was being a gloomy so-and-so when compared to my eternally romantic older brother, but I had the strangest feeling that this wedding would not go as smoothly as we all hoped. It was like an electric shock to the stomach and, as I watched the two lovers waving to one another,

I already knew that there was something unusual about the family waiting for us in their manor house near Northampton.

"We're going to have a wonderful weekend," my grandfather muttered, and I knew that he'd sensed it, too.

CHAPTER FOUR

The first leg of our trip led us to the royal town of Windsor. Grandfather rarely informed me of his plans when travelling, but I should have known he couldn't resist a stop at a historical beauty spot.

It was a stunningly bright day, and we sat on the grass next to the Long Walk, which led up to Windsor Castle. Todd had served us a top-notch picnic lunch, and we were now enjoying ice creams that we'd purchased from a man with a chilled box on a bicycle. I'd opted for chocolate flavour over raspberry or vanilla because... well, that was the best choice.

"It's just a fairy tale, isn't it?" It was my turn to be moved by something as I gazed upon the ancient monument – and relished my sweet treat. "Imagine the kings of old walking the ramparts and defending their land. It beggars belief to think of all the history that has been witnessed from this very spot."

Grandfather could always be relied upon to inject a dose of realism into our conversations. "In a sense, but the castle hasn't come under siege from an invading army since the First Barons' War of the thirteenth century... oh, and the Second Barons' War a short while later."

I'd never taken much interest in my dull-as-dirt history lessons at school, but the way Grandfather could summon tales from the past always filled me with excitement. He spoke of long-dead chapters in our nation's story much as he would describe one of the serpentine cases from his days as a police officer.

"Ah, yes, the First Barons' War. Wasn't that when..." I was hoping he would interrupt me, as I knew nothing about that particular page of the history books.

"Really, Christopher, I would hope you remember that much. The First Barons' War broke out when a number of wealthy landowners became dissatisfied with the rule of King John." He peered up at the south wing of the castle. "The concessions he was forced to make could be seen as the first steps on the road to the constitutional monarchy we have today."

"*Magna Carta Libertatum!*" I suddenly remembered a titbit of knowledge from one of my classes. "Signed by King John in 1215."

The ghost of my old history teacher was apparently still haunting me!

"Maybe your memory's not so terrible after all."

I shook my head and smiled. "The whole thing's funny when you think about it."

"What is?" Albert had finally noticed that we were talking.

"History." I tried to eat my ice cream before it melted, and the cornet became soggy. It was less than conducive to such a discussion, but I did my best. "I mean, all those people killed in wars. All those children divided from their parents—"

"You're right, Chrissy," Grandfather interrupted this time, but only to be sarcastic. "It's hilarious."

"Let me finish," I waved my hand to dismiss his cheekiness and a droplet of melted ice cream flew in his direction. "It's funny that so much that has happened over the centuries is caused by rich families who wish to become richer. For all the talk of the freedoms for which those barons were fighting, I bet they already had terribly nice lives and grand houses. You can be certain that more peasants and labourers died in the battles than aristocrats did."

Grandfather mused on this for a moment. "You may have a point, but who are we to complain? Tomorrow, we will be attending the luxurious marriage celebration between two of the oldest families in Britain. A Fairfax is to wed a Cranley. It sounds quite old-fashioned to me."

I couldn't decide whether this was a good thing or not and went back to dreaming of ancient knights and the odd dragon. Grandfather must have noticed a wistful look in my eyes as he offered up a fascinating anecdote.

"Of course, if you'd like to hear about a more exciting siege, you must go back to 1192 when King Richard the Lionheart was captured in Vienna by the Duke of Austria. His wicked brother John declared himself king and even attempted to bribe his European counterparts to keep his rival hostage. Richard was widely loved in Britain, and no one was too keen on his brother, so by the following year, an army had been raised, and John was trapped inside the castle and eventually forced to surrender."

I was immediately sucked into this tale and had to ask, "What did Richard do when he returned to England? Did he run that snake John through with his sword?"

26

Grandfather looked puzzled. "Not at all. He forgave him and confirmed him as his heir. It was all very civil. Would you have run Albert through with your sword?"

I looked at the silly groom who was terribly bothered by a horsefly at that moment and couldn't sit still. "No, of course not, but then I doubt he would pay my enemies to keep me imprisoned."

The knowledgeable lord narrowed his gaze a little and peered down his nose at his two grandsons. "You can never know such a thing until you know such a thing." I had to hope he hadn't identified some dark intention on my brother's part that I was yet to discover. "Either way, there's no time for any more chitter-chatter. We have a party to attend."

He was up on his feet before the words were out. It isn't the easiest thing to swallow an ice cream cone at speed so, to avoid choking to death, I decided not to try. Albert was a messy eater and could do nothing but stare at his sticky hands as Grandfather strode towards the car.

"Come along, Albert. You know he'll drive off if we're not quick."

In response, he waggled his dirty hands at me.

I expressed my frustration with a groan. "Wipe them on the grass and let's get going unless you want the party to take place without us."

He sighed and did as I'd suggested. "I knew I should have driven my own car. Grandfather is such an autocrat."

"That is true. But he's a benevolent one, so hurry up and move your legs."

I sped across the grass and along the path. It was my last opportunity to marvel at the sensational fortification on the hill before me (and to finish my ice cream). By the time we got to the car, the motor was purring, Todd had his hands on the steering wheel, and Grandfather was tutting at our tardiness.

"It's more often the bride who arrives late," he bellowed down the road as he caught sight of my hobbling brother. I've no idea why Albert was hobbling. I can only imagine he was hoping for some sympathy. "At this rate, you'll be lucky if you get there in time for the honeymoon."

I jumped into the passenger seat and startled our sleepy golden retriever. Approximately two minutes later, Albert climbed into the back of the car and pulled the door shut for Todd to drive away.

"You do always love to exaggerate, Grandfather," I told him

once we were rolling through the old town past elegant hotels and cheery confectioners.

"No," he bit back, "I *occasionally* love to exaggerate and, evidently, so do you." He had a good chortle and, as he was in a funny mood, I decided not to say anything for the rest of the journey.

It was almost exactly one hundred miles from Cranley to Hinwick House. Although the three-hour journey was rather long without a book to read – the fool I am for leaving it behind in my bedroom! – we arrived with the summer sun still high in the sky over Northamptonshire. After pulling onto the Hinwick estate, we passed through a pair of wrought-iron gates with two collared eagles, their wings extended on the piers on either side. It was an unsettling welcome to the place, and I felt a frisson of fear for what we were about to discover.

The very first thing I remembered my mother saying of the Fairfaxes was that they were a devious bunch, and I did not like the thought of a party with such bounders. Had I been organising Albert's *funeral of bachelorhood,* as the French call it, I would have invited his friends from university for a few games of bridge and a nice roast dinner. Instead, we were entering enemy territory. Well, perhaps that's another exaggeration, but there was something awfully discomforting about the whole affair.

"Albert, my dear boy." Lady Hinwick smiled as we stepped from the Rolls. To prove my silly brain instantly wrong, she held her arms out to her daughter's fiancé and embraced him warmly. "Samuel and I are so delighted that you've come."

She was a large, bustling woman in an elaborate Victorian dress with several voluminous skirts. I noticed certain characteristics that she had clearly lent her daughter, including her now faded red hair that sat in piles on top of her head. Unlike her daughter, she had a broad, maternal face, which I suppose is only logical, as she was the mother of the three young men who stood alongside her.

"We are very happy to be here," my brother replied with a respectful bow.

His future brothers-in-law waited to be introduced, as it was their father's turn to speak next. Samuel Fairfax, the Duke of Hinwick, looked rather like an old bear. His face was wide and round, except for his whiskery muzzle that puffed outwards like a swollen thumb. I'd never seen such an ursine human, and I was curious to know what he would sound like.

"A wedding in the Fairfax family," he mumbled in a rather restrained manner, as though unsure how he felt on the matter. "That is not something that happens every day." His voice was certainly deep enough to belong to a bear and, with this vague comment delivered, he turned to glance around the seemingly endless parkland.

"I'm Charles." The oldest (well, tallest at least) son stepped forward to offer the Marquess of Edgington his hand. "It's an honour to meet you, my lord. I'm a great admirer."

"Come, come," Grandfather replied, shaking the gaunt chap's hand with great vigour. "We are to be family. There's no need for such formality. You may call me Lord Edgington."

The others looked confused by this, but gangly Charles just smiled. "Allow me to introduce my brothers, Eric and Stanislas."

"It's a pleasure to meet you, no doubt," the shortest fellow said in a languid voice. He spoke as though he had been compelled to do so and had far more interesting things on his mind.

"So this is the man who's to marry our little Cassie?" the… middle-est brother barked in the tone of an army captain as he approached the wrong member of the Cranley family and sized me up instead of Albert. "She could have done a lot worse. A lot worse, indeed. Welcome to the family."

My brother was clearly too polite to say anything, and I couldn't think of an explanation, so it fell to the Duchess to fill in the gaps in the tubby fellow's understanding. "No, dear, this is Albert's brother Christopher. Albert is the young man next to him, whom I addressed by that name and embraced just a few moments ago."

Stanislas shook his head as though he'd just swallowed a measure of alcohol and was struggling with the after-effects. His response, when it arrived, came as a series of short staccato sounds. "What? Is that right? Oh, how foolish."

Lady Hinwick waited to see whether her husband wished to contribute anything more to the formal greeting of the Cranley family delegation, but the man remained silent. I had to wonder why she was there. From what I understood of their family tradition, the men were supposed to go to the bride's house, and the women to the groom's. I had a feeling that she had decided to stay nearby to ensure that her three sons behaved themselves.

They truly were an odd bunch, but not the absolute beasts that I'd feared. Of course, we were well accustomed to odd. Eccentricity is the bread and butter of the ruling classes, and Grandfather knew just how to handle it.

"This is a pleasure indeed, my new chums." I doubt he'd ever sounded quite so posh. He even slapped his thigh for some reason. "We can't thank you enough for hosting us this evening. My grandson here has talked of nothing else all day. Isn't that right, Albert?"

My brother managed a weak smile and, with Lord Edgington's ebullient display, there was a feeling that we could all relax.

CHAPTER FIVE

The Duchess consulted a silver pocket watch from deep within the folds of her dress and pointed us inside. As Charles placed his skinny fingers on Albert's arm to lead him across the drive, I had the chance to take in the splendid abode.

Hinwick House was extremely pretty. I really can't think of another word for it. It was like a palace in miniature – if that miniature happened to occupy an acre or two. It was constructed in limestone, and there were four ashlar pilasters dividing the façade with pairs of white sash windows between each. It reminded me of a painting I'd once seen and so, before grandfather could read my mind and tell me what it was that I couldn't quite remember, I had a guess.

"Buckingham Palace?" I said quite out of the blue, and at least the smallest of the three siblings understood what I was blurting.

"Well, Buckingham House, actually, but you weren't far off." Eric spoke in the same dismissive tone as before and took a step back to admire his family's home. "My long-dead ancestors commissioned a copy of the Queen's House that stood in London before Buckingham Palace was built. That was at the turn of the eighteenth century, and it has remained in my father's family ever since."

"It's charming." It really wasn't necessary to say this in such a smarmy tone, but something in Eric's manner made me rather competitive. By calling their house charming, I was telling him it was a great deal smaller than my ancestral home of Cranley Hall. "It's really very silly that my grandfather and I live in such an immense building. Aside from the twenty or so staff he employs, it's normally just the two of us." Delilah had been exploring the driveway but returned to object to this statement with a bark. "The two of us and our dog, I should have said."

"Fine animal, you've got there, Christopher," (possibly a captain) Stanislas replied in that clipped, martial tone of his. As he looked at Delilah, he flipped an old silver coin across his knuckles and back. He'd been at it ever since we arrived, and I was rather impressed by the way it rippled like mercury over and around his hand. "Dogs are loyal beasts. Loyal and true." He spoke like a man who had endured the horrors of battle but made it through to peacetime against all

31

the odds. The fact that he couldn't have been more than twenty-five presumably ruled out such a possibility.

"As the weather is clement, I thought we might have a drink on the patio before dinner," Lady Hinwick suggested, and her gang of boys all nodded. It occurred to me that there was something oddly obsequious about them. The Duke himself not only deferred to his wife but seemed to always await her judgement before acting.

Grandfather had a request to make. "I would appreciate it if we could go up to our rooms first. It has been a tiring journey, and we must change for dinner."

"Of course," the Duchess replied, and I noticed that Grandfather didn't correct her for not speaking in full sentences as he so often did to me. "Peterson, attend to our guests."

A butler in full regalia rushed forward from the main door of the house, and my brother, grandfather and I were placed in his care. He had a long black coat and matching waistcoat and the pained expression on his face made me think that his cravat was too tight.

"If you'd like to follow me, gentlemen." His voice was high and undulating, like a choirboy's, and Grandfather studied him as he spoke.

"You don't have to put on an act for my benefit, young man."

At first, I didn't understand what the old fellow was suggesting, but the butler breathed a sigh of relief and explained in a more relaxed tone, "I'm sorry, M'Lord. The Duchess wants us to be on our best behaviour. She's often taken me to task over my voice not being suitably servile. I find that if I squeak like a mouse, it's more to her liking."

"It seems that you're not the only one around here who lives in fear of the lady of the manor," I put to him, but to answer in the affirmative would have surely crossed a line.

"I couldn't possibly say, sir. I do my job as best I can."

The fact that he did not actively refute my supposition seemed to confirm it. With our guide leading the way, we traversed a large, airy parlour and travelled up the magnificent staircase in the main wing of the house. It was an incredible piece of joinery and dominated the elegant hallway. Made of a deep brown, glossy wood, it was as wide as some buses I'd taken and had an expansive landing in the middle of it that was large enough for two people to take tea there. A life-size marble statue of a woman from antiquity watched us from halfway up, and the walls were lined with portraiture and the odd plate or ornament.

The floor at the top was even grander and held a suite of furniture and a museum's worth of historical artefacts. I was so used to seeing large collections of weapons in such houses that a wall given over to ornate daggers did little to surprise me. However, there were some particularly interesting items on display that had been brought from every corner of the Earth.

Though the original building was relatively compact, I saw now that an additional wing had been added to one side, and so the property was deceptively large. I normally couldn't care less about the size of someone's house; I'd only been so pompous with Eric because he'd rubbed me the wrong way.

"Your room, M'Lord." Peterson the butler held the door open to a beautiful suite which contained a four-poster bed with a flocked canopy. The sunshine flooded in through six enormous windows that were divided between two walls at the corner of the house. With my grandfather deposited in his room, it was Albert's turn next.

"And this is your room for the night, Mr Prentiss." This time, the butler opened an ornately painted door that gave on to a pretty cream-coloured bedroom with fascinating documents all over the walls. "We call this the Queen Victoria suite," he explained. "She stayed here once about fifty years ago, and you can read some of the letters between the Queen and the former owner of Hinwick House."

I was truly amazed by this royal connection and would have loved to slip inside to find out what dear old Vic had said in the letters that I could see on the walls. The only thing stopping me was my eagerness to find out where I would be sleeping that night. We didn't have far to walk and, a few doors along the passageway, the butler stood in front of the final room.

"And this one's for you. We could have found somewhere larger, but we thought you would like to be close to your brother on his last night as a free… sorry, as a single man."

He pushed open the door to reveal a space much smaller than my bathroom back at Cranley Hall. They had just about squeezed a single bed inside and there was a long gap that was approximately the width of a postage stamp for me to sidle my way into the room.

"Actually, I wouldn't mind being in a larger..." I turned to tell him, but Peterson had already left. "Oh, blast."

Our possessions had been brought to the house ahead of us, along with most of the staff from Cranley who had arrived in the area that morning to prepare for the wedding. This was good as it meant that I could get changed for dinner, though it did raise the question of where I would sleep if my trunk was still taking up half the bed.

To my delight, when I opened my luggage, I discovered that I'd taken a copy of 'Oliver Twist' with me. The unusual family, Albert's impending union, and my cell-like room no longer seemed so important.

I had a book!

CHAPTER SIX

"Christopher, please tell me you haven't spent this whole time reading," Grandfather called into the room once he was ready to descend. I believe he would have opened the door and come inside, but it rather stuck on the carpet – carpet being one of the things for which my tiny room did not have adequate space.

"Not at all, Grandfather." I squeezed through the meagre gap between the jamb and the door and fell out into the hall. "I got changed as fast as I could and then spent the rest of my time reading."

"My goodness, boy," he began, and I was expecting a telling-off. "You look smarter than most counts I've known."

I had a quick peek in the mirror on the other side of the corridor and had to admit he was right. It had been months since I'd had the opportunity to wear the chic black suit he'd bought me and, in the meantime, I seemed to have developed something of a style of my own. The black, three-piece ensemble, which had previously sagged where it should have been trim and bulged where it shouldn't, looked just right on me. I had considered wearing my velvet opera cloak on top of it, but I think that would have been a mite excessive.

I turned back to my mentor, who was, for once, wearing the black attire that a formal dinner demanded, as opposed to his usual grey. "You look rather wonderful yourself, Grandfather. Where's Albert?"

My brother left his room at this moment, and he was almost as handsome as me. Fine, that's not true. He was far more dashing, but I wasn't about to tell him that.

"If you look this good tonight, Albert, I can't imagine what you'll wear for the wedding." My compliment served to wipe the apprehension from his face and he stood up a little straighter as our grandfather put a hand on each of our shoulders.

"Gentlemen? Shall we join our hosts?"

There's something powerful about a black suit that I'm sure scientists will strive to explain one day. Even my normally highly strung brother was transformed by the sleek tailoring. As we walked downstairs, I felt as confident as a film star, as wise as a librarian and as brave as a postman – I've always thought that a most frightening job, considering the number of savage dogs one must navigate on a daily basis.

When we arrived back outside, the sun was just dropping over the roof of Hinwick House. I glanced across the garden and saw a large fabric canopy on the lawn, where chairs and tables were being set out for the following day's reception. The staff from Cranley Hall were darting about the place like wasps tending to their nest. This scene inspired another smile from my brother and heartened him for the encounter with his soon-to-be in-laws.

"Now let me get this straight," Field Marshal Stanislas began, looking at Albert as though he were vaguely familiar. "You're the fiancé?" He then turned to me. "And you're the brother?"

"You've got it in two." Eric rolled his eyes and managed to make this typically contemptuous gesture all the more offensive. I really hadn't warmed to the chap, and I was ever so glad he would not be *my* brother-in-law.

"Let us have a toast," the Duchess interrupted before her sons could say anything else. "To two families, united."

We had no say in the matter and accepted a glass of champagne each in order to raise them to the cloudless sky. "To two families, united," we echoed, having already lost some of the confidence with which we had arrived.

No one knew what to discuss after this, and so we stared about at one another. Grandfather was a born raconteur, and I imagined he would regale us with the story of one of his adventures. Whenever he opened his mouth to say something, though, he thought better of it before the words could break free.

Delilah had been sniffing around the garden all this time, and her appearance from within a ring of shrubs along the side of the lawn was a welcome distraction. "Who's a good girl?" I asked to cover the not just awkward but really quite painful silence.

Well, that killed a good ten seconds, and then it was time for some more discomfort. Lady Hinwick had taken a chair and looked contented enough, but her husband had an unsettling energy about him. It was as though he wanted to order all these damned interlopers off his land, but propriety and perhaps his subservience to his wife held him back.

I eventually managed to think of a safe enough topic that could surely not offend anyone. The weather: an Englishman's first and last resort! "There is nothing like a warm summer's evening to make the world seem right."

"I agree entirely," cheerful Charles declared, and we gazed across at a copse of Spanish chestnut trees, where the warm tones of the evening light were turning the bright green leaves a touch more golden.

"Winter already feels like a distant memory, and yet it was only a few months ago that we had that late snowstorm." Lady Hinwick spoke in a rather nostalgic tone.

I believe that Grandfather considered adding something to the discussion, but three comments on the meteorological conditions were surely enough, and so he moved us on to poetry.

> **"I love to see the summer beaming forth**
> **And white wool sack clouds sailing to the north**
> **I love to see the wildflowers come again**
> **And mare blobs stain with gold the meadow drain..."**

"How lovely," the Duke declared in his gruff voice. His large, rounded shoulders rolled as he picked over the words of the poem Grandfather had recited. "That encapsulates the season just perfectly."

"It's by the Romantic poet, John Clare. A greatly under-appreciated writer, to my mind." If there is one thing that is sure to kill a conversation, it is an under-appreciated Romantic poet, but Grandfather persisted. "He came from humble stock but had an unparalleled gift for language. In fact, he worked the fields of his Northamptonshire home and became known as 'the peasant poet'."

What were we supposed to say to that? I looked at my brother in the hope that he might know something about this unusual bunch that could save us from another agonising hush.

When that didn't work, Grandfather continued his prattling. "The poor man was quite mad and died in an asylum mere miles from where we are standing."

I must now amend my previous statement; if there is one thing that is sure to kill a conversation, it is an under-appreciated Romantic poet who went mad and died in an asylum.

I could bear it no longer. "I believe dinner was mentioned?" I addressed the rude enquiry to Lady Hinwick, as it was clear that no one else had the power to help me. "I must say, I'm starving after our journey. We only stopped once for something to eat—"

"Twice," Grandfather corrected me. He really was a stickler for *the truth*. "You made Todd pull over when you saw a bakery with Bath buns."

"So I did, but that was hours ago. Would anyone mind if we jumped ahead to dinner? And then perhaps the best way to celebrate the union of my beloved brother to your wonderful Cassandra would be a nice early night."

"Christopher, are you feeling quite yourself?" His ability to read minds had let him down for once.

"It's absolutely fine," the Duchess assured him, consulting her watch once again. "If the young man is hungry, we will tell the kitchen that we are sitting down to dinner a little early." She turned to her butler, who was standing at the ready beside the French doors into the house. "Peterson, tell Cook that we'll be moving into the Crimson Dining Room forthwith."

The servant squeaked a response and hurried off to the kitchen. Albert and the three Fairfax brothers drifted after him, and the Duke helped the Duchess to her feet for the pair of them to lead us into the house. I pulled on Grandfather's arm to slow him, as there was something I simply had to whisper.

"I thought that our family was mad, but these people are lunatics."

He smiled and nodded, as though I had made some trifling comment. "What an interesting observation. And I'm very much looking forward to dinner this evening." He confirmed that no one was looking before winking to show that he more than understood my feelings.

To be fair to the Fairfaxes, things did go more smoothly after that. The dining room where we would be eating was incredibly luxurious with deep crimson wallpaper and a matching tablecloth. The walls were dripping with gold from the mirror frames to the picture frames to… well, it was mainly the frames, if I'm honest. But the effect was quite stunning and, as I settled down in a Chippendale dining chair – upholstered in crimson, of course – I was looking forward to a dinner that could almost guarantee no turnips dipped in mustard.

Instead, we were treated to Parisian salad with truffles and lobster meat, tossed in homemade mayonnaise. Next came a terrine of some sort – I didn't actually catch the description, and I was too interested in eating it to ask what it was. The main course was made up of beef fillets wrapped in bacon and stewed in a madeira sauce. There were a few smaller dishes muddled in with that lot, but I managed to save just enough room for dessert. It was a good thing that I did, as the Hinwick House cook had saved the best for last.

Quite frankly, the Crêmes à la D'Orleans was the tastiest sweet I'd eaten in weeks and would have been well worth the exercise of getting into a boat and rowing to France for a second helping. It was a sponge cake soaked in a maraschino cherry syrup with an extra layer of coffee cream on top. Even now, if I close my eyes and imagine it, I can still get the faintest taste.

My point is that the food was delicious, and suddenly the company didn't seem so bad either.

"Some of these recipes actually came from my ancestor, Diana Aster." The Duchess said this as though we should all be impressed. "She was one of the first British cookery book writers and compiled all sorts of wonderful dishes and home remedies from the kitchens of her wealthy friends. She made quite the name for herself, didn't she, Samuel?"

The Duke betrayed no emotion but nodded his agreement.

His wife sounded rather too proud at times, but she had a hearty, chipper manner. "Of course, the Aster family made their money from rags."

"I beg your pardon?" Grandfather responded in a surprised tone, which made Lady Hinwick titter.

"That's just our little joke. One of my ancestors started out as a textiles merchant before moving into publishing. Price Lewis & Aster Press was one of the first great gentlemen publishing houses and exists to this day."

At some point, whilst I was daydreaming with my eyes closed to savour every mouthful, the conversation had turned to the bride.

"Cassandra was simply the most precocious child you can imagine. From the age of three, she thought she was an adult and walked about telling her brothers what to do."

"I wonder where she could have acquired such a habit," Charles joked, and I was curious to see how his mother would react, but she nudged him genially with her elbow and continued her tale.

"By eleven, she knew that she would marry a lord and live in a palace. I know that's the kind of thing that parents desire for their daughters, but it was not my doing." She paused to think, and her plump cheeks became a little rounder. "I remember her asking whether everyone lives in big houses like ours."

"It's not that big, apparently," Eric mumbled, but he was sitting right next to me, and I caught his jibe.

The Duchess took her husband's hand before continuing. "Samuel looked at this innocent little creature and decided to tell the truth. He said, 'No, my dear. Not everyone in this world is lucky enough to live in such a big house.' To which little Cassie replied, 'Well, in that case, I'll marry someone very lucky. A lord ought to do it,' and then she clapped her little hands together and went off to plan her wedding."

If we'd been at home, I might have pointed out that Albert would inherit no title, but I decided not to spoil his moment in the spotlight.

Grandfather laughed politely before delivering his verdict on the tyke in the story. "I have known several such children myself. Albert's mother was similarly inquisitive, but it was always her mission in life to feed the hungry and rescue the downtrodden. It was a noble ambition that required me to take her to soup kitchens most weekends when I'd rather have been watching cricket."

This inspired more smiles around the table and, in the end, it was only Eric who remained glum. Even Stanislas, who normally looked as though he were struggling to make sense of what anyone was saying, appeared to be fond of his sister. "She said she'd marry me when we were very young, but only so that she could continue to tell me what to do all the time."

His elder brother raised his glass. "She didn't need to get married to have someone to puppet. She's been pulling our strings since she was born." Charles must have realised how this sounded, as he leaned across to speak to my brother in a softer voice. "In the best possible way, old bean."

"Do you remember her rabbit?" Eric had a wicked look in his eye as he addressed his family. "She'll surely want children before long if the way she mothered Flopsy Bunny is anything to go by. She loved that creature and carried it wherever she went, like a baby." It was hard to know how such an innocent comment could offend anyone, but I noticed some tensed muscles around the table as he spoke. "And now it's your turn, Albert. Let's see what she makes of you."

It was hard to say whether the Duchess ignored or really didn't notice the undertones of her son's speech. Instead of scolding him, she held her hand to her chest and breathed in with glee. "The day has almost arrived, Albert. You will be part of our family, and we cannot wait to have you."

My brother hadn't been particularly talkative since we left Cranley but managed to hide his nerves and reply with a short speech. "And I couldn't be happier to join you." He looked from face to face, and I felt rather proud of him. I know he's older than I am, and these thoughts shouldn't enter my head, but he can be a real milksop sometimes, and it was good to see him speak so confidently. "I promise with all my heart that I will love and cherish, and protect and…" Well, maybe he did revert to his usual soppiness just then, but I despatched a swift kick under the table, and he was soon back on track. "…and, indeed, love Cassandra with all my heart. So, thank you – all of you – for making this welcome such a friendly one."

CHAPTER SEVEN

Once everyone had drunk a few glasses of wine, it felt as though the frost had finally thawed. Charles was a capable host and conducted the conversation. Much like the chairman of a meeting, he went out of his way to ensure that everyone had a chance to say their piece. Although I found the relationships between the siblings and their parents hard to fathom, they ultimately seemed fairly harmless.

"It has been a wonderful evening." The Duchess consulted her watch one last time once all nineteen or so dishes had been served, plus the cheese course, a fruit course and coffee with petits fours. "It is time that I went to bed. I should rest before Albert and Cassandra's big day, and you boys must be allowed your fun."

We rose as she pulled her chair back from the table and got to her feet. She had a less-than-petite figure and, with her immense dress, such a manoeuvre was a complex procedure.

"Albert, if I may have a word in private before I retire," she continued from the doorway. "I would greatly appreciate a few minutes of your time."

Albert signified his acceptance with a smile and, as there was no footman or butler present just then, he went to open the door for her. The rest of us sat back down, but Grandfather looked perplexed by something.

Clutching his head with both hands, he explained his predicament. "I'm sorry to be so unsociable, but I have a splitting headache. I believe it would be best for me to seek the comfort of my bed."

We went through the rigmarole of standing up and sitting back down again as he exited the room. It was hard to know what had come over him. I'd rarely seen him with so much as a cold and doubted the red wine had so inebriated him that he would have left in such a hurry.

The serving staff soon arrived with cigars and cognac and, a few minutes later, Albert returned looking as pale as a "white wool sack cloud".

"We should head to the Great Hall, don't you think?" Charles suggested before I could ask my brother what had happened.

"A splendid idea," Lance Corporal Stanislas responded, and so the servants had to put everything they had just unloaded back onto a trolley to convey the refreshments to the other side of the house.

I'd noticed that Eric had been drinking faster than his brothers and snatched a crystal decanter, from which he swigged throughout the short journey. I'm not a fan of undiluted spirits but was no longer such a child that I could ask for lemonade. As a result, I'd had to make do with the odd sip of wine throughout the dinner. Thankfully, when we arrived in the Great Hall, our blue-riband retainer, Todd, was awaiting us with a batch of Duke of Norfolk Punch that he had evidently prepared on my grandfather's orders. The room was filled with the smell of oranges, lemons and, perhaps inevitably, brandy. It was far more to my liking than the pure alcohol that Eric was imbibing.

The room we had entered was surely the largest in the house and looked as though it had been transported there from a Scottish hunting lodge. The walls were covered with stags' heads, mounted on heraldic wooden shields. There was a tartan rug on the floor, and the bare walls and exposed beams gave the place a rather ancient feel. At one end was a suite of furniture, at the other a set of gaming tables and, in the middle of the room, a full-size grand piano. It was a strange mix, but I rather liked it. Had there been a nook with a few bookshelves, it would have provided everything a young man could need in life.

As Todd poured the drinks, he threw sly glances at the Fairfax men. I knew that our faithful servant was as protective of my family as his master was, and I had to wonder what he made of them. The Duke had taken the largest armchair. Stanislas was standing to attention by the bare wall, with that old silver coin once more rippling across his fingers, and as soon as Peterson had closed the door, it was as though a wave crashed over the room.

"Thank goodness that's over," Eric intoned, stretching the words out to express his suffering for longer.

"The woman's set on torturing us," his father added. "If you think that Cassandra is a puppeteer, you have no idea what it means to be married to your mother."

"Oh, we know, Father." Charles was holding a snooker cue as though it were a spear. "You're not the only one who has to endure her manipulations."

"Manipulations?" my already harried brother enquired, but Charles was not in the mood to answer questions.

"Don't worry your empty little head about it, old bean. I'm sure that our dear Cassandra will keep you far away from us. Tomorrow may be the last day she steps foot in this place. If I were she, that's what I would do." It was quite shocking to see the change in the oldest Fairfax boy. He'd been so attentive and kindly spoken before this moment, so to witness the snarl on his lips and the spite in his eyes knocked me aback.

"Eric, billiards!" he demanded, and his brother tottered over to commence the game.

It was clear from the outset who would win. Eric could barely hold the cue, and Charles split the pack with such force that several of the balls rolled into the pocket from the break. Eric didn't seem to mind and laughed in that insolent, uncaring way of his.

"I suppose it's too late to back out of it now, so we might as well tell you," the Duke began, his eyes tracing around the room to search for Albert. "You are most certainly Cassandra's ticket to freedom, my boy. If I could marry you and get away from here, I would be down on bended knee at this very moment." His large head rocked on its axis, and I could tell that he was a touch squiffy himself.

Albert looked as though someone had spent the last two minutes battering him about the head with a plank of wood. I wanted to do something to make it better, but I was almost as stunned as he was.

"Stanislas," Charles called in a piercing voice. "Entertain us."

The third Fairfax boy had been standing with his arms at his side and his chin perfectly parallel to the floor. He did not argue with the command but strolled over to the piano, placed his coin neatly on the key block and began to play. I don't know what the piece of music was, but it was the kind of dirge you might hear emanating from the unoccupied ballroom of a haunted house.

Charles launched a cue through the air as though it were a javelin, and it landed on the floor with a clatter. "I said entertain us, not send us to sleep with a lullaby. Play something jolly and find your voice, man. We don't keep you around for the company."

The Duke got to his feet at this moment and, with his glass of brandy sloshing about, stalked over to the piano. "We don't keep him here at all. That's your mother's doing."

I was eager to learn more, but it was at this moment that Stanislas struck up a jaunty allegro melody. Perhaps unsurprisingly, the lyrics he sang did not match the cheerful feel of the music.

> **"Cold blows the wind to my true love,**
> **And gently drops the rain,**
> **I never had but one sweetheart,**
> **And in greenwood she lies slain,**
> **And in greenwood she lies slain."**

As if the mood of the room wasn't sombre enough, the mournful fellow in the braided jacket had decided to entertain us with a murder ballad. The tale of a young man who spends a year at the grave of his murdered love only for her ghost to emerge was not the tonic we needed. The Fairfax men found nothing unusual about the performance, and Eric tapped his foot in time with the music as he waited for his turn at the billiard table.

I was most alarmed to see the hefty duke with his hands in the air, clicking away to himself and performing a little jig. "You see, Albert, what no one has told you is that we are prisoners here." He really was quite sozzled and released another strain of laughter before Stanislas delivered the final verse from the perspective of the ghost in the grave.

> **"My lips are cold as clay, sweetheart,**
> **My breath smells heavy and strong;**
> **And if you kiss my lily-white lips,**
> **Your time will not be long,**
> **Your time will not be long."**

As he pronounced this final word, in his deep, rich voice, he brought both hands down on the piano and his eyes locked onto his older brother. "Is that jolly enough for you, Charles?"

CHAPTER EIGHT

So that was the beginning of the soiree to celebrate the imminent union of my beloved brother to his dear Cassandra. I genuinely believed that things could not get any stranger and could only hope that morbid folk songs, confessions of family strife and a flying billiard cue would be the nadir of any such event. Sadly, I am no great soothsayer, and the worst was yet to come.

It must have been ten o'clock by the time the final members of our party arrived. A man and a woman carefully pulled the door open as though they wished to surprise everyone.

"I thought you were at that damned ball?" Charles called when he caught sight of them.

"It was too dry for words, darling, and I missed you dreadfully." The woman was young, glamorously dressed in sparkling purple, and quite captivating, whereas the man was in a real state. He was around forty years of age and had an aristocratic bearing but looked as though he'd spent the night rolling in a field. His top hat was dented, his dandyish clothes were creased and stained, and he'd clearly drunk as much as his friends at Hinwick before arriving.

"Hello, all!" He stumbled over the step into the room and only avoided falling over thanks to the pretty brunette beside him. Righting himself and disconnecting from the woman, he walked straight up to my brother. "I imagine you know who I am."

I had spent the last year learning to hone my skills of observation and to lodge the slightest detail in my memory. Thanks to this, it was no great strain to work out who this man was, but Albert remained in the dark.

"I'm Lord Ruskin!" the tatty fellow explained. "Or Damian to my friends. I'm the one who would have married Cassandra if her mother had allowed it." He had an exceedingly posh accent. He reminded me of a caricature of a toff I had once seen performed by a girl with a monocle and a fake moustache.

The pretty woman in purple went to sit in Charles's lap. Lord Ruskin glared, and Albert didn't know how to react.

"I... Oh, I see," he stammered, but the whole evening had got too much for him by now, and he had to sit down in the nearest chair.

"Don't worry, matey." Ruskin had a rather dubious grin and showed his discoloured teeth as though giving a glimpse of a gun in its holster. "I accept defeat. I'm not here to break up the wedding, just to drown my sorrows."

"That's awfully good of you." Albert's voice could barely be heard; he sounded like an invalid uttering his dying words.

Ruskin searched his pockets before giving up and taking a cigar from the bowl on the trolley. He took his time clipping the end and lighting it, but when he spoke again, his focus was still on Albert. "Please, don't misunderstand me. I despise everything about you and wish you a life of misery, but Cassandra has made her decision, and there is nothing I can do to change it."

"Awfully good of you," Albert repeated, and this time he sounded like the voice in Stanislas's song, echoing up from the grave.

"It should have been you," the Duke said as he approached Lord Ruskin. Although the music had stopped, and Stanislas appeared to be in something of a trance at the piano, the patriarch was still dancing. "Curse my wife for standing in the way of true love. Curse her for everything she has done to us."

Skinny Charles had not reacted to any of this as, from what I could tell, the young lady in his lap appeared to be inspecting his trachea with her tongue. He pulled away for a moment to raise his glass. "Cheers to that, Father. Cheers!" He took a brief swig and returned to his amorous distraction.

"Did they tell you the story of the Duchess?" Lord Ruskin swayed over in my brother's direction. He was unsteady on his feet, even on a level surface.

"We were waiting until you got here." Eric took his turn at the billiard table and the cue ball jumped up into the air and over the cushion to go rolling about the floor. "The more the merrier for any party. That's what I say."

The whole lot of them were savages. No matter how little I'd thought of them out in the garden, they were somehow worse than I had imagined. If I hadn't known what a sweetheart Cassandra was – and how very different she seemed to the men in her family – I would have suggested heading back to Cranley posthaste.

Ruskin had come to a stop in front of Albert and let out a piping puff of smoke directly into my brother's face. To his credit, the petrified fellow didn't react. He sat with the dazed look that he'd been perfecting that day – and ever since we were children, for that matter.

"Oh, yes, she puts on a good show, doesn't she?" Ruskin smouldered much like his cigar. "Dear old Begonia thinks she's Queen Victoria. But her rule is far crueller, and she certainly hasn't won the love of her people."

The Duke had been circling the room in that same shuffling step, but then, as though someone had tipped a bucket of coffee down his throat, a sober look passed over him. "That is the one good thing I can say for you, boy. You're not making the same mistake as I did." He paused to glance up at the ceiling, and I thought he must be seeing stars there. "You'll marry for love, not wealth; that's the way it should be."

Albert had no voice, but I wasn't a great deal more useful. I wanted to ask if the Duke's problems stemmed from money but, in delivering this sad, slightly romantic statement, he had exhausted his energy. He collapsed into a chair and barely moved for the rest of the night. Two of his three sons laughed like jackals at their drunken father. I'm sure you can imagine which of them stayed silent.

I went to stand beside my brother in solidarity, uncertain what new affront would be launched his way next. Perhaps Stanislas felt some pity for us, though his family had shown none. For whatever reason, he left the piano and walked over to reveal something at which the others had only hinted.

"Father may be a duke and we may want for nothing, but Mother is the only one with the fortune." I believe that this was the first fully formed sentence I'd heard from him. He normally came to a stop halfway through, as though his mind had wandered off somewhere. "She controls all of us. Every decision we make must go through her and, as she hates the thought of any of us leaving, she refuses almost everything."

Judging by his military deportment and unusual attire, I thought that I knew what Stanislas's mother had prevented him from doing, but I let him speak.

"Perhaps it wouldn't be so bad if she possessed an ounce of generosity. But she is not a woman, so much as a magpie who wishes for nothing more than to have her treasures close at hand."

This was another chance for Charles to add his voice to the

discussion and, having abandoned his passionate lip-labour, he offered some encouragement. "You tell them, little brother."

His girlfriend had her cheek against his so that, for a moment, they looked like a two-headed beast. Unhappy to be left out of the conversation, she jumped to her feet.

"No, I'll do it." From her cropped hair to the heels of her shoes, which tapped on the stones as she walked over to us, she had a very modern air about her. "I'll tell you about the woman who won't even meet me and has forbidden me from setting foot in this house. I'll tell you about Lady Hinwick, who has stunted each and every one of our lives."

The whole thing felt like a play for an audience of two. As the actors were all slurring drunk, it was hard to take them seriously.

Ruskin had gone to perch on the side of the billiard table now that Eric and Charles's game was all but forgotten. Cassandra's ex-fiancé was of particular interest to me. He had shown such venom, and yet, for the most part, he exhibited a benign expression and was happy to listen to the young woman's colourful assassination of the Duchess's character.

"If she were here now, I would claw her eyes out." She looked terribly happy with this idea and made sure to enjoy it.

"This is Sibyl, by the way," Charles leaned around her to explain. "I *am* awful for not introducing her before. What would Mother say?" He demonstrated the amiability with which he had greeted us that evening, but I knew now that it was only superficial.

"No, wait. Not her eyes!" The bottom of the girl's beaded dress swung above her ankles as she raised one hand to make a correction. "I'd leave those until last so that she could watch everything I did to her. I'd pull out her hair first. Initially, one by one, and then in great clumps until there was nothing left but a bleeding—"

"Thank you, Sibyl." Eric held the back of one hand to his forehead to feign disgust. "We have all had such fantasies, but the truth is that none of us has the courage to go through with them." He walked over to the table where Todd had set up his bar. My grandfather's long-serving employee caught my eye as he poured the man another drink, and I could tell he was as perplexed by what he was witnessing as I was. The very fact that these people would divulge such vicious sentiments in front of a member of our staff showed what callous devils they were.

50

Free from his game and his plaything, Charles got to his feet to deliver the final part of the explanation. "That's the problem *in nuce*; mother has all the power and money, and we are too weak to resist her never-subtle manipulations. She dangles disinheritance over us the way that some parents threaten to withhold their children's pocket money. So we have these little parties. We share our woes and get so drunk that we can't remember any of it the next day.

"Come the morning, we'll go running back to Mummy for whatever cash she'll throw our way. It's truly pathetic." I assumed he was talking to Albert, but I realised then that it was the mirror on the wall behind us at which he glared. "If I had an ounce of my dear Sibyl's courage, I'd start with my own eyes, so as never to have to see my mother again."

CHAPTER NINE

The one good thing about that evening was that it didn't last too long. They swigged their drinks as though they wished to pass out as soon as they possibly could.

We should have already left, of course. The Fairfax men didn't want anything to do with us and would have stopped the wedding if their mother hadn't been so strongly in favour of it. They did nothing to hide their contempt for Albert and even their own sister, who was surely 'The Ugly Duckling' of the family – though perhaps in reverse.

Now that I think of it, 'The Pretty Duckling' really wouldn't have had the same moral message to impart.

For the hour or so that we remained in the Great Hall, we had to endure the debauched antics of Charles, Sibyl and Eric and the piercing stare of Lord Ruskin. His eyes were like pools of lava, spitting out molten rocks across the hall at his enemy. The anger he felt towards my brother belied his jovial air. He reminded me of a cartoon sketch of a debonair lord, complete with pocket watch, cummerbund and Dundreary whiskers. But underneath it all, there was a fire in him that would rage until the end of time.

I had to wonder what my grandfather would have made of it all, and whether they would even have behaved in such a fashion if the eminent lord had stayed with us for the celebrations. Looking back now, I should have been cleverer about the whole thing. I should have seen what was coming and kept my eyes peeled for the slightest incriminating detail. Instead, I huddled together with my brother and found every word those despicable characters spoke offensive.

As I said, it wasn't long before they were all so drunk that they couldn't stand up straight or, indeed, keep their eyes open. The Duke finally succumbed to sleep in his chair but stirred at the slightest noise. Ruskin stumbled off at some point and we didn't see him again, and even Stanislas, who was the one sympathetic figure amongst them, fell asleep where he sat.

"Well, that's that, I suppose," I muttered to my brother, once I felt it was safe for us to speak.

The poor thing looked as though a bomb had gone off beside him and he was struggling to hear or even think.

"Come along, Albert." I thought of something rather reassuring then and decided to tell him. "I'm certain this was all done for your benefit. They probably wanted to scare you – to see whether you're good enough for their dear sister. So congratulations! You passed the test with flying colours. You weren't scared in the slightest, were you?"

He attempted to be brave for my sake. "Not in the slightest."

"Master Albert," Todd called across to us. "Would you mind if I offered you a piece of advice?" He had already packed away his equipment and was removing a large case from the room when he stopped to speak. "Don't let them burrow their way inside your head. You're better than this lot and, if you love Lady Cassandra, I'm sure the two of you will be happy together." He paused for a moment, then nodded and lugged the case outside.

"You see?" I tried again. "There's no need to worry. All you have to do is get some rest. Tomorrow is your wedding day. Cassandra loves you and nothing else matters."

This gave him cause to smile for a moment, but he had an even better idea to set his mind at ease. "Thank you, Chrissy. I definitely couldn't have got through tonight without you, but I think I'll ring Mother all the same… just to check that everything's well at Cranley."

I pulled him up to standing and put my arm over his shoulder to help him out to a spot in the hall where I'd previously spotted a telephone. "Would you rather I let you call on your own?" I asked once he'd rung the operator and was waiting to be connected.

He stared up and down the passageway, and I knew what he would say. "I think it would be best if you stayed with me."

The operator connected us to a footman below stairs, who put the call through to the petit salon where, we were frankly astonished to discover, Mother was still awake and enjoying a very pleasant evening with Cassandra, my cantankerous grandmother and a number of the bride's friends.

"Is everything all right, darling?" my favourite person asked with a great deal of concern in her voice.

"All right?" Albert replied before blowing his fringe from his forehead with one great upward breath. "I suppose it could be." He tried to inject some degree of positivity in this sentence, but it fell from his lips as a tentative murmur.

"What's happened?" she asked, and Albert looked at me as though I might have an answer.

"Don't ask me!" I whispered as he held his hand over the mouthpiece. "It was your idea to ring Mummy."

"Albert, what's the matter?" She tried once more. "Cassie is here next to me. Would you like me to pass her the telephone so that the two of you can talk?"

"There's no need to worry," he reassured her. "But perhaps you should share the earpiece. I've got quite the story to tell."

"I'm listening, Albi," Cassandra said when she joined us, and I didn't have to stand too close to the receiver to hear what was happening at the other end of the line.

I squeezed Albert's shoulder to encourage him and, to give him his due, the story just poured out. He managed to include all the major points of action, and I was pleasantly surprised at just how many minor details he'd observed. He told them about our awkward arrival and the initially awkward dinner, the flying pool cue and the pot-valiant siblings. What he didn't mention was his conversation with the Duchess, and I could only think that this was what had scared him the most.

"I'm sorry, my darling," Cassie said before he could even mention the arrival of her rejected fiancé. "My family's not like yours; the whole bunch are quite loony. I should have warned you about them, but I was afraid that, if you knew what sort of people they were, you'd never want to marry me."

Albert's voice fell quieter to match his love's. "How could you even imagine that?"

She laughed again. "The fact that you're ringing your mother at such an hour on the night before our wedding rather answers that question, don't you think?"

"Ahh, you may have a point." It was at this moment that his face seemed to melt like chocolate in a bain-marie, and I knew I was in for a bout of super-sickly mawkishness. "But nothing could stop me loving you, my sweet. Not the moon falling from the sky or the mountains crumbling. I will love you until…"

I'll cut that short if you don't mind. But let me tell you that it was milk-and-water of the very highest degree – pure lovey-doveyness multiplied by a healthy dose of saccharinity with a helping of syrupy sentiment on the top. In the end, I could take it no more and had to interrupt.

"Isn't that just lovely?" I pulled on his arm to tug him away from the telephone. "But perhaps you should save all those beautiful thoughts for the service tomorrow. There is such a thing as too much emotion, you know? You might run out."

Cassie still sounded nervous, but she found the courage to ask a difficult question. "And are you certain that you still want to marry me, Albert?" The crackling line made her voice take on an echoing, ghostly quality.

"Of course. Until the morrow, my love. Until the morrow." Though he tried his best to sound confident, there was still a touch of nervousness in his voice.

You know that something is wrong when people start using the word morrow. The one saving grace was that he hadn't read her any poetry, though, knowing Albert, he probably had something in reserve for his speech at the wedding banquet.

"There's one thing I don't understand," I said once we were making our way through the house. "You didn't tell us what the Duchess said to you when you left the dining room."

He pulled on a lock of his hair and wouldn't look at me. "Oh, we needn't worry about that. It's water under the bridge now."

This may have been the first time that night that I was actually worried about him. For all that Cassandra's father and brothers had tried to make him suffer, it was clear there was nothing they could do. We knew now that it was Lady Hinwick who held the power in the family, and so the fact that Albert wouldn't even tell me what she'd said to him did not bode well for his future.

He must have noticed how worried this made me, as he immediately changed the topic. "I have a question for you, too. Do you think I should mention in my speech how Cassandra and I first met?"

"You mean the time you dressed as a pig, and drunkenly sang 'When Father Papered the Parlour' to a bar full of your compatriots at university?"

"Yes, that's the one." He cleared his throat. "I thought it might make me look a fool."

"Why hide who you really are?" I said, without meaning to insult him. "'The course of true love never did run smooth' and all that. I'm sure that everyone at the wedding who really knows you will enjoy the story. And as for the rest, who cares?"

"You're right, Chrissy. Thank you."

We had reached that impressive oak staircase that was polished to a reddish hue. It swept around the parlour like the tail of an immense mythical beast and the curling handrail was interrupted only by the two newel posts on the landing halfway to the top. I could honestly say that the one thing Hinwick House had that Cranley Hall didn't was a first-rate staircase. I had to wonder whether Grandfather was jealous.

When we got to the wing where our rooms were situated, my brother felt the need to repeat himself. "I mean it, Chrissy. I am genuinely thankful for all you've done today."

I would have liked to share an emotional moment with my brother just then, but it was simply too late. "And I'm genuinely tired. Good night, Albert."

I managed to force open the door to my room just enough to post myself through the gap. With the last of my energy, I pushed my trunk to the end of the bed and curled up in a ball to go to sleep.

CHAPTER TEN

I slept fitfully and believed that I could hear someone out in the hall. I could not say whether it was my imagination, which had become unsettled after the tumultuous evening, or it was merely one of the maids, making a start on the cleaning before her duties at the wedding took precedence.

I probably dreamt something, and it probably wasn't pleasant, but I don't remember a thing about it. All I remember is the scream. It invaded my room and woke me up in an instant. I was still too drowsy to do anything about it, but at least I was awake. My legs were stiff from not being able to stretch them all night, and it took me several seconds to be certain that my eyes were open, but I finally found the strength to climb over the footboard and escape from the room. I hadn't taken the time to change into my pyjamas the night before, and I felt extremely odd strolling about the place at an early hour of the morning in a suit.

I heard another scream then and picked up my feet. It didn't take me long to find out what had inspired such a reaction. There were two maids standing at the top of the grand staircase, looking down from a safe distance. There really can't have been many people employed at Hinwick House, as both of the domestics were from Cranley. I was about to ask Alice what had happened when I spotted a glistening splash of red on the banisters, halfway down the stairs. I pushed through the living statues and, within a few steps, I could see the source of the blood. There was more on a ball-topped newel post and, lying face down just beyond the lower landing, was the body I knew I would find.

There was a woman in a long trailing negligee and silken dressing gown and, just before I was certain who she was, my grandfather appeared beside the two maids.

"What's wrong?"

I descended a little further to be sure of my facts. "It's the Duchess," I raced to get my words out, as he was always desperate to make such declarations. "She's dead."

I suppose it was conceivable that she was merely stunned from her fall, but the knife in her back suggested otherwise. I looked about the upstairs landing and, sure enough, there was the display of weapons I'd seen the day before with a space now visible in the middle. Whatever had cut through her had a curved, bejewelled handle, and I could only think that it had come from some distant land, like India, Japan or Torquay.

As I surveyed the scene, Grandfather issued orders to the maids. "Alice, take the other stairs and call the police. Dorie, forget about your duties in the house for the moment and tell Todd what has happened. He will know what action to take."

The two nodded and ran for the back stairs, leaving us detectives to do our job. Fine, Grandfather would do all the real work, but I was also there.

"What have you noticed?" he asked as he fished in his pocket for two pairs of cotton gloves. He tossed some down to me, though how he had such supplies to hand when dressed in a smoking jacket and silk pyjamas, I will never know.

I pointed to the two clear spots of blood, and he wandered down to look at the newel post. "There's a fingerprint visible," I revealed. "Maybe this case will be a nice quick one, and the wedding can go ahead as planned."

"Let's see, shall we?" He carefully inspected my finding, gave an ominous frown and joined me at the dead woman's side.

One of her hands reached out down the stairway and her head rested on her arm. I must admit to being fascinated by the variety of expressions we had witnessed on the corpses whose murders we had investigated. Lady Hinwick appeared to have become frozen in shock. Perhaps the look on her face was the one she wore as the knife entered her body. Her mouth was open a little way and her eyes were two small dots.

I could see from the way her gown hung lower over the steps that there was something heavy in her pocket and, sure enough, I poked my hand inside to retrieve the small, round pocket watch we'd seen her with the night before. It was not a bulky thing with a hunter case, of the sort that gentlemen tend to wear, but a small, sleek ladies' watch.

"It's a mystery watch," Grandfather explained, and I thought this sounded rather wonderful. "You can see right through it, but its workings are completely hidden."

The most interesting thing about the transparent timepiece, however, was that it had come to a stop at a few minutes after midnight.

"Could that be the time of death, Grandfather?" I held the watch out to him, but he did not take it from me and simply stared at the cracked glass and the mangled hour hand.

"It is possible. Though it's more likely that the killer thought they were being clever by disguising the real time that the murder occurred. When did the party finish last night?"

"Not long after eleven. Well, that's when Albert and I came up to bed. The others had largely passed out before we left the Great Hall. There's a whole story I must tell you."

Before I could disclose what had happened with the Fairfax men or the arrival of Sibyl and Lord Ruskin, Eric appeared from the other wing of the first floor and was about to walk down to us when he froze. Seeing me crouched there, he cautiously took the first few steps and then stopped once more when he could see what we were examining.

"Is that…?" His words wouldn't come at first, but he must have recognised the slick pink material that the Duchess wore. "Is that my mother?" His eyes were fixed upon me, his normally superior expression now absent.

"I'm sorry, my boy," Grandfather began. "From the colour of her skin, I'd say she's been dead for several hours."

He bit his lip for a moment as he absorbed the news, and then his sorrow finally rose to the surface. "I can't believe it. It's just not possible." Well, I thought it was sorrow, but after a moment, a strange whooping sound pierced the air. "She's dead… She's finally dead!" He turned tail and ran back up the stairs, yelling with joy the whole way. "Charles, Daddy, Stan. She's dead. Someone's killed Mother!"

We watched him disappear around the corner, and it was my grandfather who broke the befuddled hush. "One thing is for certain; we will not have any trouble finding suspects for this particular crime."

"You noticed that the whole lot of them had grievances with the Duchess then?"

He nodded, somehow making this simple movement incredibly long and contemplative. "It was clear that there was something wrong from the moment we arrived. I could only conclude that the men in the family were under the Duchess's control. Though I have known other members of the Fairfax clan in my life, I'd never met Samuel before coming here. From what I could ascertain, his fortunes were already greatly reduced when he married. We must assume that she controlled the purse strings and thus her family."

"There's no need to make any assumptions." I was rather proud to enlighten him on the matter. "The Duke and his sons told me that very thing. Each and every last one of them, not to mention Cassandra's former suitor, absolutely despise the woman."

He knelt to put the watch back in the Duchess's pocket. "That's very interesting."

I was about to tell him the rest of the story, but I was certain that someone would interrupt us at any moment and thought it better that we examined the scene before we lost the chance.

"Something isn't right." I was on my feet once more, trying to make sense of the picture before us. "Let us imagine that she got up in the night for some reason and was stabbed in the back by her attacker." I walked up to the turn in the stairs where a large square step held the statue of a woman in Grecian robes. "Perhaps the killer hid behind here and lunged forward with the knife as his victim came past."

"I had formed the same conclusion. What else stands out to you?"

I put my theory into practice and ran up a little higher to be able to go back down again in the Duchess's place. "She was stabbed here," I said, pausing on the edge of that miniature mezzanine to imagine the blow that would have sent her sprawling. "It seems that her head made contact with the banister just there where we can see a splash of blood, but it doesn't make sense for there to be any on the newel post. It's way above where she fell."

Grandfather couldn't conceal his pride. What I couldn't say was whether he was proud of himself for teaching me to perform such an analysis or me for doing it. "You have outdone yourself, my boy. That is exceptional thinking. Now, can you think of any way to explain what we see?"

I looked at the splash of blood and the fingerprint in its centre. There was a glossiness to it that suggested it had been drying there for hours. I imagined that it would be sticky to the touch, but none of this told me why it was in the wrong place.

Grandfather eventually had pity on me. "I think you should come down here." He beckoned me to a spot below the Duchess in order to view her from a different angle. "There's a wound on the side of her head. I believe you were correct in saying that she fell after she was attacked and collided with the handrail. But look at her clothes."

I did just that and noticed that there were fainter traces of blood visible. At first, I thought it must have seeped through from the knife wound, but it was too irregular for that. The marks were more like smears across the dressing gown, rather than further evidence of the violent attack.

"Someone has interfered with the body." I should probably have clicked my fingers in excitement that I had come to such a conclusion without too much help from my grandfather, but I didn't see how this got us any closer to saying who was responsible for the woman's death. "The dressing gown has been pulled back. So perhaps the killer was looking for something on her person."

Grandfather shuffled along the step on which he stood. "You may be right. Or perhaps—" I would not hear any more of his thoughts on the matter, as it was at this moment that Eric returned with his family in tow.

"Look!" he yelled, with his boisterous band trailing behind him. "Look at her! I told you she was dead."

Charles was so happy that he hugged his brother. "Which of you did it?" he asked, looking from one to the other. "I didn't think that you had it in you. I really didn't." Admittedly, Stanislas and their father were more subdued.

"Well, it wasn't me," the Duke groaned through his whiskers. He had the bleary eyes and pasty face of a man who had just been disturbed in the middle of a dream. "And it's hardly something to celebrate."

"I didn't do it," Eric announced, and all eyes fell on Stanislas.

"Don't look at me," he said after five long seconds of silence. "I'm not a murderer." He seemed upset to have to make such a statement.

"One of us must have done it, unless…" An idea occurred to stoat-faced Charles at this moment as he pointed to the wing where our rooms were located. "Unless…" Apparently warming to the theory, he ran in that direction, and I launched myself up the stairs to catch him.

"Wait for me," Eric called rather joyfully, as though we were embarking on a game of follow my leader.

Stanislas and his father looked more conflicted about the news. Well, Stanislas showed as little emotion as ever – he was quite disconnected from reality at the best of times – and stood shilly-shally at the top of the stairs. But as I rushed past the portly Duke, his expression was one of melancholy.

I reached Albert's room just after Charles, who knocked on the door with a pounding fist. "Come along, lover boy. We know you're in there. Come out and admit what you've done."

Albert had always been a deep sleeper and would not be woken so easily.

"Don't take too long, or we're coming in there!" Eric shouted before addressing his brother. "Imagine someone doing such a thing to our very own mother."

Charles could not even feign sorrow. "The only problem is knowing what to do with him."

"How do you mean?"

There was a comical glint in the eldest brother's eye as he banged away, and I could tell that a joke was coming. "Once we get the culprit out of his den, should we knock the stuffing out of him or shake his hand?"

Eric was about to shout again when the door flew open, and Albert appeared.

He really wasn't happy. "What's the meaning of this?" He sounded like an angry old man. "I need all the sleep I can get unless you wish me to be groggy. And let me tell you, you will not like me when I'm groggy. Today is my wedding day and—"

"You can think again on that score, chum." The arrogance had returned to Eric's voice. He spoke as though he knew something which no one else could have possibly divined.

Albert's face dropped, and he stepped back apprehensively. "What are you saying?"

The two brothers didn't reply. Their faces shaped by vicious smiles, they simply pointed at the red marks on my brother's hand.

64

CHAPTER ELEVEN

"I didn't kill anyone," Albert insisted when the charges were put to him. "I haven't got it in me. I'm more of a thinker than a fighter. And, if I'm perfectly honest, I'm not too great at thinking either."

"You killed our beloved mother," Charles persisted. "You... monster." He buried his head in his brother's shoulder and pretended to cry.

"No, this can't be right. There must be some sort of misunderstanding." He sought in vain for an explanation. "Yes, that's it. Have you considered the possibility that she's actually alive? Has anyone checked whether she's playing a trick?" His eyes jumping from person to person and floor to ceiling, he looked as though he were about to collapse. "It's my wedding day. She can't be dead."

Everything was happening too quickly. I was worried that, before we knew it, the police would appear, and the groom would spend the big day in chains at the local station. I believe that Albert was about to fall to pieces, so it was a good thing that Grandfather arrived to take control of the situation.

"Gentlemen, I suggest you wait downstairs in the morning room until the police have been called." Grandfather didn't look at them as he spoke but seized Charles's hand to inspect it in the light. To my surprise, the prickly chap did not object.

"So that you can conceal any incriminating evidence before they get here, you mean?" Eric was enjoying the chance to be impertinent, but everything he and his older brother said had a thick lathering of irony all over it.

"All right, boy," the Duke called from the landing. "That's enough."

Charles glanced at his cheeky sibling, and the two trundled back to see the others.

Now that it was just us Cranleys remaining, I thought that my grandfather might have a plan in mind to resolve the terrible situation in which my brother found himself. It was not what I was expecting.

"Albert, I'm afraid I'll need you to stand back so that I can search your bedroom."

The groom-to-be looked even more frightened than when he'd

been accused of murder. "But, Grandfather, you must know that I didn't—"

"That's not my concern at the moment," our solemn forebear interrupted. "At this stage of the investigation, I'm only interested in the evidence before us."

Feeling the weight of the former policeman's words, Albert stepped aside in silence. Grandfather gave a brief nod and walked past him into the bedroom. I didn't know whether to accompany him or stay to support my brother, but my curiosity got the better of me.

The curtains were closed, and it was still half dark inside. There was just enough light breaking through the gaps to make out the details of the room. The sheets were of white cotton for the summertime, and the red stains where my brother had slept were immediately visible. At first, I hoped that the marks I spotted were splashes that anyone could have put there to incriminate him, but they looked more like smeared fingerprints, and I had to conclude they were from Albert's own hand.

Grandfather sat down in an armchair in the far corner of the room and needed a moment to steel himself for whatever was ahead of us. "The wedding will have to be cancelled."

"But Grandfather—" I began, never expecting that I'd be allowed to finish my objection.

"I don't see any other solution. The police will come, and they will arrest your brother. This is more than circumstantial evidence. This is outright proof that, at the very least, he meddled with his fiancée's mother's corpse."

"Oh, yes." I must have picked up a little sarcasm from Charles and Eric. "Never mind the fact he has no possible reason to kill the woman just hours before he was supposed to get married. Never mind the fact that her own sons have practically confessed to the crime, let's lay all the blame on Albert."

He wouldn't look up at me but shook his head. "I'm not saying that's what I want, Christopher. I'm saying that's what everyone will think."

I wasn't panicking just yet. "That's what they'll think until you change their minds. We'll postpone the wedding and, when the police get here, you'll just have to show them that your kind-hearted, law-abiding grandson would have gained nothing from the killing."

I walked over to him as I spoke, full of confidence that the great

66

Lord Edgington would be able to put things right. But when he looked up at me, I knew that I'd made a mistake.

"That's a wonderful idea, Christopher, except for one small problem; Albert had every reason to murder the Duchess." He paused and, instead of prompting him to explain, I waited until he was ready. "Why do you think I left the dining room when I did last night?"

"You had a headache." I really am very dim sometimes.

"Have you known me to suffer such maladies?"

"Never." Really very dim. "I assumed you'd had too much to drink."

"Then you weren't paying enough attention." He revealed his frustration by smashing one balled up fist into his open palm. "I may have looked like I was glugging wine all evening, but I never moved on from my first glass. It was apparent that something wasn't quite normal about this family, and I was determined to keep my wits about me."

"So what did you discover?"

He sat up straighter and a beam of low morning sunlight cut through the curtains behind him so that all I could see was his dramatic silhouette. "I saw a group of men who – whether right or wrong – feel wounded and mistreated. I saw a woman luxuriating in the power she commanded like a tyrannical queen."

I was struggling to extract anything new from his observations. "And how does that affect the likelihood of Albert being a cold-blooded killer?"

He was quick with his answer. "Do you remember exactly when I left the dining room? Lady Hinwick had just called your brother outside for a private word." He showed no shame for his furtive behaviour. "Some element of the Duchess's demeanour unnerved me. I sensed there was something sly about her. Perhaps it was wrong of me, but I followed them. I made sure to leave just in time to see where they had gone and then listened at the door of the drawing room."

"And?" I asked, as much to offend him with my poor grammar as to hurry him along.

He exacted his revenge with a nice literal answer. "And I heard what the Duchess said to your brother, obviously."

I gasped in irritation and constructed the full and precise question that I had meant to put to him in the first place. "And what did she say?"

He pushed himself up from his chair in one dramatic movement in order to pace in front of the window. "She said that, by marrying into this family, he would be accepting her rules."

"Is that all?" I was frankly disappointed. "I'm certain that Granny said far worse to your daughter when she married my father."

"No, Christopher, that's not all." He shook his head, and I was no longer certain whether it was my dubious detective work or Albert's dilemma that most disturbed him. "She said that she had tried to control Cassandra just as she had her sons, but she was too wilful, too independent to influence. And then, in an ever so ruthless voice, she told Albert that if he didn't agree to live the life that she'd planned for him and Cassandra, she would call off the wedding and make a spectacle of him in front of everyone."

At first, this seemed so farcical that I struggled to understand it. The very idea of a duchess putting such an ultimatum to her daughter's fiancé was impossible to imagine, but then I thought about the way she had treated her sons and I knew it had to be true. She was hoping to cultivate yet another subject and rein in the one who was trying to escape.

When I wouldn't say anything, Grandfather continued. "The woman was a monster and, if he wanted any hope of a successful marriage, Albert might well have decided that the only option was to remove her from the equation."

My body felt cold then as I imagined this terrible scenario coming to pass.

"Hello? Grandfather?" a voice came from the doorway and Albert poked his head into the room. "Is everything all right in there?"

CHAPTER TWELVE

The world had been turned upside down, which is never a good thing when I haven't had time to change out of my old clothes and there's a wedding due to start. There were so many questions to resolve, so many threads of the case to unpick, that I didn't know how or even where to start.

Luckily for my brother and me, our grandfather had some sensible ideas on the matter and, once we had regrouped in the hallway, he laid out his plan.

"Albert, I'm not giving up on you yet. I think I have a solution."

Actually, wait just a moment. I should probably tell you what happened in the ten minutes between learning that my brother might be a killer and now. First and foremost, Albert had done a lot of crying. I don't just mean he'd had a bit of a sob at his misfortune; he cried oceans. Standing beside him as the floods came gave me a whole new sense of what it must have been like to stroll along the shores of the Red Sea on the day that Moses went there on holiday.

It quickly became clear that there was nothing we could do to reassure him, so we gave up trying, and I explained to my grandfather everything he had missed when he went to bed early the night before. Something in my telling set his mind at ease, and he went from consulting the calendar in his head in order to work out approximately when my brother would hang, to seeing some glimmer of hope. And that was when he said…

"Albert, I'm not giving up on you yet. I think I have a possible solution."

Finally, after six hundred seconds of tears, Albert managed to dry his eyes. "You have?"

"You might still have to spend the day in a cell…" Grandfather was not always the most sensitive person when it came to delivering bad news. "…but I will do my best to distract the police's attention from the sheer weight of evidence there is against you."

Albert had stopped crying and was now shaking instead. "Thank you, Grandfather. You're too kind."

He ignored his grandson's fears (and his still-wet tears, for that matter) and began to lay out his master plan. "Christopher will find Todd and get him to pass the message around that the wedding is postponed until as late as possible this afternoon. It will be down to Cassandra, of course, to decide whether she wishes to go ahead with it. I've no doubt that the Duke has some influence with whichever cleric is performing the service, and what could be more romantic than a wedding on a summer's evening (with the mother of the bride recently slain)?" He didn't say these last eight words, but I was certainly thinking them!

"The point of this being…?" I asked as, even for him, this seemed a circuitous way to clear Albert's name.

"The point of this being that it gives the impression that we are not worried about Albert's imminent arrest for the violent murder with a ceremonial Indian dagger of the woman who could have tormented him for the rest of his life. And it also gives us the time we require to find the real killer."

There was a point I felt he was overlooking. "But how can you explain the blood all over his sheets and hands and what may well turn out to be his fingerprint on the banisters?"

"Yes, how can you explain that?" Albert was close to tears again, and the fact that he had just argued against his own innocence seemed to tip him over the edge.

"From the brief glance I had of it, it is quite likely that the fingerprint on the newel post belongs to Albert," Grandfather revealed to comfort precisely no one. "To my knowledge, everyone in the Cranley line has a rare tented arch on our thumbs. Of course, I no longer keep records of every member of our family," he said, as though such a thing were standard practice, "but the chances that anyone in the Fairfax clan would have the same feature are extremely low. Looking at Charles's hand just now, I saw no such pattern."

"Are fingerprints hereditary then?" I was quite surprised by this. "I really had no idea."

Grandfather was cheered by my question, as it gave him a chance to show off his immense knowledge on the subject. "It is not the fingerprint itself, as each person's is unique, but certain patterns are passed through family lines." He held his hand up to show off the tented arch in question. "You both have this tiny pyramid shape in the middle of your thumbs because I have it, and whatever quirk of nature dictates such things must be dominant as it has been passed down to both of you."

It was often hard to know how to react to grandfather's proclamations, but this was a particularly difficult one for my brother to absorb. "There we go then. All the evidence points to my involvement in the crime."

"Yours or Chrissy's," he clarified. "Or mine, for that matter." It was at this moment he indulged in an inappropriate chuckle.

My brother sat down on the floor, put his fingers in his ears and, one can only assume, prayed to God to wake him from this bad dream.

"You still haven't told us how you will explain the situation to the police." I crossed my arms and gave Grandfather a stern look. Sometimes that was the only way to deal with eccentric former policemen.

Instead of answering, he marched back to the landing to look at the wall of weapons and the empty space where the exotic dagger had previously been. "That is not our biggest problem," he said, his pace suddenly increasing. "All we have to do is tell them that the real killer wished to incriminate Albert and that he is entirely innocent and, if we're lucky, the policeman isn't too bright, and I also speak very fast, just like this, there's a good chance that your brother won't be charged with murder."

Though he had stayed behind to pray, Albert must have caught a snatch of what Grandfather had said as he let out a tortured moan. I thought that, for his sake, I would not raise the question of what our biggest problem was if that wasn't it. In fact, as the old man's brain was working at three times the speed of sound, I decided that the best action I could take was to stop asking questions altogether and trust that wise old Lord Edgington knew what he was doing.

"Fine, I'll find the staff and get them to rearrange the whole wedding," I told him. "I'm sure that Cook will be thrilled."

For the first time since the Fairfaxes had left us, Grandfather looked a little uncomfortable. "Ahh, yes. Cook. I'm glad that you'll be the one to tell her rather than me." He could not be faulted for his honesty.

"May I at least change my clothes before I go down?"

"Of course, dear boy." He gave a florid bow. "Which reminds me,

Albert should do the same. The police will need to examine the outfit he's wearing."

Another cry wafted over to us, and I nipped into my room to change before my brother could become more distressed.

I wonder whether whoever first said, "Clothes maketh the man", had lived through a murder investigation and realised the impact a new ensemble can have on a young detective. I felt a great deal better after I'd swapped my crumpled black suit for my uncrumpled grey one. There were some angry noises coming from one of the neighbouring rooms, and so I steered away from my brother and headed downstairs to do as I'd been asked.

I followed the corridor at the bottom of the second staircase in order to access the extensive lawn at the side of the house, where I knew the staff from Cranley would be hard at work. But when I went to push the French doors open, I found that I couldn't quite bring myself to do it. I'd only been up for half an hour and so much had already happened. Whilst I admit that finding a body first thing in the morning is at least a biannual event for me, on top of the wedding and Cassandra's manic family, it wasn't just a bitter pill to swallow but a massively large one that only just squeezed down my windpipe... if that is where food goes... which, now that I think about it, doesn't sound quite right.

And so, before I raced on with our new tragic adventure, I closed my eyes for five seconds and tried to steady myself. I took a deep breath and attempted to recall all the things we had not yet learnt in our nascent investigation. It was easy enough to remember the clues we had found, but staying conscious of all that we still had to discover was a far more complicated endeavour. Grandfather hadn't explained to me why there was blood higher up on the banisters than where the Duchess had fallen. He hadn't given me the first idea of how Albert's thumbprint had ended up in the blood. We didn't know what the killer might have been looking for in the Duchess's pockets and, now that I thought of it, I couldn't say that it made much sense to find a lady walking around in her dressing gown in the middle of the night with a watch on her person.

With these doubts neatly stored for later, I stepped outside. Though the sun had put on a good show throughout the first weeks of summer, the mornings were still crisp and there were drops of dew visible on the bushes and atop each blade of grass. I could see a number of Grandfather's employees already attending to their duties. Our footman, Halfpenny, was nervously doddering about the place – which was his usual state, whether he had a wedding to organise or a cup of tea to produce for his master. Dressed in smart green Cranley Hall livery, the gardeners were there to move furniture and, if the banquet were ever to be held, serve drinks to the influx of guests. I caught sight of Todd directing his colleagues and was about to shout across to him when someone spoke to me.

"Woof," went a voice. Very well, it wasn't a voice so much as a dog and, as the Fairfaxes didn't appear to own one, I was fairly confident that it was Delilah.

"What are you doing there, girl?" I foolishly enquired. I say foolishly not because the dear creature couldn't understand me, but as I couldn't make sense of her replies.

She responded with another "Woof" which rather killed the conversation. I really didn't know what to say to that but walked closer to the spot next to the house, where she was half hidden behind a rose bush. It turned out that she was not alone. Lying on the ground with his arms wrapped around our golden retriever was Damian Ruskin.

In the light of day, he was even scruffier than he had looked when I'd first seen him. He was also a fair bit older than I had first thought and must have been more than twice the age of the young lady he'd intended to marry.

"Lord Ruskin?" I began, as I do try to address people by their appropriate title. However, when good manners fall short, I'm not averse to barking. "Damian! Are you alive?"

There was a brief groan – so at least I knew he hadn't succumbed to the same sad fate as the Duchess. Nor, however, could I wake him. I was delighted all the same. My discovery meant that we had an extremely suspicious sort of suspect who could be placed on the premises at the time of the murder, thus narrowing the chances that my brother was to blame. Furthermore, in the state Ruskin was in, it seemed very unlikely he'd be going anywhere soon.

"Delilah, keep an eye on the man. He is a potential murderer and not to be trusted."

She seemed happy with the arrangement and gave a gentle moan. I took this as confirmation of my plan, though she might equally have been demanding breakfast. For a moment, I forgot all about the task I'd been given and wished that I was still the kind of boy who had time to worry about that most fortifying of meals. I remembered a period in my life, not so very long ago, when I would have spent the next few minutes dreaming of eggs on toast, bacon, pork sausages and black pudding.

"Todd," I called without knowing where he'd got to. It was as much to pull me out of my culinary reverie as from any hope that he would hear.

Wherever he had been before, the man in question popped up beside me. "Yes, Master Christopher? How may I be of service this morning?"

"I imagine you'll have heard of the Duchess's death?"

"Indeed, sir. It is a real tragedy. The staff have been informed, and we have started to implement certain measures that I had formulated in case such a circumstance were to arise."

"You mean to say—"

"That's right, sir. I had created an emergency plan on the off chance that someone should be murdered, and Lord Edgington would be required to investigate." The man knew his master awfully well. "After what we witnessed last night in the Great Hall, I thought it a wise step."

I was really very impressed. "Jolly good. It sounds like you have everything under control." I almost forgot to pass on the message that our superior wished me to impart. "Oh, Grandfather thinks we should postpone the wedding until this afternoon to give us time to investigate the murder."

"I had come to the same conclusion. In fact, Dorie has obtained a list of the invitees to the wedding and Halfpenny is calling everyone he can. Inevitably, some guests will have already begun their journey, and we can expect people to arrive in time for the original service at midday."

"Excellent work, Todd." I tried to think what my grandfather would say in such a situation. "Really, it's top notch." It took me a while to land upon something useful. "Perhaps you could station young Timothy at the scene of the crime to prevent anyone interfering with the body before the police arrive."

"The page boy, sir?" Todd looked a little concerned. "He is only fourteen."

"Is that too young? I was sixteen when I found my first corpse and I doubt it's done me any harm." I had a little think on the matter. "Having said that, I am now almost entirely insensible to violence, and the very presence of a murder victim on my morning route to the breakfast room seems as normal these days as noticing that my shoelaces are untied. You may be right, Todd. We'll save Timothy from such horrors for a while longer and send Driscoll in his place."

"Very good, sir. There is one other thing." He'd held his hands behind his back until this moment, in what I thought was a humble stance, but he now presented me with a small parcel of waxed paper.

"You crackerjack!" I exclaimed as I opened it to reveal a floury bap filled with everything I could want on a breakfast plate. "Truly, Todd, you are *nulli secundus* in your field. If Grandfather hadn't just given you a promotion, I would demand that he do so."

He nodded to me. I nodded to him and, already eating my sausage and bacon stuffed roll, I turned to walk back to the house before throwing one last instruction over my shoulder. "And, Todd, make sure you keep an eye on the Fairfaxes. I don't trust them one bit."

"I'm already ahead of you there, Sir. Alice has been 'cleaning' the morning room ever since they went in there. She will report back to one of you if she hears anything incriminating."

"Stupendous!"

I occasionally wondered whether Grandfather's staff had been trained in basic detective skills when they commenced their jobs at Cranley Hall. They were all more than capable in that department. In fact, their efficiency left me at something of a loose end. Normally, I would have eavesdropped at the window of the morning room and, short of a small bird coming to distract me, hoped to glean some significant detail that could confirm the identity of our culprit.

The police had been called, the wedding arrangements had nothing to do with me and so, short of inspiration, I returned to see the detective in charge of the case – or, Grandfather, as I like to call him.

CHAPTER THIRTEEN

To my surprise, when I returned to the first floor, I was accompanied by the grieving widower. Perhaps grieving is a little strong for the Duke's state, but he was certainly more affected by his wife's death than his sons were.

"Lord Edgington, you asked to see me," he said when we arrived at the space at the top of the stairs where Grandfather was sitting in quiet contemplation.

"Yes, Your Grace." As a peer himself, it was not often that Grandfather had to show deference to another aristocrat, but dukes are superior to marquesses, just as kings trump jacks in a game of cards. "There are some questions I would like to ask you before I speak to the rest of your household."

The Duke looked around the open lounge area as though he had never laid eyes upon it before. I believe that the very concept of passing time in such an informal spot was quite beyond him. Instead of taking the seat opposite my grandfather, he waved one hand for us to follow him.

We strode across the landing towards the long Victorian extension which had been tacked onto the main house. Grandfather followed obediently, – which is not a sentence I often have to use – and we soon came to a door that was covered with padded green leather.

"This is my reading room," the Duke explained as he held the door open for us to enter. "I come up here to get away from…" He paused then, as though deliberating on the most polite term to use. "…everything."

"A reading room!" I said rather cheerfully. "What an exceptionally good idea."

Although, in most respects, it fulfilled the role of any library – an example of which could undoubtedly be seen on the ground floor – the reading room was brighter and more spacious. The same large windows that characterised the house were arranged in pairs on two sides of the room, and acres of blue sky were visible through them. There were two tall bookshelves behind wooden doors with lattice wire to stop the books from escaping, but the opposite wall was bare except for some stripy white and duck egg green wallpaper.

The room was simpler than much of the rest of the house. There was no excess of portraits on the walls, and the only furniture was a Chesterfield sofa in green leather with two matching armchairs, which we now occupied.

"This is obviously a trying time for you," Grandfather began once we were settled. "I do not want to make this tragedy any more difficult than it already is."

In his usual bear-like fashion, the Duke growled. "I'm sure you know by now that her death was not the tragedy that some may assume. The day of my daughter's wedding may not be the best circumstances for a murder, but I'm afraid that Begonia's demise was long overdue."

Though the men of the family had shown no love for the Duchess, it still came as a shock to hear her husband state this so bluntly.

"I did have some sense that matters were not as cordial here as one would wish." Grandfather really should have become a diplomat. Have you ever heard such a respectfully constructed sentence? "I appreciate your honesty on the matter. May I ask what caused the schism between your wife and the rest of the family?"

"Her black soul," was the answer that came shooting back to us. "Oh, and I sold mine when I married her."

The Duke was not a man of a humorous bent, and yet there was something oddly amusing about his words. I had to look away to avoid giggling.

"My father was a profligate rogue and left this family on the point of bankruptcy," he continued. "I had no other option than to marry the richest woman that my mother could find in order to save our estate. Sadly, we did not consider any other criteria when choosing my bride."

It was hard for Grandfather to respond to such a confession, and so I took control of the discussion on his behalf.

"I'm sorry, Your Grace, but the fact that she was rich does not explain why someone would kill her."

He pulled at the hairs on his chin before replying. "Very true, boy. And yet, in many ways, that is the case. When I married Begonia, she promised to restore Hinwick House to its previous high standards. In exchange, it was agreed that our finances would not be merged; my wife was allowed to retain control of her fortune. My family thought this mere capriciousness but, as soon as my father died and we inherited the estate, she made it clear that her generosity came with many conditions."

"So she manipulated you?" I suggested, to summarise the issue.

"In a sense, yes." He sat back in his chair. "From the time the children were born, everything had a price. Cassandra was allowed a pony if she behaved a certain way in public and said the exact things that her mother had prescribed. Charles gained her permission to go to boarding school as he wished, but every visit we made there was a piece of elaborate theatre which Begonia directed and, after a year, she called him home again."

"Why would she act in such a fashion?" Grandfather asked, and I was happy to hear that I wasn't the only person who found this strange. "What did she hope to achieve?"

The Duke put his immense, muscular hand to his mouth. He had presumably been asking the same questions for decades. "She was not a simple person to understand, and she certainly never confided in us. Being married to Begonia was like having a scheming intruder in the house at all times. She was as sly as Iago and as treacherous in her machinations as Richard III."

As I've always said, there's nothing like comparing your enemies to Shakespearean villains if you really want to insult them.

"However, I came to believe that her main motivation was the cultivation of the way people saw her. She bought her duchy – she had the title she desired – but that wasn't enough. She was trying to cultivate the image the world had of her in much the way that other people grow orchids in their spare time."

He stopped his explanation, and I think that the three of us required a few moments' silence to make sense of it all.

Grandfather eventually decided to break it. "This may not sound a pleasant or nurturing way in which to raise a family, but could it really explain her death?"

"My apologies. I evidently wasn't clear enough. That was just the beginning." He sighed then, as though merely recalling the events required great effort. "As with all despots, the power she possessed made a bad person worse. It went to her head, and she revelled in the torment she could inflict. I didn't care about myself so much. I am old and have accomplished most of the things I wished to do in life. It was my children whom I hated to see suffer. She tortured them. There's no other word for it. She took great pleasure in playing her wretched games with them, knowing that I had no power to intervene. Every penny that we own belonged to her."

It was interesting that, whilst detailing his wife's wickedness, he kept returning to the financial question as if that was even crueller than her other behaviour. "Money isn't everything," I said, a little naively. "There must have been a way for you to turn the tables on her."

"Don't you think we considered that?" He sneered then, but even this angry reaction was subdued. "The children spent their adolescence trying to charm, trick and overwhelm her. Nothing worked. The choice was clear; either we could leave this house to live on the streets, or we had to do what she demanded."

He breathed in deeply to lessen the pain of this statement. "We stayed, and she doled out punishments for each and every indiscretion. When Charles wanted to go to university or Damian Ruskin asked for Cassandra's hand in marriage, there was nothing Begonia enjoyed more than denying them. She kept her boys particularly close to her. Each of them was denied the path they wished to walk. And yet, in our daily interactions, she was cheerful and light, as though we all got along perfectly. Her flair for the theatrical was astonishing; she should have been on the stage."

I felt his suffering then. I really did. I could see how much the man had endured throughout this strange existence.

It was Grandfather, of course, who found a contradiction in his tale. "Which prompts the question of why she allowed Cassandra to go to university or get engaged?"

The Duke had evidently been sitting for too long and pushed himself up to standing to walk over to the window. As he replied, he looked down at the wedding preparations on the lawn.

"Cassie was the only one of us who could turn off her feelings and pretend to be the person her mother wanted her to be. The boys tried, but their anger and rebelliousness would come to the surface before long, and they'd fall from her graces." He looked back at us with a snap of the head. "Have you read Dickens's 'Great Expectations'?"

I practically jumped out of my seat and waved both arms in order to answer his question. "Yes! Yes, I have."

His response was less enthusiastic. "Then you'll know how Miss Havisham shaped Estella to be like her. I'm glad to say that my Cassandra resisted such manipulation but, as far as her mother knew, she was the very image of the obedient daughter. It would have been funny if the whole thing weren't so tragically sad."

Grandfather returned us to the crime itself. "The coroner will give us a more accurate picture of what happened. From my inspection of the body, however, it appears the Duchess was killed in the early hours of the morning. Do you know why she would have been out of bed at such a time?"

The Duke's answers had come fairly quickly until now, but this question had him at a loss. "I don't think... You know, we have separate bedrooms. Mine is across the corridor from hers, and I really can't say what she was doing."

"That's interesting," Grandfather said, perhaps to unnerve the suspect further. "Did you hear anything outside your room at any point?"

"I'm a light sleeper, and so I would have..." He hesitated over this point before revealing something which he should have already remembered. "I'm sorry. I don't know what I'm thinking. I wasn't in my bedroom last night and evidently couldn't have heard anything. I fell asleep in the Great Hall as your grandson here can attest."

Lord Edgington looked puzzled by this sudden recollection. "So what time did you go up to your room?"

"I didn't. I mean, I haven't been back there yet. I was woken by Eric when he came to the hall with the news of Begonia's death."

Grandfather followed up his perfectly simple question with a perfectly treacherous one. "Do you suspect one of your sons of the murder?"

"I'm aware that they each had a strong motive, as did I." Lord Hinwick worded his response most precisely. "However, I have no reason to believe them capable of such a crime."

I'd had a sense throughout this discussion that the Duke was hiding some significant fact. The thought occurred to me again now. I could only conclude that, if he did not know for certain that a member of his family was capable of murder, he was aware of something that could make one of them a likely suspect.

My mentor bothered his lower lip with his teeth before deciding on his next approach. "So you all had the necessary motives, and yet no one had previously taken the opportunity to put an end to the Duchess's reign of terror. I wonder what was different about last night."

The Duke stuck to his previous strategy. "I've already told you; I don't believe that my sons had anything to do with the killing."

The detective wouldn't give up. He was on a scent and pushed for more. "Perhaps you had never had a perfect sap in the house to take the blame before. Although I love my eldest—"

"Second eldest," I whispered, as he often forgot the odd grandson or two.

"I love my second-eldest grandson very much, but I am under no illusions as to his strength of will, intelligence or the malleable personality he possesses." He paused to reflect for a moment. "I wonder whether Charles is the killer. He presented such a welcoming front to Albert last night and then showed his true face as soon as his mother had gone to bed. Did he befriend Albert to learn as much as possible about him? Did he identify an easy mark and plot his mother's downfall even as we sat around the dining table enjoying one another's company?"

The Duke did not reply this time. His gaze had hardened, and his muzzle-like lips had pursed together.

"I think there's a certain logic in that scenario," Grandfather answered his own question. "Charles is the strongest of the three boys, don't you think? Stanislas is a shy, faint sort of fellow. Eric is all snide comments and angry looks, but not the type to take action. Surely your firstborn son is the likely suspect."

"No." The Duke's patience was wearing thin.

"I can only imagine that he saw his opportunity to be rid of the Duchess, found some way of incriminating Cassandra's fiancé, and then woke his mother in the night to do the deed."

The Duke's resilience broke, and he turned away from us to look out of the window once more. "You're talking nonsense, man. In fact, it's worse than that. You're abusing your position as a self-appointed detective to divert suspicion from your own kin. I won't have it, and you can be sure that the police won't either."

"I see." Grandfather crossed his arms at this point. There was a finality to the action, and I think he wished to communicate that this line of thought had run its course. "In which case, the only alternative I can imagine at this juncture is that you yourself were responsible for your wife's death. You had a greater reason to wish the woman out of your life than anyone. After all, your four offspring were the ones she had mistreated."

This certainly got the man's attention. He threw one hand in the air in dismissal, and I thought he might launch himself across the room to strike my grandfather. If the truth be told, it was surprising that more suspects didn't attack the old stirrer. He really was a genius at putting our suspects' backs up.

"I won't stand here and listen to such insults." The Duke marched to the door as he spoke. "What I will do is make sure that the police hear our side of the story when they arrive. From what my sons tell me, that will not put Albert in a particularly good light."

With this said, he glared at us for a few seconds longer, then stormed from the room.

"Wasn't that fascinating?" Grandfather muttered once we were alone.

"No. I'd say it was just the sort of behaviour I would expect after you insisted on riling the man."

"Perhaps, but you must remember that he'd already admitted that he and his sons hated the Duchess. At the beginning of our conversation, he seemed happy to accept that they were all suspects. By the end, he claimed to be offended by the very idea." His elbows resting on the arms of his comfy chair, he put the tips of his fingers together in front of his chest. "Tell me this, Christopher; what changed in such a brief period?"

CHAPTER FOURTEEN

The police would surely arrive at any moment and, as we never knew in advance whether they would be happy to have our assistance or eager to chase us off the property, we had to make the most of their absence.

"There's somewhere we must go while we still can." Grandfather was on his feet and out of the door before I could ask where we were heading.

I had an idea, of course. We'd looked at the body. The suspects were grouped together downstairs, and Albert had been stashed away carefully in Grandfather's bedroom to stop him incriminating himself further. There was really only one obvious place to look, but I awaited Grandfather's explanation, nonetheless.

"We're going to the Duchess's bedroom."

Fine, there were two obvious places to look, but I was still fairly confident we would have to inspect the Great Hall at some point to see what had gone on there after we went to bed.

Grandfather had a sixth sense when it came to navigating old houses and led us along one corridor after another towards the family's enclave of bedrooms in the Victorian wing. "We must establish whether the killer visited this part of the house in order to attract the Duchess's attention."

Admittedly, I could not have guessed this, though it did seem a good idea to have a poke around the Fairfax brothers' bedrooms if the chance arose. We eventually found ourselves in the right part of the house and, to make things a tiny bit simpler, the first door we tried was the Duchess's. I used all of my most developed skills of deduction to divine the ownership of the room. Not only did the place smell of a highly sweet and floral perfume that matched our hostess's, the furnishings were ever so soft, the curtains a shade of pink that would normally only be found in a little girl's nursery, and the bed had recently been used, so I could rule out the possibility that it belonged to Cassandra.

I was about to inform my partner of my success when I realised that it was a fairly basic conclusion to form and decided not to say anything. Instead, I stalked about, looking for the smallest clue – or any big ones, for that matter. There was no blood anywhere, what with the victim being murdered on the stairs. I spotted no muddy footprints, either, though that would have been far too convenient for one of Grandfather's cases. By the time I'd completed few laps of the room and not discovered anything out of the ordinary, I took a peek through the window and noticed two drab, boxy cars pulling to a stop on the front drive.

"We must be quick. The police have arrived."

He was on his knees, skimming the carpet under the bed for clues. "It doesn't look as though there's much to find, although that *is* interesting…"

He was looking at me, and I worried for a moment that I'd disturbed some vital clue and it was hanging from my face. I checked my cheeks and the top of my head before he signalled to a point just over my shoulder.

"The window, Christopher. Look at the window."

It turned out I'd been looking straight through the clue we needed. In the upper right-hand pane of the sash window was a large crack that spread out from the centre like a spider's web.

"What does the damage to the glass tell you?"

I took a step back to consider the possibilities. "I would say that it was hit by something. A bird maybe?"

He'd seemed happy with my answer at first, but his expression soon changed. "Is it common for a bird to have such an impact?"

"Well… maybe if it flew directly at the window with its beak at just the right angle."

Despite his best instincts, he was compelled to ask another question. "And what particular species could cause such damage around here?"

"Now, that's not fair. You know I'm not good at identifying birds. If I said a sparrow, it would probably be a seagull. And if I said a duck, it would definitely be a goose."

He opened his mouth to respond before realising the depths of idiocy that we were plumbing and changing his mind. "No, Christopher, I do not believe that a bird flew at the window. If you look at the size and shape of the crack, it is clear that something hit it."

"That's what I said." I thought I might be able to get away with this whisper, but he glared at me all the more keenly.

"Something like a stone, perhaps."

I craned my neck to look at the ground below the window but only ended up banging my nose. "You mean that someone could have thrown a stone to get the Duchess's attention." I couldn't fault his logic, but there was one thing I doubted. "That crack could have happened at any time. We don't know for certain that—"

Rushing across the room to inspect the carpet, he stopped me before I could say anything else that was instantly disprovable. "There, just by your foot! Do you see it glinting in the light?"

I half hoped it was a fragment of diamond and that this find would take us off on an interesting tangent involving smugglers, international travel and a wicked criminal mastermind, but it was just a speck of glass.

"So the break was recent." I felt I was on safer ground with this statement. "A maid would have cleared it away otherwise."

"That's the stuff, boy." He put his hand on my shoulder. Sometimes he was nicer to me when I was making a fool of myself than when I was marginally cleverer. "It seems that my hypothesis was correct. The killer didn't come up to the room here but found a way to get the Duchess to leave it of her own accord. Then all he had to do was hide on the stairs and wait for Lady Hinwick to pass."

Realising something that he hadn't, I calmly walked over to the door to the bedroom and peeked outside at the stairs that led to the Great Hall. "Why would the Duchess have walked halfway across the house if there are stairs just in front of her door?"

He raised one finger to dismiss my point and then realised it was not so easy. "Well, I suppose the killer shouted up to the Duchess to tell her to meet on the main staircase, then bolted over there before she could put on her gown and arrive at the agreed location."

I wrinkled my nose up as I wasn't entirely convinced. "So that means we can at least prove that the victim knew her killer, which did seem to be the case from the beginning. However, that still doesn't explain why anyone would go to so much trouble."

"How do you mean?" He looked out of the window as, I could only imagine, the police officers had left their car and were approaching the house.

"Why didn't he just kill her here? Why tease the Duchess out of her bedroom when the simplest thing would be to murder her as she slept?"

He smiled such a smile at this moment that I knew how Da Vinci felt when painting the Mona Lisa. "You tell me, Christopher. You already have the information you require." Instead of explaining his thinking, he rushed past me out of the door.

I chased after him, and we took the aforementioned non-bloody stairs to the ground floor. I had already made mental notes of so much that we did and didn't know that it was hard to know what was important and what I should have ignored in the first place.

We were halfway down by the time it came to me. "The killer couldn't risk killing the Duchess in bed because the Duke is a light sleeper and might have been in the room opposite hers."

"Excellent work, Christopher." I believe this was the second piece of praise he'd offered that morning! I was evidently doing something right. "And what conclusions can we then draw from this vital piece of evidence?"

I actually think I was a step ahead of him for once. "It shows that the Duke didn't kill his wife as, if he had, he wouldn't have needed to worry about the noise."

"That's exactly it. Well done."

I was feeling rather elated. We hadn't found the killer, but we'd narrowed our field of suspects mere hours after discovering the body. "And so that means we can rule out the Duke as the killer. We know for certain that he didn't do it."

His smile disappeared, and he looked puzzled and perhaps the tiniest bit worried about me. "Why on Earth would you say that?"

"Because it's a perfect conclusion. There's no room for doubt. If the Duke was the killer, he wouldn't have needed to keep quiet and could have happily murdered his much-loathed wife in her bed. The real killer lured the victim to the stairs to do the job. Ergo, the Duke isn't to blame." I thought this a rather persuasive argument, while at the same time worrying that I'd misused the word *ergo*. I'd never been any good at Latin.

We'd left the stairs and were following the hallway through the house to a small entrance hall at the end of the more modern wing.

"Again, Christopher, you have displayed some truly insightful reasoning. The only thing you have overlooked is that, by mentioning the detail that he was a light sleeper, the Duke himself may have been leading us down this winding path. Perhaps he wanted us to have this very conversation, knowing that we would think it impossible that he was the killer."

I was frankly lost in his foolproof logic and, as we stepped outside, he finished the discussion with a nice resolute, "The Duke could be the murderer, just as you or I or even that man asleep in the flowerbed could be."

CHAPTER FIFTEEN

"Lord Edgington, I heard you were here." Detective Inspector Lovebrook was a handsome man of around thirty with an air about him that was quite distinct from most of the provincial police officers we'd had the chance to meet. "I cannot express how much of an admirer of your work I am."

It was always a roll of the dice to know what sort of assistance we'd get from the boys in blue. Competence did not seem to be a stipulated condition when it came to appointing policemen out in the provincial wilds. This made our meeting with Lovebrook all the more encouraging.

"You really are too kind," Grandfather luxuriated in the adoration for all of three seconds before concentrating once more. "But whatever you have heard about me doesn't change the fact that we have our work cut out here."

"No doubt, my lord." The fresh-faced officer with a wispy fringe and neatly clipped sideburns hesitated for a moment. "But please let me say what an influence you've had on my life. You see, I followed in your footsteps somewhat. My father wanted me to look after the family estate and marry and all that sort of thing, but I wasn't interested. I read all the stories about you when I was a child and enrolled in the police force the day I turned eighteen and a half."

"And how's the life of an inspector treating you so far?" I was curious for my sake as much as his. Though I very much doubted I would end up joining the police, I didn't know what other paying job I might be able to do and thought I should keep an open mind on the matter.

He turned to smile at me. "Well, it's certainly a varied life. I'll say that for it." He had a cheerful, honest manner, and I instantly liked him. "I couldn't possibly have imagined that I'd arrive at work this morning to discover that the Duchess of Hinwick had been murdered. That is what happened, isn't it? The boys at the station haven't sent me here as a joke?"

"I'm afraid not," I replied, then thought I'd leave it to Grandfather to fill him in on what had occurred.

I could go through everything he said to the inspector, but it's more or less what I've been prattling about for the last however long. You know the sort of thing: dead matriarch, blood on the banisters, broken watch, etc., etc. There really is no need for me to go over it again, and so let's skip ahead a few minutes to the inspector saying, "My men and I are at your disposal, Lord Edgington. I cannot officially put you in charge of the investigation, but as far as I'm concerned, you're a darn sight more likely to solve this case than anyone else in the county."

Grandfather put his hand out for yet another shake. He clearly approved of Lovebrook's singularly agreeable disposition. As a general rule, the great Lord Edgington admired men who admired the great Lord Edgington. The one thing of which Lovebrook had not been informed was the extent of the evidence that we had accumulated against my brother. I knew exactly why Grandfather had chosen not to divulge such information, but I doubted it would be long before the inspector discovered the truth for himself.

Whilst we were talking, two pairs of bobbies had exited their Austin Seven and were already guarding the perimeter of the house.

"Have your officers keep any prying wedding guests outside," Grandfather told the inspector. "People should start arriving soon, and we do not want any evidence to be compromised."

Lovebrook looked surprised at this. "Is the wedding going ahead, then?"

Grandfather considered the likelihood of such an event. "That remains to be seen. My staff are calling as many people as possible to delay things, but some are bound to have already left home or stayed nearby overnight."

"I'm sure my officers will look after them and, in the meantime, if you have no objections, I'll take a look at the body."

The more experienced detective seemed pleased with the idea. "Excellent work, Lovebrook." I tried not to show my jealousy. "Two pairs of eyes are always better than one." I must have failed in my task as Grandfather caught my surly look and added, "Or three even," before Delilah released a short bark from her flowerbed and the peeved lord had to amend his statement a second time. "In fact, everyone's contribution is welcome."

Looking a little puzzled by the exchange, Lovebrook nodded politely and headed towards the house. Delilah was still making a fuss to get her master's attention and so he went over to see her.

"Who have you got there, girl?" my companion asked. "Have you apprehended a suspect?"

"In a way, I suppose." Obviously, this was me talking. Delilah's diction wasn't nearly so clear. "This is Lord Ruskin, the man who wished to marry Cassandra before the Duchess objected and Albert ended up pipping him. I saw him here when I came looking for Todd a little while ago."

Grandfather wasn't impressed. "You mean to say that there was another man on the premises with a particular grudge against our victim, and you didn't mention it?"

"I haven't had many opportunities to do so. I was hardly going to interrupt your interview with the Duke to tell you that it might be a waste of time, as there was a more likely suspect hugging our dog down among the pansies."

"Christopher," he said with disappointment dripping from every syllable, "they're not pansies. They are clearly Torenia fournieri." Trust him to be distracted by such an entirely irrelevant detail.

"I'm terribly sorry," came an exceedingly well-spoken voice from down in the dirt, "but some people are trying to sleep here. Would you mind taking your argument elsewhere?"

Grandfather wouldn't stand for such insolence. "*I'm* terribly sorry, but would you mind taking your hands off my dog?"

Ruskin opened one eye to see who was on top of him. "To be quite honest, I've woken up beside less handsome young ladies in my life. And she's certainly a better kisser than many."

Delilah appeared to smile at this. I'm sure she didn't, but that's how it looked.

"Here, girl," Grandfather commanded, and the obedient beast jumped off the tatty lord and came to heel at his… ummm… heel.

Ruskin took his time to stand up and made a brief attempt at brushing off the dirt, but his clothes had already been in quite the state when I'd met him. I noticed that he'd lost his top hat too, though he had bigger things with which to concern himself.

"Ruskin, I imagine you know who I am. I have some questions for you," the imperious detective began. "Can you tell us at what time you left the house last night?"

He looked up at the sun as though this might help. "No, can you?"

Grandfather glared at him and so he glared back. Not seeing how this could get us anywhere, I decided to intervene. "He left the Great Hall at around half-past ten. I don't know where he went after that."

"How interesting." My favourite investigator was in full detective mode by this point. "You left a party early without explanation, then hung around the house until the following morning. Can you tell me what you've been doing here until now?"

Ruskin smirked a little. He was that kind of person. "I remember arriving last night and falling over in the garden when I made use of the facilities." He pointed to a nearby tree. The man really had no shame. "After that, I went inside to see the Fairfax boys. Sadly for everyone involved, your man had prepared a refreshing yet wicked spirit that I shouldn't have imbibed but evidently did in rather large quantities. Oh, and I woke up approximately two minutes ago in a flower bed. Does that answer your question?"

Grandfather didn't look as though he could say one way or another. "I don't suppose you popped back inside in the middle of the night to murder someone?"

"Murder?" That wiped the snide grin from his face. "Why would I murder anybody?"

"Oh, I don't know." His inquisitor pretended to consider the question. "Perhaps for revenge on the woman who prevented you from marrying her daughter? Or did you kill Lady Hinwick to stop Cassandra's wedding to my grandson?"

"She's dead? The Duchess is dead?" If he'd had a hat to hold just then, I feel he might have dropped it.

"That's right. She was stabbed through the back in the middle of the night."

His face was still grim as this fact sank into his consciousness. "Do the boys know?"

Grandfather nodded in reply, and the man's cheerily arrogant demeanour faded... for approximately four seconds.

"Then why is there no music playing?" He released a high-pitch chirp of laughter. "Wind up the gramophone, open the champagne. This should be a celebration. The harpy has crowed her last caw."

Grandfather would not be distracted by the colourful display.

"Did you do it, Ruskin? Was it your handiwork with the dagger that felled the Duchess?"

"No, but I wish I had. I'm surprised I didn't hack her up months ago, actually. The woman was a monster."

"The exact time of death remains to be established, but you've already admitted that you were on the property. Your motive is widely known and you're clearly happy that Lady Hinwick is dead. So what is there to stop me arresting you right here?"

His ebullience subsided, and he looked a little reflective for a moment. "As far as I know, you're no longer a police officer. But apart from that, nothing." His lips curled up ever so slowly as a new possibility formed in his mind. "In fact, go ahead. I'll hand myself in to the nearest officers and they can look for bloodstains on my clothes or whatever it is they do these days to incriminate innocent men like me."

"You look as innocent as a wolf on a rabbit farm." It was unusual for Lord Edgington to show such anger towards a suspect until we'd found sufficient evidence to prove he was guilty. What's more, under normal circumstances, he would never have employed such an obvious simile; I had to wonder what had unsettled him.

"Wonderful." Ruskin remained unmoved. "Perhaps if we've finished this little game, we can do something about breakfast. I haven't eaten anything since I left the Horseshoe Ball last night, and I'm half starved."

I hated to agree with the horrid sort, but he did have a point. "We're certainly not going to solve this case on an empty stomach, Grandfather. And I'm sure the other suspects will be hungry, too."

He looked down at his dog, who was even more adept than me at delivering pleading looks. "Very well, Ruskin. Wait with your friends in the morning room, and I will have a servant bring you refreshments."

Lord Ruskin clapped his gloved hands together. "Exceptional. Strong coffee all around, of course. And if there happen to be any Viennese pastries floating about the place, I am rather partial to them."

Damn the man! He spoke such sense.

He gave a cheery wave and wandered past a uniformed officer who was standing guard at the door that was closest to the main staircase. We stood watching him until he disappeared inside.

"I'm sorry, Christopher, but I've known men like him before.

In my mind, he's the wrong kind of aristocrat. A man who thinks nothing of abusing his position to have the easiest existence possible and hang the consequences."

"I can't say I'm too keen on him myself, but would he really have stayed here if he'd killed the Duchess? He could have done the deed, then left the house last night, and none of us would have been any the wiser."

"You may have a point." He took a few steps towards the house and then stopped himself. "Or perhaps he banked on the idea that his absence would have incriminated him even more than his continued presence." He took another few steps forward, and then another pause, and I got the impression that he was not quite himself. "Perhaps a hot drink *would* be a good idea. Tea, not coffee, of course. I am a British marquess, not an Italian Marchese. There is nothing like a cup of Earl Grey in the morning to diminish one's problems."

He finally found the impetus to make it all the way inside the building and then muttered the whole way to the morning room about coffee and "the slow erosion of British society".

CHAPTER SIXTEEN

The handsome salon was just the place for us. Though smaller than several of the rooms we had visited, it had a warmth and familiarity that I found appealing. In this bright, unimposing space, all the furniture was pointed towards the windows in order to welcome in the day. The walls were lined with paintings of prize bulls, cows and sheep, which gave something of the feel of a schoolroom, and I can't say that I minded one bit.

The only drawback to our arrival was the sour looks we had to endure as we entered.

"The heroic duo return," Eric mumbled in a harsh voice. He was the sort of person who was happy to make disparaging comments, but when it came to actually standing up for something in which he believed, he would fall strangely quiet.

"What a comfort it is to know that we have Britain's finest detective working to find our dead mother's killer." Charles was almost as bad, but there was a little more bite to him, a little more intelligence behind each barb.

"Quieten down, both of you," their father demanded, and I thought he must have recovered somewhat from his interview in the reading room. "Have you discovered anything more, Lord Edgington?" Although his transformation was hard to accept, at least he had assumed a more co-operative attitude.

Instead of responding, Grandfather went for a tour of the room, taking in whatever he could about our suspects. Ruskin had propped himself up against the mantelpiece, and Stanislas stood motionless in the corner with his usual distant expression. I couldn't help thinking that he looked like a standard lamp that no one had taken the time to illuminate.

With his task complete, Lord Edgington finally answered the question. "We are still at an early stage of the investigation. I have no doubt that the Duchess was murdered by someone she knew well and so, unless some rancour existed between Lady Hinwick and the staff here, I can only conclude that one of you was responsible for her death."

The five men glanced about at one another, and I must say that it was a shame to have such a limited cast of suspects. Four members of the same family and an extra aristocrat thrown into the pot for good measure? To be perfectly honest, I preferred more variety and harked back to our visit to Mistletoe Hall the previous winter, when we'd had people from all walks of life to blame for a nasty murder or three.

Just as Grandfather asked this question, the butler, Peterson, entered the room with a tray of cups, saucers and the usual paraphernalia. We turned to look at him with great suspicion before Stanislas dismissed him from the investigation.

"No, the staff here had never clashed with my mother." He seemed sure of his facts, though this, in itself, was hardly proof. "She took great pleasure in telling everyone who would listen just how much our cook, butler and maids adored her. It certainly didn't hurt that she paid them above the going rate of most employers."

On cue, Peterson spoke up in his fake squeaky voice to address my grandfather. "If I may say so, M'Lord, the Duchess was a kind and generous mistress. She paid for my children to go to school, indeed she did."

"Which was more than she would do for me," Eric grumbled, but no one turned to see what had got his goat this time.

The butler disappeared, and we took our seats on an aged suite of brown leather furniture. Grandfather and I were afforded the sofa, and I must say that it was pleasantly springy.

There was the requisite amount of nervous staring, some fidgeting of hands, and the odd suspicious look exchanged between the brothers. Peterson soon returned with coffee, tea and a selection of cakes, and I stopped paying attention to the suspects for a maximum of fifteen seconds as I worked out which shiny lacquered pastry I most desired. Though there was a good chance that a member of the Fairfax family was the killer, they weren't complete savages and allowed their guests the first choice of sweet.

With my raisin whirl procured, I could concentrate on the case once more.

"As I was saying," Grandfather continued once he'd had a refreshing sip of scalding hot infused water, "it is too early to share our findings, but I thought I would take this opportunity to offer you the chance to defend yourselves."

"That is very kind of you, Lord Edgington," the Duke replied, continuing his act as the good egg of the group. "Isn't that kind of him, boys?"

There was some light murmuring in reply, but nothing definitive, and so Grandfather spoke again. "Do any of you possess any information that could rule you out as suspects?"

"Stanislas and I were asleep in the Great Hall for most of the night," Eric put forward. "He was asleep on my shoulder."

I looked to the corner for confirmation. "Is that true, Stanislas?"

"Yes, but that doesn't mean we couldn't have slipped out to kill her. Surely an alibi holds no water if the person giving it was asleep."

I looked at his clothes and noticed that he was the only one who had got changed that morning. The Duke and his other sons were in the same formal attire as the night before, but Stanislas was neatly dressed in a summer outfit of white slacks and a cotton sweater. "What time did you go up to bed?"

He opened his mouth to reply and then changed his mind and came to collect a cup of coffee. "It was light outside. Perhaps seven o'clock, if I had to guess."

"And you didn't go back to sleep?" Grandfather asked.

With Stanislas, it was hard to know whether he was weighing up each word he delivered to ensure that he wouldn't say anything that might implicate him in the crime, or it was merely his usual slow manner. "No, I…" I wondered if he'd been dropped on his head as a child, or an adult for that matter. "No, I didn't go back to sleep. I don't like to waste the day, and I thought I might be able to help with the wedding preparations."

Grandfather's eyelids closed just a fraction. "Are you in the habit of assisting your staff with such tasks?"

He looked at his family to see if they might have something to say in support. "No, but… Well, it's a special occasion. I wondered if the staff had everything that they needed."

"How generous of you." This was sarcastic Eric, obviously.

"That's enough," the Duke began before clearing his throat pointedly. "This was supposed to be a chance for the boys to give their version of events, not weave more rope with which to hang themselves."

I could tell that Grandfather hadn't finished his questioning, but there would be time to talk to Stanislas on his own, and he chose to accept Lord Hinwick's intervention.

"Very well. What else can you tell me?" He held his cup to his lip but did not drink as his eyes travelled about the room to direct the question to each suspect.

Lord Ruskin had already finished one helping of coffee and refilled his cup. I have no idea how his insides weren't on fire. Either way, it did not look as though the drink was the restorative he required, as his face was quite pale, and he held one hand to his head as though bracing himself.

"The whole thing is ridiculous." Charles attempted to mount a vague defence, but there was little passion in it. "The thing that should rule every last one of us out of your investigation is the timing. We've had our whole lives to kill the old crone. Why would we do it now?"

Grandfather responded as though he hadn't even heard. "Fine, if you have no defence for your own behaviour, perhaps there is something you can say to clear your companions' names."

Charles seemed particularly enthused by this. "An excellent idea; I'll start." He took a moment to decide who most deserved his help. "Stan is the baby of the family and wouldn't hurt the lice in his hair if he could help it."

"That is quite the weakest form of evidence," Grandfather responded. "If such testimony were admissible in court, no one would ever be convicted."

"You didn't let me finish." For all the duplicity he had shown, his smile could still be quite charming. "It is not just that he is a good person, but Stanislas, more than any of us, believed that there was goodness in our mother. I refuse to accept that he could have killed her. He simply doesn't have it in him."

"Oh, yes?" It was my turn to show a little cynicism. "Just like Benjamin couldn't have stolen Joseph's silver cup in the Bible, I suppose?"

Grandfather leaned over to me on the sofa to whisper in my ear. "Benjamin didn't steal the cup. Joseph placed it among his possessions to see how his treacherous older brothers would react."

"Fair enough," I replied. "I'm happy that Stanislas is innocent. Who's next?" I didn't mean this, of course, but I was eager to move

100

on from my faux pas.

The Duke stood up from his chair. I would guess that he was only in his fifties, but his immense frame turned even the simplest movement into an impressively drawn-out process. He went to serve himself another drink, and Peterson rushed forward to assist him, only to receive a tut and an impatiently swatted hand for his trouble. With the tea poured, the Duke walked over to a set of doors which gave onto the garden and stood staring at the sky.

We all waited for him to speak. "I know that everything we've told you weighs against us. I'm aware that you have every reason to blame us for Begonia's death. But there is a difference between wishing she were absent from our lives and taking a weapon and murdering her." He turned from the window and the full strength of his gaze was directed upon us. "You must see that my children are incapable of such an act. We were prisoners in this house – rarely allowed out of Begonia's sight if we wanted to keep her favour. But there are worse forms of existence."

"Father is right." Eric wasn't nearly as persuasive and leaned back in his chair with his legs sticking out straight in front of him. "Come the funeral, we won't be crying, but that doesn't make us monsters."

The Duke propped himself up against the window frame, as though he suddenly lacked the strength to support his weight. "Someone else is responsible for what happened; you mark my words. So please find the killer, for all our sakes."

To be frank, I was quite moved by his entreaty. It was just the kind of thing that normally won me over in an investigation and, more often than not, such requests for help had turned out to be honest pleas, rather than some attempt to throw us off the killer's scent. Of course, there are exceptions to every rule, and I couldn't say for sure that the Duke was telling the truth or that he even knew what such a thing might look like. As Grandfather had already explained, he had more reason than anyone to kill the Duchess and, if he hadn't done it himself, he was just as likely to be lying to protect one of his sons.

I realised just then that there was another, even more salient point that I'd been ignoring. I may not be a mind reader, but from their shifting glances, I imagine that the brothers Fairfax were thinking something along these lines…

Dad might have a point. But if we didn't do it, who did? Hang on a moment! There's someone else in the room who looks extremely uncomfortable and has said very little.

At which point, all eyes swivelled to the fireplace, where Damian Ruskin was now massaging his temples to relieve the pain.

"Wait just one second." He had plainly realised the same thing that I had. "Now, listen to me. I'm not responsible for what happened."

"Then what are you still doing here?" Charles demanded.

"I fell asleep in the hydrangeas, just as any man could."

"They're Torenia fournieri." Grandfather tutted, but no one was listening to him.

Eric had straightened up in his chair and was evidently contemplating the possibility that their old family friend could have killed the Duchess. "You hated mother."

"So did you!" Ruskin shouted back.

"You said it on an hourly basis. If it weren't for her, you'd have married Cassie and none of this would have happened."

"If it weren't for the Duchess, Cassandra would never have been born." Grandfather was just being pedantic now.

Charles stalked around the coffee table with its glimmering silver tray and matching tea set. "You always said that Mummy ruined your life, and it's no surprise that you should want to stop the wedding. You're as guilty as a wolf."

You see, I told you it was an unoriginal simile.

"I barely remembered it was happening today," came Ruskin's poorly considered reply.

"That's not true." Stanislas was getting in on the act. Although he remained in his corner, he directed this accusation at the bounder at the hearth. "Sibyl told me last night that she'd bumped into you at the Royal Horseshoe Ball, and you'd convinced her to come here to, as you put it, 'mourn Cassandra's passing'."

The morbid nature of this comment was not lost on the audience, and I believe there was even a gasp of shock from the Duke.

"Is it true, Damian?" Charles was right next to him by now. "Did you finally get even with Mother?" He didn't give his friend the time to respond, and Ruskin looked more nervous by the second. "I may have considered her a black shadow over this family, but that doesn't mean we wanted you to stab her to death."

102

"I didn't kill her." Ruskin's voice reached a high note. "Anything I said to Sibyl was a joke to get her here. Speaking of which, where is she right now? I drove her here last night, so she must still be about somewhere."

I did feel a little silly not to have kept track – or even count – of our suspects, but this was surely a diversion on Ruskin's part and wouldn't get him off the hook.

"Tell me the truth," Charles continued in a quieter voice, but his anger was just as noticeable. "Did you kill her?"

Ruskin had avoided his challenger's gaze until now. To snuff out the fuse that Charles had lit, he took a step forward and looked him dead in the eyes. "No, Charles. No, I didn't kill your mother." I could barely hear his response, but it did the trick. The eldest Fairfax boy collapsed back into the armchair.

Except for the exaltation they had initially exhibited, it was the first real sign of emotion I'd seen from the brothers. Charles had exhausted himself in the confrontation and sat looking dazed. As a somewhat impartial observer, I kept bouncing between sympathy and suspicion towards every last one of them.

The resultant silence was interrupted by a loud knock on the door and, a moment later, Lovebrook entered with a curious look on his face.

"Lord Edgington?" He sounded just as polite as before. "My constables found a young woman in one of the bedrooms. She says she slept through all the commotion this morning and didn't wake up until now. I thought I'd better tell you that you've another suspect to add to the list."

CHAPTER SEVENTEEN

"How could you forget that there was another potential killer lurking about the place?"

I was frankly a little disappointed that he could blame me for this. "I didn't know she was still here. I assumed she left after I went to sleep last night."

"Which would be all the more reason that you mentioned her as a potential suspect."

The one thing saving my blushes was that Grandfather had taken me out into the hallway to tell me off, although this also made me feel like a seven-year-old boy.

"We have been rather busy this morning," I thought it fair to mention. "You're still wearing your pyjamas."

He looked down at his clothes and laughed. "So I am! You know, it quite escaped my mind that I hadn't taken the time to change. What must the inspector have thought of me?"

"You see, we've both forgotten things today. I think that makes us even."

He silently debated the equivalence of the two acts before shrugging with some resignation. "Well, fine. But are you certain there are no other possible suspects concealed about the place whom you have failed to mention?"

"I am certain." I was approximately fifty per cent sure.

"I won't find out later that the Duchess's brother is hiding in the drawing room?"

"Definitely not."

"And there's no way that the Duke's secret lover is really one of the maids?"

I had to consider the possibility. "It seems very unlikely, though we should perhaps put that to him when we speak again."

"Excellent thinking."

"Thank you."

It appeared we had reached something of a stalemate. I was expecting him to tell me what vital part of the case we should pursue next, whereas he was staring down at his silk pyjamas and sheepskin moccasins.

"Grandfather, there is one other thing we might have forgotten."

"Oh, yes? What's that?"

"The bridal party."

"The bridal party?" It took a few moments before his words had their desired effect. "The bridal party! My goodness! They'll be on their way here. If they set off early, they may already have arrived."

There was a clock on the wall above the telephone where Albert had called our mother the night before, and I realised that it had already gone eleven. "The service was due to start at midday. I'll call Cranley, just in case, but where was Cassandra supposed to have gone when she got here?"

Grandfather was clearly torn between this pressing detail and the state of his appearance. "I… I really don't know. You'll have to ask one of the staff." He began to ascend the second staircase, but then ran back down to me. "Call Cranley and, failing that, find Cassandra and your parents. I'll be upstairs getting changed."

He'd gone before I could complain that he'd told me to do the exact thing I had suggested. It was at times like this that it was worth having our dog with me. I did consider sticking my head out of a window to say, *Typical. He spends his whole time complaining that I don't have the right priorities when I put my hunger ahead of finding a killer, and then he runs off to change his clothes at a key moment in the investigation.* I suppose it was lucky that there were no windows in that long corridor, as anyone outside would have thought me a madman for attempting to initiate a conversation with a canine.

The operator connected me to Cranley Hall, but there was only a single footman left behind to guard the fort. He said that my parents, Cassandra and all of her friends had set off in convoy three hours earlier and had most likely already arrived. This was good news in one way as, should we manage to clear my idiot brother of murder, there would be someone on hand for him to marry. At the same time, if Cassie was now in Hinwick, that would make it my job to tell her of the bloody fate that had befallen her mother. It was hard to know which was less appealing: the bride not turning up to her own wedding or arriving to such terrible news.

I began the journey to find someone who knew anything about anything or, if I happened to bump into Todd, everything about everything. My route led me past the Great Hall, and I couldn't help peeking in at the destruction that Albert's cocktail-fuelled send-off had caused. There were still dirty glasses everywhere, and – what with the wedding they'd had to organise and everything else that had occurred that day – I think it was fair to spare the staff criticism when it came to general tidying.

The snooker cue that Charles had launched across the room was in pieces beside the wall, and the balls from his game with Eric were spread out around the billiard table. In fact, I could still smell the alcohol and cigars from the previous night, and that evocative mix triggered my recollection of the strange scenes I'd witnessed. I thought of Eric's unstinting smugness, Lord Ruskin's stumbling arrival, and Sibyl's clear hatred for the Duchess. I pictured poor distant Stanislas, rolling that old coin over and over again across his knuckles as his cruel brothers laughed and told their nasty stories. I thought of Albert in some adolescent state, shocked into silence by the gang of bigger boys amongst whom we'd found ourselves.

And that was when I saw it: Stanislas's coin. It was between two cushions on the sofa where he'd fallen asleep beside his brother. It didn't mean much to me at the time and I don't really know why I took it, but I dashed across that large space as though this would be the key to the case. What I did realise at that moment was that it was no ordinary pocket-burner. On one side was a laurel crown and, on the other, were the words 'Napoleon Empereur' and the likeness of the famous military leader. I had to conclude that Grandfather would have been able to link this to our case via references to the French revolution, Admiral Lord Nelson's death at the Battle of Trafalgar and, if he were feeling indulgent, Charles Dickens's "A Tale of Two Cities'. To me, though, it was just a coin, and I put it in my pocket to give it back to Stanislas the next time I saw him.

It was probably a good thing that the wedding was delayed. If not for the murder, we would have been heading to the church within the hour, and it didn't appear as though much was ready for the day. There were no flowers arranged beneath the canopy. The head table hadn't been set, and the staff looked very strained indeed.

"Would you happen to be looking for the bride and your parents, Master Christopher?" Todd was almost as clairvoyant as his master.

"Yes, I would happen to," I replied, a little impressed. "Or rather, yes."

"I believe they are in one of the cottages on the far side of the house. That is where Lady Cassandra has chosen to prepare for the wedding."

"I'm very grateful for the information," I told him then somewhat optimistically asked, "I don't suppose anyone has informed her of what happened during the night?"

He smiled his always welcome smile. "I'm afraid not, Master Christopher. In fact, you'll have to inform everyone that the latest the wedding ceremony can start is five o'clock. I had a discreet word with your father, and he's going to plead with the vicar at St Mary's, but I doubt it will do much good. However, I'm sure you'll do a fine job of breaking the news." Another thought occurred to him. "Oh, and your mother will be there for moral support."

He knew just what to say to make me feel better about the calamity we were facing. All a young detective really needs is his mother there to help when times get hard. Of course, this did mean I would have to break the news of her elder son's role in the case and Grandfather's subsequent attempt to hide Albert's involvement from the police. Oh well, life would be boring if it were too easy.

I don't mind telling you that I did not sprint to my next port of call so much as trundle. Delilah spotted me traversing the garden and, as she didn't have any suspects to manhandle (or, indeed, doghandle), she accompanied me to the run of cottages that were in a line parallel to the main house. Sure enough, I spotted my father's Bentley pulling away as I approached. I called to attract his attention, but he didn't hear me over the noise of the engine and merely returned my wave.

Not much further along the path was Cassie's Amilcar CGS – she shared my brother's fondness for sporty French vehicles. It was parked in front of the first cottage, which certainly wouldn't be classed as such by most people. With its clock tower and turreted spire, it was larger than some manor houses I'd visited, and I could see now why this was where the bride had chosen to ready herself for married life.

I peeked in through the front window to see my mother and several young ladies keeping Cassandra company. It was nice to watch her for a moment. She was so happy, so free of cares in her oblivious state that it took more than a little courage for me to step over the threshold.

The door was unlocked, and I realised as soon as I entered what this cottage must once have been. There were painted murals on the walls of clowns, dolls and teddy bears and, everywhere I looked, the furniture was a few sizes smaller than it should have been.

"Chrissy, you've come to play," my (if Albert was lucky) soon-to-be sister-in-law teased. "Welcome to my doll's house. Eric and I spent half our childhood in here. Mummy had it converted for me, but the boys tended to invade whenever they were bored. There's champagne open if you'd like a glass."

I was happy to let her chatter, as an older woman with a serious face and no neck attended to her hair. For as long as Cassie was talking, I didn't have to say anything. I'd practiced in my head what to say, but now that I was standing in front of her, I couldn't remember the words.

Her voice faded out, and she studied me for a moment. My expression must have done enough, as her face fell to match mine and she asked, "What is it? Not Albert? Please tell me Albert hasn't changed his mind?"

I suppose it was a natural conclusion to make. Especially after the telephone call he'd made late the night before. It was only logical to think he'd be having second thoughts after spending a night with her disagreeable family.

On this account, at least, I could set her mind at ease. "No, no. It's not Albert." Well, it was also Albert, but I didn't want to say anything about him just yet. "It's your mother. I don't know how to tell you this…" I had to swallow down my emotions then. I'd only known the Duchess a short time and, from everything her family had told me, she was not the most sympathetic character, but my insides were all in knots as I finally uttered the key sentence. "She was murdered in the night. The police are here and they're investigating what happened."

I had rather hoped that getting the bad news out in one quick burst might make it easier to bear. I don't think it turned out that way.

Cassie's hands shot to her face as though she wished to hide. After a brief fight for breath, she erupted in tears. My mother came to comfort her, and the line of girls in matching dresses stood by ineffectively, uncertain what to do to make it better.

"I don't understand." As she wept, Cassandra kept her eyes dead ahead. She was pleading for me to take it all back. "This doesn't make any sense. I know my mother could be a truly impossible woman sometimes, but who would have killed her?" At least, I think that's what she said; it was hard to know through the sobs. One thing I definitely caught was her closing question. "Why did it have to happen today?"

"Grandfather has all sorts of theories," I replied to reassure her, and instantly wished I'd kept my mouth shut. "Your brothers seem…" I abandoned this sentence just in time. "But it's more likely to be Lord Ruskin or Charles's girlfriend Sibyl. In fact, I very much doubt anyone in your family had anything to do with the wicked crime."

This was when her friends finally worked out how to help her. Like a tide, they lunged forward to wrap the bride, my mother and the unfortunately positioned hairdresser in a clothesline embrace. That was when I judiciously decided that the news of Albert's bloody fingerprint could wait until later.

"According to the vicar, the latest you can get married is five o'clock. That should give us plenty of time for us to find the killer and, unless the shadow hanging over the wedding is too much to…" I hadn't previously considered the possibility that a woman might not want to get married just hours after her mother had been murdered, but I certainly did now.

I caught sight of Cassie's tragic expression through the mangle of bodies and managed to say, "I'm sure everything will turn out well in the end. I'll report back if I have any news."

"Where's Albert, Chrissy?" she shouted, but I was already outside.

That was one question I was in no hurry to answer but, unlike the heart-stricken bride, my mother managed to escape from the house and caught up with me. "Christopher Prentiss, slow down."

I hated it when she used my full name. It was as if, with those two words, she threw a net over me, and I couldn't move.

"Hello, Mother. How are you?" This wasn't the most obvious question to ask at that moment, but nothing else came to mind.

"I was very well until two minutes ago when I discovered that Cassandra's mother had been murdered."

I should probably have turned around to her. If I'd just turned around and acted like there was nothing more to the story than the sudden murder of a megalomaniacal duchess, everything would have been fine.

"Christopher? What are you hiding?"

110

"Hiding? Me?" I think I whistled a few notes before giving in and telling her. "It's Albert. There was blood all over his bed and his fingerprint was found at the scene of the crime. The only reason that he isn't in handcuffs already is that Grandfather didn't tell the really very sympathetic inspector all the details."

I finally turned to look at her. I never lost sight of the fact that she was her father's daughter, but I'd forgotten how strong she could be. "I see. Well, in that case, you'll have to help your grandfather find the real killer, won't you?"

"Yes, Mother."

I could see she was considering the best course of action. Just occasionally, I spotted a look in her eyes that was so close to that of the great detective who'd raised her that I knew she was flipping through the same mental instruction manual that he himself often consulted.

She was surely wondering whether it would be best to come with me to aid the investigation or stay behind in the cottage to look after the bride. Her conclusion, when it came, was, *Too many cooks spoil the broth!*

She nodded and said, "I'll be here with Cassandra. Her friends have nothing but feathers for brains, and so it's probably better that I make sure she's all right."

"We'll call if we need you," I promised, and I was happy that Delilah stayed behind to keep her company. Mother took a deep breath and returned to a task that was more difficult than anything I would have to do that day.

CHAPTER EIGHTEEN

It was hard to know which way to turn or to whom we should be speaking. With the discovery of Lord Ruskin and Sibyl, the possibilities had only multiplied, and I had to wonder how big a pool of suspects we would have by the time the wedding took place… If, in fact, it was still happening, which was yet another thing I did not know.

I cut into the house through a well-stocked drinking room. I doubt that's the name by which anyone referred to it, but it was a room with stools, glasses, a wall covered in bottles of alcohol and little else, so it seemed an appropriate moniker.

Before I reunited with my grandfather, I decided that it would be a good idea to form my own opinions on the case. When he was with me, the pressure was often too much, and I was prone to spouting first-class nonsense. But when I had the time to consider all the evidence, I occasionally came to some interesting theories. The obvious culprit was Lord Ruskin, of course. He had the most apparent motive for killing the woman who had prevented his marriage to the girl he still loved. He had also changed his plans the night before Cassandra's wedding in order to be there at the house. My only reservation was that, in our past investigations, the obvious suspect so rarely turned out to be the killer that it seemed unlikely to be the case this time, either. Unless, of course, Ruskin being the most obvious suspect actually made him the least obvious and thus a possible killer after all…? It was all very confusing.

I would like to have ruled out Stanislas's involvement for the simple reason that he was a damned sight nicer than his brothers. However, there was something not quite right with him and it was the sort of *not quite right* for which juries just loved to convict odd characters in racy trials. His brother Charles seemed to have the wherewithal and resources to carry out the crime, but we'd yet to discover a compelling reason why he would have killed his mother. Eric was a nasty cove, and the Duke's behaviour had been unpredictable ever since we arrived. The question now was whether any of this was enough to prove who stabbed the Duchess in the back? I don't feel I need to add, *both literally and metaphorically* here, as it is so obvious it doesn't bear saying.

By the time I'd drawn the conclusion that I hadn't any conclusions to draw, I was back in the drawing room with Grandfather and the suspects. Sibyl had joined the party, no longer in the glittering dress she'd worn the night before but wrapped up in one of her boyfriend's perfectly white shirts and a pair of short trousers. She was so glamorous that, with her orchid bob and kiss curls, she looked rather stunning even in this strange get-up.

Grandfather was holding forth as I arrived. "I have given you all the chance to explain why I should rule you out as suspects, and I'm afraid to say that I remain unconvinced by your arguments."

"*Quelle surprise.*" Ruskin looked less peaky than before but was still leaning against the fireplace for support.

Grandfather ignored the troublesome fellow and continued with his speech. "Instead, I will interview you one at a time, starting with—"

"Charles," I interrupted, not entirely sure why I felt this necessary but convinced that it was the right choice.

"That is correct: Charles." Grandfather hadn't sounded particularly pleased with me for some time, so it was nice to hear that note of surprise in his voice.

Detective Inspector Lovebrook had been observing the scene, but Grandfather nodded to him, and he moved to escort our chosen suspect out of the room. I lingered for a moment to watch Sibyl's reaction. She had a relaxed, almost conceited air about her. She lounged in one of the armchairs looking out at the garden as though this were her house, and we were all intruding.

It seemed to me that we knew very little about this woman beyond her first name and the fact she was in some way intimate with the oldest Fairfax boy. If the Duke were to be the next to die, my money was on her and her boyfriend killing their way to the top of the chain. Murder is always easier in a team and, though she was utterly charming in many ways, her sideways glances and nervy stance spoke of underhandedness. Or, to put things in a slightly shorter form, I didn't trust her one bit.

I followed Grandfather, Lovebrook and Charles out of the room, but they had come to a stop and looked uncertain where to go next.

"Do you have any suggestions?" the inspector asked our suspect, who sighed and walked across the parlour to a door I had not yet peeked beyond.

I noticed that Charles cast a glance at his mother's body on the stairs as he went. It was hard to know whether he was checking that the Duchess was still dead or mourning her fate.

On the other side of the door was the library, of which I had so cleverly predicted the existence when interviewing the Duke. Like most rooms in Hinwick House, it was a bright, airy space. It didn't have the palatial splendour of Grandfather's immense and gothic sanctuary at Cranley Hall but was no less comfortable for it. If there was a theme to the room, that theme was burgundy. It was everywhere from the tied back curtains to the rug on the floor and the large squishy sofa and armchairs that dominated the centre of the room.

Mahogany bookshelves lined the walls. One of them was given over to cookery books, with special pride of place for the work of the Duchess's famous ancestor, Lady Diana Aster. I'd never heard of her, but the family were clearly proud of their connection, and she'd evidently earned a few inches of space on the library's shelves.

None of this held interest for Charles, who plopped himself down in a chair by the window, as though wishing to avoid us as much as possible. That smart butler, Peterson, was good at his job and arrived with more tea as soon as we sat down. I wondered whether they had some sort of bell that rang whenever someone entered a room in order to know when refreshments were required.

Charles was certainly a talented actor. He managed to utter sarcastic expressions without a hint of sarcasm. "How may I be of help today, detectives?"

Former Superintendent Edgington looked at Detective Inspector Lovebrook to see whether he wanted to ask anything, but the man was clearly in awe of the legend in our midst and signalled for my grandfather to speak.

"Perhaps we should start with what happened last night."

"Oh yes, perhaps we should." The light of the midday sun caught Charles's fair hair and gave him a faint halo, but there was no reason to believe this angelic transformation went any further.

"What time did you go up to bed?"

"I didn't."

It was hard to know what Grandfather was thinking as he selected the appropriate questions and manoeuvred from one point to another.

"You stayed in the Great Hall all night?"

"That's correct. Sibyl fell asleep against me. And I didn't like to wake her, so we stayed where we were." He cleared his throat as though wishing to apologise. "If the truth be told, we all had a bit too much to drink last night. I'm afraid that, in my family, we like a bottle of wine or three."

"So you were still there this morning when the body was found?"

He reached into his pocket to extract a cigarette from a slim silver case. "I didn't say that. I said that I didn't go to bed. As it happens, Sibyl woke me at around six and we retreated to my bedroom, but we did not go back to sleep."

"Was there anyone else still in the hall when you left?"

"Let me think." He put one finger to his lip to symbolise this process more visually. "Just Eric and Father, as far as I remember."

I suppose he must have been lulling our suspect into a false sense of security with these simple questions before changing tack in a heartbeat. It was quite stimulating to watch. "Did your mother know about your friend Sibyl?"

Charles had to pause for just a second and there was a look in his eyes as though he realised the need to adjust his approach in order to deal with the slippery detective. "No, she certainly did not. I tried to introduce them once, but she refused and forbade me from seeing the woman I love."

"What would the Duchess have done if she'd known you had ignored her demand?"

"She would have definitely disowned me, probably killed me and perhaps chopped me up into tiny pieces and thrown them in the lake."

Grandfather's hand slid along the arm of his chair as though it was moving of its own free will. "I thought as much, and yet, *the woman you love* is still here in the house."

"I doubt Mother will object anymore." Charles tapped the cigarette against the case but did not light it. "What you don't seem to have understood about my mother is that she was particularly controlling over my brothers and me. It wasn't merely that Cassandra knew how to act around Mother and so got her own way; she was never our mother's priority. Beyond dressing Cassie up in pretty dresses and showing her off in public, Mother was far less interested in her for some reason."

116

"And yet Lady Hinwick stopped Cassandra marrying Lord Ruskin. That would seem to contradict your theory."

"Not at all." He moved the white paper tube from one finger to another. "That might have been the only thing my mother did with which I agreed. Damian is too old, too drunk and too debauched for my dear little sister. He's penniless, too, and had I been the one making the decisions, I would have opposed the marriage."

Lovebrook had apparently found the confidence to ask a question. "It would appear that you don't have a particularly high opinion of Lord Ruskin. Is that correct?"

"I have a perfectly high opinion of him when it comes to organising a party or needing a friend with which to drink away my sorrows. Damian is a wonderful bachelor, but he'd have made a terrible brother-in-law."

I felt just a trifle left out so added something to the conversation. "How did Lord Ruskin come to ask for your sister's hand in marriage?"

Charles rolled his eyes as though to say, *I thought we were supposed to be talking about me.* "His father was a friend of the family. We saw a lot of him when I was a child. And then, after the war, he found himself enamoured of the beauteous ingenue whom we all adore. In his defence, he at least waited until she was old enough to have an opinion on the matter before popping."

"Popping?" My grandfather injected so much disapproval into the word I'm surprised he didn't just growl at the man.

"The question, dear fellow! He asked my sister to marry him just months before she left home."

"And what did Cassandra think of him?"

He looked across at my grandfather even as he answered me. "I imagine she saw him as a way out of this bedlam. To be frank, I would have married him myself if I could have escaped my mother's clutches."

Lord Edgington took the reins once more. "But the Duchess refused the match, and the engagement was called off for good."

"It was never on, in fact. Mother wasn't about to let Damian get his grimy hands on Cassie. I truly believe that she saw her daughter's only value as the marriage she would make. Damian could offer neither high rank nor a connection to a wealthy family, and so Mother thwarted his plans. To make up for Cassandra's disappointment – and avoid any tantrums – she allowed my sister to go to university."

Though the other detectives had taken a seat on the sofa, I stood behind them, watching the interview unfold. There was a point I considered making just then, but the words wouldn't come, and Grandfather said it for me.

"It's a little contradictory, don't you think? Your mother stood in your way at every turn but allowed your sister to wander off into the wide wild world to meet new people, learn new things and fall in love without her supervision."

"Not if you'd been listening to me, it's not." His skinny face grew even longer as his thin lips fell open. "She treated Cassie differently from the rest of us. By allowing my sister to move to Oxford, she could win her daughter's favour and simultaneously nettle her sons. She didn't just want our love, you know. She enjoyed controlling and stunting us. I think her ultimate dream was to breed a pack of Peter Pans who would follow her around like footmen and never say a word against her. That must be why she liked the servants so much; they always did as she told them."

"What of your father?" Lovebrook asked. "Didn't he object to your mother's cruel treatment? I hope you don't mind me saying, but she seems like something of a despot."

"I don't mind you saying that at all, but Father would never have allowed such a slight in her presence. He may love us – he may even like us – but he was not the man to stand up to her. He is a great believer in the best sort of life being a quiet one. He might have disapproved of the way Mother acted, but he liked his cigars, hunting trips and expensive cognacs too much to say no to her. In fact, he became something of a disciple. Without him, we wouldn't have fallen in line so readily."

"That is very interesting, and I appreciate your candour." Grandfather sat waiting for whatever came next. There was an amiable smile on his face and his head was angled curiously, but his lips remained pursed shut.

"Listen, I know what you must be thinking," Charles began, though I doubted he did. "I don't blame you for imagining that I wanted rid of Mother because I absolutely did. When she allowed Cassie to go to Oxford, that was a direct rebuke to me. I'd begged her to send me to university. I had dreams of becoming an engineer and changing the world. I wanted to build bridges, trains and aeroplanes, but she simply

118

said, 'no'. All I wanted was a chance to make something of myself in my own way, but that tyrant told me that I had everything that I needed here and, if I really wanted to make a life of my own, I could do it without her money."

"She was a rotter," I said out loud, almost without realising.

·"Thank you." He had waved the cigarette around so much by now that tobacco had flown out, the paper was squeezed, and one half was now at an angle. He lit it all the same, and the end glowed as he took a puff. "Normally when I tell my sad tale, my friends tell me that I should have left home and never looked back, but that's easier said than done."

Grandfather maintained that same ingenuous expression. "So you stayed here at Hinwick House. You bided your time, knowing that her reign couldn't last forever and then – would you believe it – someone came along and did you a favour."

"Yes, something like that." Charles was not intimidated by his insinuations. "You do realise that if my father or one of my brothers is responsible for what happened, there is no way you will catch them."

"Oh, no?"

His dangling cigarette waggled as he spoke. A tiny rain of ashes fell onto the carpet in front of him, turning from red to black as it tumbled. "Of course not. Just think about it. If one of us is to blame, we will have spent years planning how to get away with the crime. We would have to be complete ignoramuses to fail now."

"And yet, if one of you is the killer, you made a mistake the moment you plunged the knife into the Duchess's back."

"Why do you say that?" He seemed less certain of himself and kept his eyes locked onto his inquisitor.

"Because you killed her with a detective in the house. (The greatest detective Britain has produced in the last fifty years.)" He didn't actually say that second sentence, but he was probably thinking it.

"Or perhaps we needed you here to fall for our trap. Perhaps you are the person who will keep the real killer out of gaol."

Lovebrook and I remained silent as the two warriors battled. Charles was a smooth sort of fellow, and clever with it. For his part, Grandfather made no attempt to hide just how much he enjoyed sparring with such an opponent.

"Perhaps." He crossed one leg over the other. "Perhaps you will be the criminal geniuses who finally get the better of former Superintendent Edgington, the bane of London's criminal underclass." He actually said all that out loud!

Charles finally looked away. "Has it entered your mind that we're not actually guilty? Have you even considered the possibility that your grandson upstairs or the bounder Damian Ruskin will turn out to be the culprits?"

Lovebrook's eyes twitched at the mention of my brother, and I had to wonder whether he was more suspicious of Albert's involvement than I'd initially assumed.

"Dear, dear." Grandfather tutted loudly. "It sounds as though you've overlooked one suspect who had the motive and opportunity to kill your mother on the stairs last night. Tell me, how did you meet your little girlfriend?"

"My *little girlfriend's* name is Sibyl Podence."

Lovebrook moved forwards in his seat at this moment. "*The* Sibyl Podence?"

"The very same."

"Well, I never." Even Grandfather was impressed.

Inevitably, I would be the only one who didn't know this essential fact. "Who's Sibyl Podence?"

"Peter Podence's wife," Charles partially explained, and before I could ask who Peter— "You must know the story. He was as rich as a Tsar, made his money in copper or some such and married a much younger woman."

"And that woman was Sibyl." This was a nice, easy sort of mystery that I was more than capable of solving. "What happened to the happy couple?"

"That would depend on who you ask." Lovebrook still looked taken aback by the revelation. "The prosecution—"

"Prosecution!?" Just about everything surprised me that day.

"Yes, the case went to trial. The prosecution said that she had been poisoning him over months before the man died. They claimed that his body was riddled with morphine. The defence, on the other hand, said that he was merely an old man with a fondness for poppyseed bread. They said he died of natural causes and Sibyl had been a loving wife to him and stayed at his bedside to his final day."

120

"And what does Sibyl say?"

On hearing my question, everyone turned back to Charles. "You'll have to ask her yourself. I can't possibly speak on her behalf."

Grandfather couldn't let such a juicy discussion pass without comment. "The case was thrown out of court, and the widow Podence inherited a fortune. And now she's here at the scene of another suspicious death."

"That's right." Charles Fairfax was apparently quite amused by the scandal of the thing. "Though I very much doubt that stabbing is her style. She's rather a lazy type. I can't imagine her skulking about in the darkness to jump out on someone. Poison is a far more efficient way to get rid of one's enemies."

"Is she in love with you?" Grandfather had mastered the art of the hard stare and employed a particularly penetrating one at this moment to put the fear of God into the man.

It might have worked for a moment or two, but Charles soon recovered. "She may well be, but you're talking to the wrong person. Half of these questions would be better put to her."

Grandfather was impervious to our suspect's deflections. "Yes, I think that makes a lot of sense. If Sibyl is in love with you, and you've already told us that your mother would not have tolerated her presence in your life, it wouldn't have been a terrible idea for her to kill the Duchess. Poison would be off the menu, of course, as everyone would have known she was responsible. As you say, a dagger is not her style, thus making it the perfect weapon with which to throw off suspicion."

"For goodness' sake, man. Why don't you talk to her yourself instead of bothering me with this infernal chatter?" He put his hand to his head then, and I believe that his alcoholic exertions from the night before were still haunting him.

Lord Edgington remained perfectly calm even as Charles frothed. "I'm sorry. Perhaps I didn't make myself clear. It makes sense a lot of sense that, if Sibyl Podence was responsible for the murder, you were her accomplice."

This sent Charles to his feet as though someone had lit a fire under his chair. "I thought you were supposed to be a master thinker. Where's your evidence? What could possibly suggest that I was involved in my mother's death?"

I had the sense that Grandfather was willing him to ask this very question.

"Aside from the fact that you and your brother Eric celebrated the discovery of her bloodied body as though you'd just made a boundary in cricket, Sibyl was still here this morning."

Charles didn't have anything to say to this. He puzzled over the significance for a few moments but would not respond.

"If you didn't want your mother to discover the nature of your relationship with the woman, what was she still doing here?" Grandfather's voice was so rich and so resonant it seemed to fill the room. "The only conclusion I can make is that you knew your mother was dead, and no longer had to worry about her discovering your secret."

I thought that our suspect would yell and complain again, but he was smarter than that. He could tell that Grandfather had caught him out, and any explanation he might offer would sound like an excuse. So, instead of railing against the truth as the great detective had presented it, he fell back into his chair and would not utter another word.

CHAPTER NINETEEN

When we left Charles behind in the library, I was tempted to fire off a list of my usual questions. You know the sort of thing: *Is that it, Grandfather? Do you really think that Charles and Sibyl worked together to kill the Duchess? Can we think about lunch now?*

I'd learnt my lesson from all the other cases in which he'd been too clever for our suspects and left them speechless. I knew that the eldest Fairfax boy's reaction was not a confession of guilt so much as the consequence of a run-in with Lord Edgington. If he wasn't the man we were hunting, he was back where we had left him, thinking, *how on earth did he tie me up in knots like that?*

And so I didn't ask any such precipitous questions, but Detective Inspector Lovebrook did. "Is that it then? Do you really think that Charles and Sibyl worked together to kill the Duchess?"

We came to a stop a few yards from where the victim lay. A police surgeon or what have you had inspected the scene but, so far, no one had come to remove the body.

"No, I do not believe that is the most likely outcome." Grandfather was always more diplomatic with other people than he was with me.

"But the Widow Podence is famous. Even though nothing was proved against her, there were all sorts of doubts. Perhaps she got a taste for killing and couldn't stop." For all his calm and composure, it was nice to see that the officer was just as naive as I was.

"Or perhaps the press blew the trial out of all proportion, and an unfortunate young woman was vilified for something she never did."

Lovebrook looked a little disappointed. "So then you don't—"

Before he could finish this thought, a shout went up from the morning room and we rushed back to see the main congregation of ne'er-do-wells. What we didn't expect to find was the bride-to-be, yelling her lungs out.

"I want to know what he's doing here." She addressed her father, but it was obvious to whom she referred.

"Calm down, Cassandra," was all the Duke could think to say, and his typically passive nature came to the fore. "Damian is an old friend of the family, as you know."

"How can I calm down? Mother is lying dead on the stairs and Lord Ruskin just happened to turn up at the house shortly before she was murdered. Send him away, Papa."

Ruskin was still propping up the mantlepiece, still looking pale and tired. I watched him as Cassie talked, and he couldn't even look at the woman he claimed to love. His gaze remained on the unlit fire, and he didn't respond to any of her entreaties.

"I can't do that, my love," her father attempted once more. "Damian is a suspect, just like all of us. The police will not allow him to leave."

Seeing that she would have no luck with her father, she turned to Ruskin at this point and, with fire in her eyes, demanded, "Why are you here on my wedding day? How could you think that anyone would want you here today?"

His gaze still wouldn't shift from the cold hearth, but he shook his head as though he was the one who deserved our pity. I really didn't know what to think of the man. He was old enough to settle down with a family and devote his free time to gardening or the odd spot of fishing. Instead, he was made up like a rather rumpled peacock, chasing after a girl who was young enough to be his daughter. I'm sure I sound terribly close-minded when complaining about such things, but I simply didn't like the chap.

"I don't know what I was thinking," he finally mumbled, and I thought that Cassandra might hit him.

"Lord Ruskin," Lovebrook intervened, "I believe it would be better for you to go into the room next door until we have time to interview you."

His grim countenance barely reacted to the detective's suggestion, but he marched straight past us out of the room. Grandfather watched the events without reaction, much as a spectator at an opera sits mutely as the soprano sings her songs of heartache.

Cassandra had achieved her first objective but would not rest there. "Thank you, Inspector. Now, where's Albert?" She looked at her two brothers before turning to me. "Chrissy? Where is the man I'm due to marry?"

I was rather hoping that my mother would have broken the bad news. "Well, he's up in Grandfather's bedroom."

"Because…?"

124

"Because we found his fingerprint in the blood on the handrail beside the Duchess's body, and we've kept him away from the evidence until we can prove who really killed the Duchess."

If the bride hadn't been distraught before this point, she certainly was now. "How can this be happening? I thought my wedding day would be a celebration, not a disaster."

"Wait a moment. His fingerprint?" The fact of our obstruction was finally clear to Lovebrook. "You didn't mention that, Lord Edgington. The boy should be in handcuffs already. This doesn't seem right at all."

"Exactly," Eric shouted across the room. "This whole situation is ridiculous. The killer's identity was evident from the very first moment. Albert Prentiss should be locked up in a cell. He will not be marrying my sister."

Cassie fell back onto a sofa as though someone had pushed her over. I don't know whether she heard anything after this moment, or the shock had overwhelmed her, but she sat staring into the void of her future, which had previously seemed so clear.

I could tell that my grandfather was unhappy to see the case spiral out of his control. It was a rare situation which forced him to go on the defensive. "What's ridiculous is the idea that my grandson would have murdered the mother of the bride. It's hardly the perfect wedding present now, is it?"

Lovebrook at least seemed willing to listen to both sides of the argument and turned to the Fairfaxes with a point to raise. "Lord Edgington is right. If Albert's the killer, why did he do it?"

Self-satisfied Eric couldn't summon a motive that quickly, and his father looked just as blank. I doubt that I was the only person who was surprised to see Stanislas think of something where the others had failed. He stepped forward to stand in front of his quick-tempered brother. "At dinner last night, Mother called Albert outside to talk to him. He was particularly quiet afterwards, and I can imagine what she said to him." He spoke with a note of reluctance, as though he had no wish to incriminate my brother but felt compelled to tell the truth. "I believe she told him what he would become if he married into our family."

"Oh yes, and what was that?" The detective kept his eyes fixed on the strange fellow as Stanislas stared out of the window in his usual listless manner.

"Another young man to add to her collection. You see, this was her doll's house, and we were her toys. She just loved to take us out and play with us. I have no doubt that she explained the choice Albert had. It's the only reason she agreed to the wedding in the first place. Either he could marry the woman he clearly adores and fall under mother's sway, or the wedding would be cancelled. That was the power she had over him, and if I know anything about my mother, I believe that she used it."

I'd heard this story from my brother himself, but I still found it hard to stomach.

The inspector looked conflicted. "I'll talk to Albert," he said and was about to fly from the room when the Duke approached him.

"Do you really think it is necessary for us to stay in this room? To tell you the truth, I think we'd all like a change of clothes. It's not as though we can interfere with anything now that the scene of the crime has been examined."

"Very well." Lovebrook seemed happy to accept this, but Grandfather had something to whisper in his ear. Whatever was relayed, it ended with the inspector saying, "Change your clothes and hand them over to one of the officers at the door for forensic inspection."

With this done, he marched from the room, and we wouldn't see him again until another catastrophe had occurred.

CHAPTER TWENTY

The suspects dispersed about the house like flies and, for the first time that day, I pictured my brother swinging from the gallows at Wandsworth Prison. I must admit that it terrified me, and I could no longer contain my fears.

"It's a calamity," I complained. "Nothing has gone to plan, and the family has turned against us."

Grandfather was pacing the length of the morning room, and I doubt he needed me to pile criticism on top of everything else he was enduring. "The circumstances are not what I would like them to be; I will admit that. But calamity is a terribly strong word. This is a mere disaster." Our perilous position had, at the very least, provided him with a chance to be pedantic.

"What can we do now? Albert's for the police station. Cassandra's heart is broken. There's a dead duchess on the stairs, a woman who may have murdered her husband is loitering about the place, and every last suspect had a reason to kill the Begonia Fairfax."

"Yes, it's exciting, isn't it?" This was not the reaction I expected.

"Grandfather, can you please take this more seriously?"

He seemed quite frantic as he buzzed about the place. "I am never less than serious, Christopher. I thought you would know that by now."

I perched on the arm of a chair, as we clearly weren't going anywhere just yet. "In which case, will you tell me how to make sense of anything that has happened so far?"

He stopped dead still and, his eyes on me alone, asked a key question. "Do you believe that your brother could be to blame for the killing?"

"No, of course not." I was about to mount a defence of Albert's name, but he spoke once more.

"In which case, how did his fingerprints end up at the scene of the crime?"

"Well, that's obvious, isn't it?" I thought this was true at first, then swiftly changed my mind. "Actually, no it's not. I haven't a clue."

"Then what about the Duchess's pocket watch that we found on her body. Have you considered why she would have been carrying it at that time of night?"

"I have indeed." I was rather proud of this fact.

"And what was your conclusion?"

"I concluded that I hadn't the faintest idea why she was carrying it."

It came as something of a shock that he approved of my response. "Very good, boy. That is just the position to take on the matter. I'm pleased with your work."

"Smashing," I replied, as what else could I say?

"I find it highly improbable that Lady Hinwick would have picked up her pocket watch when called from her bedroom. It seems likely, therefore, that the killer placed it on her body to suggest she was murdered at midnight, when it was really either earlier or later than that."

"So wouldn't that have benefitted Lord Ruskin?"

"How do you mean?"

"Well, I saw him leave the house before midnight and he claimed to be asleep outside all night. Perhaps he wanted to suggest the murder happened later than it did."

He considered the possibility, but I knew what his answer would be. "No, I'm afraid I doubt that could be the solution. Shifting the time by an hour or so when the suspect is still close at hand is hardly proof that he couldn't have committed the crime."

"And what about more generally?" I asked. "Do you know yet who is our most likely culprit?"

He began his pacing once more. "Sibyl Podence might know something, but I very much doubt that she was the one to plunge the knife into the Duchess. We still have to talk to Eric and Stanislas, and Cassandra may know something significant, but it's Lord Ruskin who most intrigues me. Had you heard of him before this weekend?"

"No. Should I have?" I thought that he might turn out to be a popular bête noire of the newspapers, or perhaps an unpunished killer like Sibyl Podence. I was wrong on both counts.

"He's a war hero. He flew countless missions over the channel and was famed for his skill behind the controls of his Sopwith Camel. It's rather sad to see the state of him these days."

Nothing made sense to me just then. "So does that make him more or less likely to have killed Cassie's mother?"

"I don't know." He stopped moving again and took a moment to consider the question. "He killed people for a living throughout the war and is known to have shot down a great number of enemy aircraft. Perhaps such an experience left him numb to violence. Perhaps he felled the Duchess just as he would a German flying ace. It's impossible to say."

"Well, there is one way." I was out of the door before he could respond.

Situated between the morning room and the library, there was one final door that led off the parlour. I anticipated that we would find Lord Ruskin in the drawing room and, to my great surprise, another one of my guesses proved correct.

At the risk of sounding like the brochure of a home decorator, I can tell you that the drawing room was larger and grander than any other we'd visited. It had a collection of paintings of past monarchs, several tall stands with huge Chinese vases set upon them, and two immense chandeliers dangling over the sofas in the middle of the room. It was quite pretty.

Ruskin was lounging across one of a trio of immense and immensely comfortable sofas. He was still clutching his head and looked as though he wished there were no such thing as alcohol in the world. Just as we arrived, Peterson appeared behind us with a cup of coffee for our suspect, which he placed on the table in front of him.

"Oh, hurrah," Ruskin said in that toffee-nosed voice of his. "Refreshments and entertainment. I must have been a good boy to deserve this." He sat up to welcome his drink rather than us. "And to what do I owe the pleasure, gentlemen? Have you found the *corpus delicti*? The key piece of evidence that will seal my fate?"

"For the moment, we will make do with the corpus itself," Grandfather replied almost as sniffily before taking a seat on the sofa opposite our suspect. "My first question for you echoes one that the understandably irate bride voiced a few minutes ago. What are you doing here?"

"Me?" he said, raising the cup to his lips. "Why, I'm merely in need of a strong drink after a long night. And, oh my goodness, that is strong! I've drunk less bitter wormwood liqueurs than that." He shook his head to get rid of the taste, then pouted and drank it down all the same. "I like it!"

Grandfather was content to observe the man as he recovered from his strong (not to mention hot) beverage. It seemed to rush through his body like a snifter of alcohol, and I was glad that I was not the one drinking such a substance.

"Would you care to answer the question now?" Lord Edgington asked after a good long silence had passed.

Apparently invigorated by his libation, Ruskin shot to his feet for a silent turn about the room. I was far less patient than my companion and wanted to shout at him to get on with it. In time, he returned to his seat, and there was a light in his eyes that hadn't been present before.

Sitting up ever so straight, he made a to-do of clearing his throat before finally replying. "What was the question?"

"Why are you here, man? What made you leave the Horseshoe Ball and drive two hours from London in order to intrude upon the preparations for the wedding of a woman who rejected you?"

This touched a nerve. "Cassandra did not reject me." The words rose up in one great burst of anger, which soon subsided for an explanation to take its place. "She never had the chance to reject me. Begonia made sure to stand in the way of love."

"So you believe that you were in love?"

Ruskin's face had become quite stern, and I could see how much the topic affected him. "I loved Cassandra Fairfax from the first moment I saw her, and she would have married me if her mother hadn't been such a despicable harridan. If you're looking for a suspect, I am a fine pick; I despised the woman from my very core. Unfortunately for you, I did not kill her."

He seemed less a figure of fun than he had all day. There was something rather sad about him, in fact. The fading lothario – a war hero, no less – who had passed his prime.

I must have taken pity upon him as, when I asked a question of my own, it was in a less hostile tone than my grandfather had adopted. "We heard that Cassandra would have married anyone to escape her mother's control. Would you really have wanted a union forged out of desperation rather than love?"

"You can think what you like, boy. I choose to believe that our love was true." He turned away from us and stared at the mirror above the fire.

"You still haven't answered my question, Lord Ruskin." Even

130

Grandfather had softened his approach. "Why did you come here?"

"I came because last night was possibly the seventeenth Royal Horseshoe Ball I have attended, and I found it terribly depressing. All those young people full of life and love and me all alone."

"Then why did you persuade Sibyl Podence to come with you?"

He looked up at the ceiling for a moment as though this question was beneath him. "To make sure that I didn't crash the car, I suppose. I'd already had a lot to drink and thought her conversation would help distract from the boredom of the drive."

Grandfather smiled at this. "It seems that it did the trick then." He needed a few seconds before introducing his next point.

I can only imagine that he was unsure what to make of the man. Ruskin really was a bundle of contradictions and, though he was still the most likely killer, I genuinely hoped he was innocent. With this in mind, I decided that I would try to be more cynical as, if he were guilty, this whole tragic act could have been put on for our benefit.

"Did you really think that it was a good idea to come here?"

This provoked a burst of laughter. "I didn't think at all. Alcohol tends to have that effect on me. Back before the war, I never used to drink, and I was a better man for it. But I have to do something these days to help me forget all that I witnessed; a good old bout of stupefaction usually does the trick."

"You mean to say that you don't remember your actions last night?" I asked, thinking this might bridge the gap between the almost admirable, shabby figure in front of me and the violence of the scene in the parlour.

"You could put it like that. But then again, I've been drunk any number of times and never done anything terrible before."

We must have strayed from the topics that Grandfather wished to address as he now seized the reins of the conversation. "You've known the Fairfax family for some time. Would it surprise you if one of them was responsible for the Duchess's murder?"

Whatever good the coffee had initially done, its effects appeared to be wearing off as Ruskin was slower at answering by now. "The... the boys, you mean? Oh... Yes, I suppose it would. All three of them are well-meaning types. They've had a thousand opportunities to kill their mother before and not taken them. Waking her up in the middle of the night to do so seems a bit odd, if you ask me."

"How do you know someone woke her up?"

"Well, I…" Once he'd got going with an answer, he was fine, but it was beginning to take longer with each one he was asked. "I… I don't. All I know is that she was in bed when I arrived, and so I assumed that was the case." A look of some fear appeared on his face for a moment, but it wouldn't stay for long. "As you are someone who uses logic on a daily basis in your job, you surely can't condemn me as a murderer for doing the same thing."

I couldn't begin to understand why, but he smiled broadly then. It was quite excessive and certainly did not fit the subject we were discussing. He had become rather restless as well, and his feet were shifting from side to side in quick, fidgety movements.

"Returning to the Fairfaxes, I believe it was the Duke with whom you were originally acquainted. Is it possible that—" Grandfather had noticed the man's strange behaviour. "Lord Ruskin, is everything all right?"

The smile on his face suggested that life was wonderful, but his eyes told a different tale. "I'm… Sorry, I'm… I don't know what to say. I'm not quite feeling myself." He got up at this moment and commenced another tour of the grand salon. "I really must have overindulged last night; this is not the 'Monday head' from which I tend to suffer."

"Should I call for some water, Grandfather?" I had the definite feeling that this was more than a mere hangover. I'm not a great drinker myself, but I'd seen such states in certain family members, and this was quite different.

Lord Edgington looked just as worried as I sounded and, instead of answering, he ran from the room, shouting, "Peterson, Peterson, where are you?" I went to poor Ruskin and took his arm to guide him back to the sofa.

"No," he objected. "I need to move. The muscles all over my body feel like they're being pulled at both ends."

I supported him as he performed the necessary exercise, the rictus grin still present on his weathered face.

"Peterson, Lord Ruskin is ill," I heard my grandfather say out in the parlour, as evidently the sprightly butler had appeared. "Go to the medical cabinet and look for tannic acid, or anything containing bromide of potassium. You may find it in headache powders. And quick about it! A man's life is at stake."

The elderly sleuth was back with us in a moment, by which time Lord Ruskin no longer had the strength to stand. He fell back onto the sofa and stretched his whole body out in the most curious way.

"His shoes, Christopher." Grandfather had noticed it too. "Remove his shoes. That may ease his pain a little."

I did as instructed and unlaced the man's black leather Oxfords. With them off, I could see that the muscles in his feet were curling up in the most unnatural fashion. The soles of his feet were bent in on themselves to resemble Marble Arch.

"What is it, Grandfather? What's happening to him?"

He had sat down beside the poor chap and was peering into his eyes as Ruskin cried out in a tormented moan.

Lord Edgington was quick with a diagnosis. "Strychnine poisoning. I've only seen the after-effects before, but I'm fairly certain that's what it is. Someone must have put it in his coffee to disguise the bitter flavour. The question is whether the killer knew what he was doing and added enough to end a life."

Ruskin's head jerked in our direction then and, though he evidently couldn't form the words, I knew what he was thinking. Whatever he'd caught of our conversation, the inference was clear. *Poison? Is this how I go?*

If Hinwick House's medical cabinet was anything like the one back at Cranley, it would contain half a pharmacy's worth of bottles, sachets and jars but, before five minutes were up, Peterson returned with what we needed. The man really was a competent butler.

"I brought bromide of potassium, just as you asked, M'Lord." He was carrying a silver tray with a jug of water, a glass and a number of small white packets from a chemist.

"That's good," Grandfather replied, and he tore open the first packet of headache medicine to pour it into a glass of water.

Even as we were speaking, I heard a shout from the parlour. I was fairly confident it was the inspector's voice, but it was drowned out by the beat of heavy footsteps on the floor above. One thing I know for certain is that the next words out of his mouth were, "Stop, do you hear me? Get away from there!"

CHAPTER TWENTY-ONE

There was nothing I could do for Lord Ruskin and so I ran out to see what had caused the commotion. By the time I left the drawing room, Lovebrook was jumping down the stairs over the body and was about to enter the corridor into the Victorian wing of the house when he came to a sudden stop.

"What happened?" I called as I ran over.

"Someone was interfering with the Duchess's body." He was peering down the dim corridor as though he still hoped to spot the unidentified figure. "He must have taken a turn off here."

"Or shot up the other staircase," I suggested, and opened the first door off the corridor. "Quick, he may be hiding somewhere."

We each took one side of the corridor and briefly searched a silver room, a smoking room and several small spaces reserved for the staff. There was no sign of whomever the inspector had seen, and so we came to the second staircase that led up to the main wing of bedrooms.

The inspector drew level with me but looked hesitant to go any further. "I don't understand what good it would do anyone to meddle with the corpse at this stage. The police surgeon has come and gone. There are no secrets left to hide, bar whatever the coroner finds in the post-mortem."

"Perhaps the killer didn't know that," I replied as I began the ascent. A thought occurred to me, and it seemed a little strange that my companion from the police had failed to identify the man. "What was he wearing?"

"A long black cloak that covered his head," he explained. "I don't mind telling you, Christopher, I am quite in the dark." This seemed rather too apposite, considering the shadowy stairs we were navigating. "I originally thought the killer had to be one of the Fairfax boys. Soon after that, it seemed Ruskin was the obvious choice because of his connection to Lady Cassandra. Then I discovered that much of the evidence pointed towards your brother, but I was talking to him when someone came to rifle the poor Duchess's pockets. It doesn't make a jot of sense."

"Unless the person on the stairs wasn't the killer," I replied, before realising that I'd just reopened a path to Albert's guilt. "Or rather... I mean..."

We'd reached the top of the stairs and were walking along the corridor where we'd interviewed the Duke what now felt like many hours earlier. There were bedrooms on either side and a window at the far end through which the sunshine poured into the house. The inspector knocked on the first door and there was a grunt from inside.

He peeped in, then murmured, "My apologies, my lord," as evidently the Duke was there, and he was unhappy with the intrusion. "It couldn't be him," the officer explained in a whisper. "Whoever I saw was a little more..." He searched for a term that would not inadvertently imply that Lord Hinwick was overweight. "...agile."

I looked in the dead woman's bedroom, but it was empty, and so I knocked on the next door along. Eric responded with an angry, "What do you want?" I took this as an invitation to come inside, which was definitely a mistake. I had no interest in seeing the man's bare buttocks, but that's what happened.

"Oh, I'm... dreadful... I mean, dreadfully sorry."

He grabbed a pillow for his own discretion. "What the deuce are you doing in here?"

"My apologies, Eric. I was just looking for..." I'd quite forgotten what I was doing there and could only count my blessings that he'd been facing away from the door as I entered. "...for the killer!"

From the look on his face, I could tell that he wanted to throw something at me. To be perfectly honest, I wouldn't have blamed him.

The inspector was already in conversation with someone in the opposite room when I nipped back out to the corridor.

"Charles is in the bath," a woman's voice replied.

"Has he been in there long?" Lovebrook asked.

"Why? Is Scotland Yard policing water usage now?" Sibyl's tone was typically sharp.

"Don't worry, madam. I apologise for disturbing you." He closed the door and shook his head despondently. "This is getting us nowhere. Short of finding one of them with the cloak wrapped around them, what are we hoping to discover?"

There were several more rooms to inspect, but I agreed with his assessment. The first was empty and, from the look of things, it must have once belonged to Cassandra, though I couldn't imagine she had slept there very recently. From what I'd heard, she and Albert had been joined at the hip – or at least the hand – ever since they'd met at university in Oxford. She'd moved to her own apartment there the previous year, and we knew she had little interest in returning home.

We inspected several guest rooms before the corridor snaked around to a lone suite set away from the others. The inspector knocked, and Stanislas was the only member of the family who seemed unflustered by our intrusion. He was sitting at a small desk reading a book that looked to be some sort of military history. It certainly fitted with the rest of the room. There were old sabres, pistols, tricorn hats and any amount of army memorabilia, though I'd seen no sign in the house of anyone in the family having served in the armed forces. Stanislas and his brothers were just a little too young to have fought in the war.

"Is there something I can do for you?" he asked in his usual slow, faltering manner.

"Someone interfered with your mother's body," Lovebrook answered truthfully. "Did you hear anything?"

"Not a sound." He looked surprised but not disturbed by the explanation. "But then I don't tend to hear much of what goes on from here."

"Thank you for your time." This was all the inspector had to say on the matter, and we left the room once more. "Perhaps it wasn't someone from the family," he said to himself as much as me. "I should have stationed an officer with the body instead of at the door. If we hadn't had to deal with the guests at the same time as everything else…" He didn't finish that sentence but seemed genuinely upset by the decisions he'd made.

As Grandfather's assistant, I knew exactly how he felt. "Perhaps we should search their bedrooms for the cloak. If you tell them it's necessary, they surely can't refuse."

We'd reached the main wing now, and something caught my eye through the window at the end of the corridor. It was not the guests who were milling around the seats and tables on the lawn, or my beloved friends from Cranley Hall who were still finding tasks to keep themselves busy over an hour after the service was supposed to have started – it was a small pile of black clothing just beyond the perimeter of the house.

The inspector saw it too and shouted across to one of his uniformed officers. "Grigson? Did you see anyone at this window recently? Did you see who threw out that cloak?"

Grigson was as much use as a one-legged chair, but at least he collected the cloak from the garden as evidence.

"Well, we found the cloak." Lovebrook's expression turned yet glummer. "For all the good it does us."

"There's something you don't know," I told him. "While you were talking to my brother, someone put strychnine in Lord Ruskin's coffee. He drank the whole cup down while we were interviewing him."

"That puts your brother in the clear, then."

I managed to resist saying, *unless he had an accomplice.* I sometimes think that my grandfather had trained me too well; I simply couldn't ignore a potential solution to a case!

"Ruskin was still alive when I left, and Grandfather was attending to him."

We were already walking in that direction, and Lovebrook had a confession to make. "I didn't say it earlier, but it's not just your grandfather I've followed in the press. There was an article about you in the Hue & Cry."

This was news to me. "I'm sorry, the Hue & Cry?"

"Yes, you know, the Police Gazette. It was only a short piece about the future of policing in Britain, but someone in Scotland Yard obviously thinks highly of you. I wish I'd had your abilities at such a young age."

I felt a little proud to hear a real officer talk about me in complimentary terms. "I'm sure you wouldn't be so impressed if you'd heard the nonsense I spouted on our early cases. I was as green as a leaf."

"We all have to start somewhere. The way I heard it, you were just as much to thank for apprehending the Condicote killer as your grandfather. By all accounts, you prevented a great injustice to boot."

"I wouldn't go that far."

It was lucky that we'd made it to the drawing room. I was so red by this point I could blend in with the drapery. Inside the room, it was clear that Ruskin was in a lot of pain, but at least he was still breathing.

"Did the medicine do the trick, Grandfather?"

The old wizard was still checking the patient, but his face was not so grave as it had previously been. "It does look that way, and I'm

138

happy to say that we interrupted the progression of his opisthotonos."
I had no idea what this word meant. Fortunately for me, he explained.
"That's what leads to death in cases of strychnine poisoning, you
know. Convulsions through the body lead the spine to curve in on
itself until the sufferer can no longer endure the pain and soon expires.
A most agonising and awful way to go. I've only ever seen unhappy
cases before today, but I believe that we got to Ruskin in time."

Even this did not appear to relieve the victim, but he managed
to mumble an "I am grateful" through clenched teeth. He still had
that look of being stretched all over, but the substances that had been
administered appeared to have halted, or at least slowed down, the
effects of the poison. Ruskin was still reeling from his own personal
earthquake, but it was only the aftershocks that were left to endure.

"I'm amazed." Lovebrook certainly showed this through the
wide-eyed expression he wore. "I thought that strychnine was always
lethal. You saved the man's life." If he'd previously been a fan of Lord
Edgington's, he was now a devotee.

"What we don't know is how much poison was added to his drink.
It might well have been a non-lethal dose. And considering how bitter
the stuff is, the killer may have erred on the side of caution to avoid its
detection. Anything from one hundred and forty milligrams would be
enough to kill a man of Ruskin's weight."

I had no idea whether this was a little or a lot, but I nodded and looked
impressed. My first chemistry teacher when I was at school believed that
the metric system was part of a clandestine papist plot to infiltrate Great
Britain and, in his words, "turn us all foreign". As a result, I'd never
known the difference between a litre, a metre and... that other one.

My knowledgeable grandfather had evidently twigged to my
confusion. "It's really quite simple, Christopher. A little under sixty-
five milligrams is equivalent to one grain. In the apothecaries' system
there are twenty grains in a scruple, three scruples in a drachm, eight
drachms in an ounce and twelve ounces in a pound... unless of course
it is an avoirdupois pound, in which case there are sixteen."

"I see," I lied. "It's all quite simple." A more pressing concern
came to my mind just then. "But what we really need to know is how
it was administered. Assuming that Peterson didn't do it, how did it
get into Ruskin's coffee?"

All eyes turned to the butler, who looked a little ruffled by my less-than-polite phrasing. "I did set down the tray in the hall as I fetched cups and utensils from the drinking room. Someone could have slipped the poison into it."

My goodness, it really was called the drinking room. How many more of my predictions would come true today?

"When did Ruskin even order the coffee, though?" Grandfather asked. "How would the killer have known for whom the drink was intended?"

The red-haired retainer peered back and forth between the two policemen. As Ruskin couldn't produce an answer, Peterson spoke for him. "It was as everyone was leaving the morning room. Lord Ruskin opened the door here and asked for refreshments. Anyone in the family could have heard."

Grandfather clicked his fingers out of annoyance for once as opposed to celebration. "At least this puts some light between my grandson Albert and the trail of violence."

I believe that he knew full well this was not the case, but Lovebrook seemed convinced.

"I've called for a doctor already," Peterson explained to calm everyone's nerves. "However, you have done such a good job, Lord Edgington, that I doubt any quack could do better."

Grandfather nodded his thanks, but he was thinking of where the inquiry should next take us. Well, I assume that's what was on his mind. Perhaps he was wondering whether there was enough food to provide a lunchtime snack before the possibly still happening banquet. That's what most concerned me just then, and I liked to believe that our way of thinking had grown a little closer over the two years he'd been teaching me.

"We still have several witnesses to interview," he eventually declared. "We will leave you in Peterson's capable care, Lord Ruskin."

He stood up from the stricken man, who was experiencing another mild convulsion, though the strength of his symptoms seemed to be abating. His eyes had closed, and he hadn't reacted to anything that had been said for the last minute, so I had to conclude he was under the influence of the medicine that had been administered.

Lovebrook looked uncertain whether to accompany us into the

parlour or stay with the second victim, but finally decided to leave the room to check on his men.

"I imagine you'll tell me if there are any new developments," he commented, before slipping through the front door and out to the gardens beyond.

I looked at my mentor and life seemed a little calmer all of a sudden. It had been a good half an hour since anyone had been murdered or poisoned.

CHAPTER TWENTY-TWO

"Who should we see first?" I asked my grandfather as, whenever I picked the next suspect to interview, I was normally wrong.

"We still don't know what part Sibyl Podence and the two younger Fairfax brothers played in any of this. They were all present at the party last night and have been here throughout the day. We cannot yet rule out anyone's involvement."

"Except Albert's," I said, with good reason this time.

"On what evidence?"

"He's my brother, and I know he's more likely to invent a new type of plane that can fly to Mars than murder someone."

He stopped in the parlour and frowned. "As much as I agree with the sentiment, I'm not sure that the British justice system will take our word that your brother is a good egg."

"I suppose you're right," I reluctantly accepted. "And there's still plenty of evidence against him. We haven't proven how his fingerprint could have got onto the banisters. Nor why the Duchess's blood is all over Albert's bed."

"I would have thought that was obvious." This was one of his favourite phrases, and he delivered it with just the right level of arrogance to make me feel terribly dim.

"Not to me, it isn't. But then, I am a noted ignoramus."

He laughed at my comment and mounted the stairs. Someone had placed a sheet over the body, which our cloaked interloper had evidently pulled back. I couldn't understand what the Duchess was still doing there… Well, I knew what she was doing there; she was lying dead on the floor, but I was about to ask why no one had come to take away the body when two men in overalls appeared at the door with a stretcher. I could only assume they were there from the coroner's office.

"Sorry we're late, guv'nor," the first grey-faced worker told my grandfather. "We were called to a car accident on the other side of Northampton. It was a real mess, actually. Body parts everywhere there were. Some rich idiot driving too fast through a village smashed headfirst into a lorry. Ruined his Lancia Lambda. It took us ages to find the chap's head. Sorta makes a dead Duchess look sedate." With this gory picture painted, he set about his work.

My grandfather shuddered at the story. It was hard to say whether it was the driver or his car that he was mourning, but I had to hope that he had learnt his lesson and would drive more carefully in future. Of course, there was no guarantee that would be the case.

"As I was saying…" he continued, the interruption not fazing him.

But instead of saying anything whatsoever, he stepped around the body and continued up the stairs to the newel post where we had spotted the bloody fingerprint. It was now covered in iron filings, and I had no doubt some genius with a microscope would be in the Northampton police station at that very moment comparing it to the inky prints the police would have taken from my brother.

Grandfather donned his gloves, presumably to keep his hands clean rather than to avoid interfering with any evidence, as the scene had already been examined by the police. With this done, he turned the wooden ball at the top of the post to see if it would unscrew. How such thoughts entered his mind, I really can't say, but, sure enough, the top of the banister had a carved thread within it, and the ball rose up some way on a metal bolt.

"We both knew that Albert wasn't responsible for the murder, but I couldn't explain how his fingerprint came to be here. Unless he had crept down here in the night and foolishly handled the body, it just didn't make sense. But I now see that the blood is not limited to the fingerprint itself."

I looked to see what he meant. The well-defined print was in the centre of a congealed splash of red, and he soon explained the significance.

"It is not uncommon for a killer to touch the victim's body and thus get blood on his fingertips. On fleeing the scene of the crime, it is conceivable, therefore, that he would touch the banister and transfer his bloody fingerprint onto it. What we see here is quite the opposite. It is a large amount of blood with a print in the middle. Furthermore, as you previously indicated, there is no reason for it to be so far above the spot where the woman was murdered. It is clear that the killer removed the wooden ball, wiped some blood onto it, and pressed Albert's finger on top to link him to the crime."

"That's amazing," I said, although it was probably very obvious to any normal person. "So the killer unscrewed the ball and stuck my sleepy brother's finger into the blood?" I was still trying to comprehend the gall needed to plan such an act. "It would explain the stains on his bedclothes."

"Precisely. If Albert was the killer, he would have hidden the evidence by washing his hands before getting into bed."

With the first part of the ever-so-complex puzzle solved, new ideas formed in my mind. "The real culprit must have banked on the fact that Albert had drunk enough at the party and wouldn't wake up." Ping, ping, ping went the synapses in my noggin. "In fact, I heard someone. I know I did. There was someone moving around in the hall last night. It's hard to say what time it was, but it had to be a few hours after we went up to sleep."

"That is very interesting." Grandfather was still staring at the banister, and I wondered if the evidence we had discovered that morning would be all we needed to find the guilty party. "It brings me back to the idea that this whole thing was planned for last night because of the wedding. My first thought was that someone was trying to prevent it from happening. But Lord Ruskin's poisoning would seem to undo that possibility."

"Unless he had an accomplice," I thought it best to mention. "Perhaps Ruskin was working with one of the Fairfaxes, who then decided he couldn't be trusted and so poisoned his coffee."

Grandfather was in an easily amused mood and smiled at my quick response. "Yes, that is one consideration, though I find it a little too dramatic to be a likely solution. Thieves and murderers settling scores are fine in the pages of a young man's adventure novel, but I doubt it would happen around here."

"Are you saying that criminals never murder one another?"

He shook his head and, apparently reflecting on something, moved on up the stairs. "No, of course not. But a second murder, in the closed confines of Hinwick House, is a risky endeavour with the police present." The proud expression on his face – one eyebrow raised, his lips turned up just a fraction – suggested that he was aware of another obstacle to the killer's plan, and that obstacle was wearing an elegant grey morning suit. "There is nothing to say that, if Ruskin is involved, he was about to tell us the name of the murderer. Which makes it unlikely that an accomplice was trying to kill him."

He seemed ever so sure of himself, but I didn't see how he could rule out such a possibility. Of course, whatever *I* thought was irrelevant. Once I'd solved as many cases as he had, I would have the right to doubt him. As I'd still only identified approximately one murderer, though, I decided to accept his theory. We followed the corridor through the upper floor of the house to the bedrooms I had previously visited with Detective Inspector Lovebrook. I couldn't guess which door Grandfather would pick, but perhaps I should have.

"Mrs Podence?" he said rather politely as he knocked on the door. "May I have a word with you?"

It was Charles who opened it for us. He looked just as out of sorts as he had the last time we'd spoken and, with all that had gone on that day, I could hardly blame him. His hair was wet from his bath, but that was hardly proof that he hadn't been the cloaked figure on the stairs.

"Sibyl doesn't like the police." If he thought this would be enough to get rid of the tenacious Lord Edgington, he would be sorely disappointed.

"I can't say that's the worst attitude to have." The famous detective walked right past him. "I, however, am not here in any official capacity, and she should have no fear of me."

I generally had a lower capacity than my mentor for such bold actions, and I felt a little self-conscious as I tiptoed past Charles to find a nice dark corner in which to skulk.

Sibyl was standing beside an open window, smoking a long, white cigarette. She didn't look back at us as she took drag after drag on the glowing tube and released each puff of smoke up into the atmosphere in desperate exhalations. It was clear that she was upset by our presence there and, as Grandfather had opted for his usual brooding silence to kick off the interview, I decided to say something.

"I can quite understand why you wouldn't want to speak to us, Mrs Podence." See, I can be polite when I have to be! "But it's in everybody's interests that we catch the killer. He just put strychnine in Lord Ruskin's drink."

Charles was the first to react. "Gosh, poor Damian. Has he snuffed it?"

Grandfather made no attempt to respond, so I answered the question. "Thanks to Lord Edgington's quick thinking, it looks as though he'll live."

"We gave him bromide of potassium," he explained, as showing off about his achievements trumped the chance to be mysterious. "It helped control his convulsions, and I'm pleased to say that the worst effects of the poison never took hold."

Charles opened his eyes as wide as they would go so that his eyebrows climbed high up his large, pale forehead. "That's wonderful news." He needed a moment to make sense of events. "Really, Lord Edgington, I'd like to shake your hand. My brothers and I might have got carried away when we crowed over Mother's body, but we don't want to see anyone else hurt. You'll talk to the detectives, won't you, Sibyl?"

The stylish young woman turned to us as a puff of smoke danced around her. "Do you know what I spent the last two years doing?" I suppose we all took this as a rhetorical question, as we allowed her to continue. "I nursed my dying husband, as his health slowly deteriorated. He died in my arms, and the only interest anyone showed in me after was to question whether I'd murdered him."

Her words faded, but they were so uniquely powerful that they rang in my ear for some time.

"No one offered me any sympathy. No one came with flowers or sent me cards. I was the heartless opportunist who had killed my trusting spouse and taken his every penny. No one cared that we'd actually been deeply in love or that I'd supported him the whole time he was ill. The way the newspapers talked about me, you'd think I'd spent the time drinking and dancing as poor Peter perished."

The presumably accidental alliteration put a rather emphatic exclamation mark on her sentence. She pouted then, as though to play up to the lascivious picture the newspapers had painted of her. "I met Peter when I was still very young. It took him a year to convince me that we should be wed but, by the end of that time, there was no other man for me."

She looked at Charles as she said this, as though to apologise for the sentiment. He did not seem concerned and sat down on his bed with one bare foot resting on the quilted coverlet.

It was about time that my grandfather took charge. "I'm truly sorry for the violent language that the gutter press used to describe your case. I followed the trial and did not think you guilty. In fact, I was greatly relieved that justice was done, and the charges were dismissed."

I thought she might expound upon the same theme, but Sibyl just nodded. She was framed against the window and the bright sunlight behind her. It was the perfect day for a wedding, were one ever to take place.

When she said nothing, Grandfather continued. "But I am not here to talk about your married life. I'd like to know what happened last night at the Horseshoe Ball."

It wasn't easy to make out her expression, as the sun was blinding, but she seemed surprised by the focus of his interest. "Well, I have far more money than I know how to spend, and so I like to go to fashionable events. People probably think I'm looking for a new husband to murder, but it's not that at all. I go because I can't resist making a scene. I go to see the toffs squirm." If her cigarette hadn't burnt down to nothing, I'm certain she would have puffed on it to make the most of this revelation. "Occasionally, I'll meet someone a little different who isn't terrified of my notoriety. From time to time, good folk come out of the woodwork and are interested in me for who I really am. That's how I met Charles."

Grandfather was unmoved by this part of her tale and responded in a voice that was dryer than Tempranillo wine. "That's fascinating, of course, but I was more interested in what happened last night with Lord Ruskin. How did he convince you to come here?"

She looked across at me before speaking and tucked a lock of her glossy brown hair behind one ear. "There's nothing nefarious about it. I know Damian through Charles, and neither of us was having a lot of fun at the ball last night, so we decided to cut out early."

"Did you know that Cassandra's wedding was today?" I jumped in to ask.

"Yes." She walked over to Charles and draped one arm around him but stayed on her feet. "I knew all about the wedding to which I wasn't invited."

"And yet you thought it was a good idea to come here on the eve of Cassie's nuptials with a man who was in love with her?"

148

Sibyl shook her head in mild amusement so that her hair danced about her ears. "I didn't think it was a good idea, exactly. I just thought it would be more pleasant than spending any more time with a legion of snobs once I'd had my fun terrorising them. You know, Princess Mary was there, and even she looked terribly bored by the whole event."

Grandfather had allowed me to ask a few questions but seized his moment to take us off on a useful tangent. "How is your relationship with Charles's sister?"

For his part, Charles had been listening intently. His weaselly little eyes darted about to look at whoever was speaking, and I felt that he was making careful notes in his head of all the most salient points.

"I've only met Cassandra once or twice." She caressed the hair at the back of Charles's neck as she spoke. "We visited her in Oxford, and she seemed perfectly nice. I'm sure her brothers would be less generous in their assessment of their little sister's character, but I rather like her."

"And so you had no reason to disturb her wedding to my grandson?" This was the big point towards which my grandfather had been driving. "After all, you just told us how you like causing a scene and scaring all the toffs. What bigger occasion is there than a wedding to achieve your goals?"

Far from being intimidated by the implication, Sibyl roared with laughter. "You know, you're right! It would have been wonderful to destroy such a precious and pretty event. Imagine the faces of all those earls and countesses and what have you."

Grandfather closed his eyes then, as though tired of the interview. "I'm asking whether you brought Lord Ruskin here intentionally, knowing that it would cause drama in the family."

"No, I didn't." Her whole being seemed to harden. It was no longer a laughing matter. The old man had accused her of something, and she would have to stand up for herself. "I came here with Damian because I wanted to see Charles. I happen to love him an awful lot, even if his mother wouldn't accept that."

The woman was full of contradictions, though that didn't necessarily make her a killer. I felt great sympathy for all that she had endured with her husband's illness and the harrowing trial. And yet, there was so much anger within her, it was hard to believe she was entirely blameless. The fact that she had not killed her husband didn't rule out her capacity to kill. Perhaps her experience in the dock had changed her – not to mention her simultaneous trial in the court of public opinion.

I remembered the display she'd put on when she'd arrived the previous night. "You said that you hated Lady Hinwick. Did you ever actually meet her?"

She needed some time to compose herself. "No." Even with this said, she would take a deep breath before explaining further. "I came here to see her with Charles a few months ago, and she refused to grace me with her presence."

"The woman was insane," the Duchess's eldest son informed us, but his paramour had more to say.

"I was willing to give her the benefit of the doubt, but she didn't even have the courage to insult me to my face. There's a reason that no one in this family could abide her. She made Eric bitter, Stanislas a nervous wreck and turned her own husband into a shadow."

I thought perhaps she would say something about her own lover at that moment, but whatever impact the Duchess's behaviour had made on Charles would remain a secret.

"If you want my opinion on who killed that witch, then I'll tell you that Lady Begonia 'Too Good for Anyone' Fairfax killed herself. She might not have wielded the knife, but it was her cruel manipulation of all those around her that led to her death."

CHAPTER TWENTY-THREE

"Don't you think that was fascinating, Grandfather?"

Out in the corridor once more, he looked at me as though what I'd said was hard to decipher. "No, boy. I didn't think it was fascinating in the slightest. I found the whole interview hugely frustrating." So that told me.

I strolled after him, wondering what had got his nanny-goat.

"Must you think so loudly, Christopher?" I knew it wasn't worth arguing with him when he was in such a mood and kept my mouth tightly sealed. "If you must know, the reason I found our discussion with Sibyl Podence frustrating was because it did nothing but reveal new possibilities."

"Oh." At first, this was the most I could summon in way of a reply. "Is that a bad thing?"

He shook his head like a dog who doesn't like the rain. "At this stage of the investigation, it is."

"We've only been at it for a few hours, Grandfather. Don't you think you're being too hard on yourself?"

He came to a stop beside the open window where I'd spotted the cloak. "No, of course I'm not. I always apply the exact right amount of self-criticism at all times. The fact is that some investigations take years, and some should be completed in the time it takes to eat a fine meal."

At my grandfather's house, "a fine meal" could take anything between seven minutes – as he barks at me to eat faster – and a day to consume.

"There is a shape to every investigation. We start by building slowly – gathering evidence and information, postulating theories and considering who our suspects might be. Then there is a turning point at which everything must fall into place. I believe that Lord Ruskin's poisoning was that moment, but instead of narrowing down our field of suspects and the possible motives for the crime, we keep stumbling across new ideas."

He really was infuriated, and I doubted there was much that I could do to calm him, so I changed the topic entirely. "Look, Grandfather," I said, pointing out of the window to where a small flock of birds was chirping past. "I think they must be linnets."

He looked quite bemused by this. "Gosh, Christopher. I believe you're right."

"No, I can't be." I am singularly dreadful at identifying birds, and I had to swallow in surprise, though my throat was quite dry. "I was only saying it to distract you from your disappointment. I thought we could have a good laugh at how far off I was."

"Then I must offer my condolences, as you have failed in your task. The birds we saw were definitely linnets. The chirruping song gives them away, and I caught the faintest flash of pink on the breast of the male birds."

I had finally identified a garden bird on the thousandth time of trying. I can only assume that the complete lack of pressure on me to be correct – I certainly hadn't expected to get it right – robbed me of my usual apprehension.

We took a moment to acclimatise ourselves to this new reality and glance down at the site of the would-be wedding. Plenty of guests had arrived by now and staff were milling about with trays stacked with glasses of sparkling champagne.

"You don't think we should simply call the whole thing off until another day?" it occurred to me to ask.

"If I were in Cassandra's shoes, that is what I would do. However, with the exception of her well-paid staff, no one actually liked the deceased. Even the bride couldn't abide her mother and, if we can find the killer before it's time for the service, then cancelling her wedding will be one less tragedy that poor Cassandra has to endure."

I took a moment to consider this idea. "I suppose you're right. If she and Albert do decide to go ahead with the celebration today, it will be a nice way to improve an otherwise gloomy experience. And think of the stories they can tell their grandchildren."

There seemed to be something of a paradox in what we were saying. If Cassie and her family didn't like the Duchess, there should have been nothing to inspire gloom in them. Of course, life is rarely so simple, and I was certain that, whatever they claimed, the Fairfax siblings would have conflicted feelings about the whole sorry affair.

"You know," I began as a new possibility formed in my mind, "we've never before faced a case in which everyone was so eager to show us how much they disliked the victim."

Grandfather's nostrils flared as he snorted out a laugh. "You're right there. It's most unnerving, and that must be part of the reason I'm so flustered. It should be a great deal easier to prove who the killer is when so many people had a good reason to want her dead."

"Yes, I've been thinking about that for most of the day, and I might have an explanation."

"Oh, really?" It goes without saying that he sounded surprised.

"Perhaps they're protecting one another."

"Continue." I believe that I'd piqued his interest.

"Think about it. What if they all know who's to blame and, to prevent the real killer from ending up in a cell, they're offering a blanket of evidence that applies to each and every last one of them?"

I watched him chew the inside of his mouth for a few moments as he, well... chewed over the matter. "Christopher, that is a very interesting hypothesis indeed. That would be a wonderful way to distract attention and muddy the picture we have to investigate." He clapped his hands together and explained my theory back to me. "Yes, I can see it now. They have all expressed their loathing for the Duchess in order to protect their own. Sibyl hated Charles's mother because she wouldn't accept her as a potential daughter-in-law. Ruskin was in a similar situation. We haven't found out exactly why Eric is such an angry young man, but I'm confident that we will. What's more, the Duchess held the Duke's purse strings, and she held them tight."

"In fact," I interrupted, as I already knew all this, "the only person who hasn't shown great hatred towards the victim is Stanislas. He's been oddly distant the whole time we've been here, and I get the impression that he's the person who cared for her most."

"You're quite right, Chrissy. And that is why we must talk to him next." He didn't wait for me but walked back along the corridor towards the older part of the house.

It took me a moment to realise that he hadn't a clue where Stanislas's room was. "Excuse me, Grandfather? You're going the wrong way."

CHAPTER TWENTY-FOUR

I wasn't certain that the youngest Fairfax boy would still be up there, but it did seem as though the whole family were in hiding after their time in the spotlight. We followed the snaking passageway to what must have been the final extension to the house. The hallway was narrower here, and no light broke through. There were cupboards leading off it and a door I hadn't noticed before, with a third set of stairs behind it that led down to the ground floor.

It seemed the perfect place for Stanislas to have his room. He'd been so removed from most of the scenes of family life we'd witnessed. Right from our first meeting on the drive, he'd been aloof and oddly emotionless. It was hard to connect him with his sly brothers and even his strong-willed sister. He was an outsider in a family of already unusual characters.

There was no need to knock this time, as the door stood ajar.

"Come in, Lord Edgington," our next suspect murmured from his desk.

He was still sitting in the exact same spot as when Lovebrook and I had left him. The book was still open on his desk, but I had the distinct impression that he hadn't been reading it. The view from his window showed nothing but the forest that brushed against the property, and I wondered whether he'd been staring out at the soft green leaves as they were buffeted by the breeze. Without evidence, I concluded that he'd been daydreaming, just as I was so prone to do.

"Thank you for seeing us." My grandfather adopted a different attitude for each interview. With Sibyl and Charles, he'd come prepared for a confrontation, and that was just what he got. But upon entering Stanislas's quiet refuge, a more thoughtful approach was required. "I'm sure today is a trying time for you."

The man turned his head a fraction. He looked like a child trying to make sense of some exotic new object. "That's not what my family would have you believe. They must have told you how dreadful our mother was. I would be a fool to mourn her."

"I don't think it's foolish to feel attachment to one's relatives," his questioner replied. "I had a perfectly strange relationship with my parents. They were singularly unfeeling people and, to this day, I am uncertain whether I loved or loathed them."

I wondered whether Stanislas would think that Grandfather was making up a story to curry favour, but I'd heard him speak of his emotionless Victorian parents on any number of occasions.

"I suppose there's a difference between being standoffish and actively cruel." There was intelligence to the way he spoke, though it was not the normal kind. He was slow in some ways, but perceptive in others. "And my mother prized cruelty above almost any other human attribute."

"You might think that, but I'm sure there were times in my childhood when even cruelty would have felt like a blessing compared to neglect. At least if my parents had teased and tormented me, I would have felt as though they knew I existed."

Stanislas shook his head, clearly doubting this statement.

"I'm sorry," Grandfather continued. "Perhaps I've misspoken. It is hard to comprehend the emotions and experiences of another family, as we are so attuned to our own from such an early age. Could you tell me what, in particular, your mother did to hurt you?"

The young man's chair swivelled on its metal base, and he moved about restlessly as he looked for an answer. "For a long time, I didn't think that she was so terrible. I believed her when she told us that everything she did was for our sake. She knew that I'd wanted to join the army since I was a little boy and, when she told me that I couldn't do so, I accepted it quite meekly. That wasn't enough for her, though. She didn't merely want to quell my ambition, she wished to rob me of it entirely."

A tingle of sadness passed over me, and I doubted in that moment that Stanislas could be the killer. "What did she do?"

It wasn't just his chair that spun from side to side; his head mirrored the action. "She was unhappy that I should still read my books and collect my artefacts, even after she'd forbidden me from going to the Royal Military Academy. Last year on Guy Fawkes night, she took half my possessions away and burned them. I didn't know anything about it until I saw a helmet my father had bought me burning in the fire. I was so incensed that I put my hand in to pull it out."

He held one arm up and pulled his sleeve down to show us the faint scars that reached across his skin like cracks in porcelain.

156

"Was your mother there at the time?" Grandfather's voice had fallen even quieter.

Instead of answering directly, Stanislas carefully set the scene. "We'd been having such a happy time; whatever my brothers and sister might say, such moments did exist. Charles danced around the fire like a caveman, and Eric sang a song. It was some time before I realised what my mother had done. She must have gone up to my room when I was in the forest collecting firewood. Father lit the bonfire, and I didn't know anything about Mother's treachery until I saw that blackened helmet. I pulled it clean out in one movement and it wasn't just the flames that hurt me, but the burning hot metal. For the briefest of seconds, I thought that it was fused to my skin, but I managed to shake it free."

As he recounted the tale, he stared halfway between us at that invisible point where stories come from. "Eric pulled me screaming to the lake and plunged my hand beneath the surface. It was so cold that I wondered what was worse between the fire and the icy water, but it might well have saved the skin on my hand. Eric can be grumpy and hostile, and he loves to tease me, but I'll always love him for what he did that day. He held me there as I yelled and insulted him. He lay on the ground with half of his weight on top of me to make certain that I wouldn't run away. When the doctor came fifteen minutes later, I'd barely taken my arm out for more than a few seconds at a time."

He let the silence fill the room then, but it didn't last long. That expressive hush was replaced by the linnets' song and the chatter of wedding guests in the distance as our ears adjusted and went searching further afield for something to fill the void.

"I cried of course. I cried the whole time, but so did my mother. Her tears came from anger while mine were of pain. She called me an idiot and an embarrassment. She told me that she'd never wanted me in the first place. When the doctor had anointed the wounds and bandaged me, she hit me again and again and wouldn't stop until my father pulled her away. I had bruises across my chest and a great red welt on my cheek from where she'd struck me, but it didn't change anything. When it was over, none of us were more likely to stand up to her. We didn't turn our backs on her money or the luxury of living here. We accepted our roles, and everything returned to the way it had always been."

"Why did she hit you?" I found myself asking almost without knowing that I'd spoken.

Each answer required a breath, a pause. For Stanislas, each word deserved its due consideration. "Because she'd failed." His leg made a soft rustle as it jiggled up and down as he spoke. "Even though I couldn't join the army without her permission, she hadn't changed me. She hadn't taken my dream away as she wanted, and she hated me for it."

Grandfather took his time to formulate a response. "I'm beginning to see why so many of you disliked her. Until now, all I'd heard were the easily dismissed complaints that any child could make of his parents, but she truly was despotic in her behaviour."

"I'm glad you understand. Mother could never forgive us for not loving her as she needed to be loved… for not considering her the most important thing in this world, just as the ancient Egyptians worshiped their rulers as gods." More than at any time that weekend, Stanislas exuded a sense of hard-earned calm. "And that's why I don't think Charles or Eric are to blame for what happened. We were used to our subjugation. If the events of that night in November didn't spark a rebellion, I don't think that anything could."

Once again, one of our suspects had presented us with evidence and motive, whilst swearing that there was no way that anyone in the Fairfax family could be responsible for the crime. It was either a clever strategy or further proof of how bizarre the case was.

I realised then just how readily we had fallen into Stanislas's way of doing things. The conversation progressed at his plodding rhythm, and it was hard to move away from it.

I decided to ask a less poetical, more straightforward question to return us to the facts. "What time did you go to bed?"

"You've already asked me. I slept for most of the night in the Great Hall and then came up here at around seven this morning."

"Do you remember seeing the time?" I pointed at the carriage clock right next to his bed. It was probably an unnecessary gesture.

"That's right. It was a few minutes past seven when I arrived."

Grandfather had realised something and set to work unpicking his answer. "And yet, your brother told us that you were not in the Great Hall when he and Sibyl woke up an hour before that. Would you care to explain?"

158

Stanislas didn't panic. He maintained his slow, serene manner and provided an answer. "He must have got the time wrong. I was there until seven, and then I came upstairs to get changed."

"And where are the clothes you wore last night?" Grandfather had set his sights on him the way that a falcon targets its prey.

"I put them to be washed. Would you like me to ask Peterson to fetch them?" There was a moment's hesitation between sentences, a slight extension of that final word that told me he was less sure of himself than he had been before.

"That won't be necessary." Lord Edgington studied the strange young man before us. He wasn't ready to pull apart any discrepancies just yet, but that moment would come. "In fact, I think that's all we need for now. We won't keep you any longer."

"I appreciate you taking the time to talk to me." To my surprise, Stanislas sounded quite sincere, and I wondered whether his biggest problems stemmed from being in a family of large personalities where he would always be overlooked.

"I have one last thing to ask," I said, to halt my grandfather's retreat. "I wondered what it was about battles and armies that so appealed to you."

Grandfather might have faulted me for saying I was going to ask a question and not actually forming one, but Stanislas was happy to respond. "My father read me books about the Napoleonic wars when I was a child, and I thought they were the most wonderful fantasies I could imagine. It didn't seem real to me at first and, when I grew up and discovered that such events had truly occurred, it was almost impossible to believe." He smiled for the first time since we'd entered his room. "I'm aware that every war is filled with cruelty and suffering, but I believe that my childish perception of battle as a noble adventure changed the very concept for me. Even the Great War fascinated me when I was younger, and all those things made me who I am."

It was another contradiction. Stanislas was the most peaceful, self-contained member of the Fairfax clan. It was hard to imagine him fighting in a war or leading a squadron of soldiers.

"Will you join the army now that your mother can no longer stand in your way?" Grandfather asked.

He leaned back in his chair to consider. "Almost certainly, but we'll have to wait and see."

Grandfather fixed his gaze on the unusual character, then nodded and turned to leave.

"Oh, I forgot to give you this." I took the old French coin from my pocket and tossed it across the room. It sparkled in the sunlight on its arcing journey towards him. "I found it in the Great Hall. You must have left it there last night."

Grandfather watched the coin spin and Stanislas catch it, but that's not all we saw. When the youngest Fairfax boy opened his hand to examine his prize, there was a look of pure relief on his face.

CHAPTER TWENTY-FIVE

"That was enlightening in its own way," Grandfather informed me, and I found this comment almost as transparent as the last two interviews we'd undertaken. "We'll send up one of the constables to see what happened to Stanislas's clothes from last night. You can never be too careful with these things. Just because someone may not appear to warrant suspicion, that doesn't mean we should abandon standard investigative protocol."

"You consider him free from suspicion?" I said with some doubt in my voice.

"Not literally, perhaps, but I doubt he will be the one standing before a court when this is all over." He followed his response with another question, and I could only think that there was something in my tone which had alerted him to my true feelings on the matter. "Why? Don't you?"

"I find Stanislas a very interesting person," I replied noncommittally. "Eric and Charles are the brothers who instantly arouse suspicion but, overall, I believe that Stanislas has more to say for himself."

We opened the door to the servants' stairs and descended without saying anything more.

"That is a succinct summation of the three brothers," Grandfather commented once we'd come out on the ground floor beside the kitchen and another set of stairs that led to the cellars. "What's more, it's hard to imagine what it would have been like for Cassandra to be part of such a family. She seems more settled in herself than her brothers do. It must be true what Charles told us about their mother paying more attention to her sons. Cassandra was given the freedom to grow where they weren't."

"Up to a point," I replied. "As soon as she attracted the attention of the wrong man, her mother put her foot down."

"That is true, but having spent some time with Lord Ruskin, I believe I would have done the same thing if he'd wished to marry one of my daughters."

The conversation would go no further as there was a shriek from the kitchen, and we rushed in to see what had happened. The large, modern space looked quite out of place in such a grand old house. There were countless cupboards on the walls, all painted white, and several maids were rushing about the steamy room.

"What's the matter, Henrietta?" I asked, running over to the cook from Cranley Hall.

It was clear that her shriek had been one of frustration rather than pain. I'd been imagining another case of poisoning.

"It's the food. You can't just delay a wedding by several hours. It's impossible, no matter who's been killed." I could see that she was mourning her overcooked pastries more than the death of the Duchess of Hinwick. "I've no idea what we'll end up with by dinner time. I just hope it's edible."

I considered responding that such concerns had never worried her in the past, but I didn't want that fine woman to turn her ladle on me.

"Come along, Christopher," Grandfather called from the doorway. "We've wasted enough time today. It's already three o'clock, which means we must solve this case right now if we wish to salvage the day."

There was no chance of salvaging the day for the departed Duchess, but I didn't argue with him. Instead, we wandered from the kitchen and through the foyer beside the Great Hall to make our way to the gardens.

I felt that there was something just out of reach in my head, and I knew it was connected to Stanislas's part in the whole affair. I was certain that he'd been lying to us in some way, but I couldn't say how, and I couldn't say why. He was such an ill-defined sort of person that it was hard to get a sense of who he really was. Could his comparative softness be a veil for the darker side of his nature? Could he have murdered his mother, knowing that no one would suspect the only gentle member of the family?

My grandfather seemed to have accepted the idea that Charles had got the hour wrong when he told us at what time he had gone up to his room that morning. But if Stanislas was lying, it meant that he could have left the Great Hall at any hour, thrown a rock against the Duchess's window to lure her from her room, and waited for her on the stairs.

I didn't want to believe this, but it was an attractive idea. I could imagine the Duchess getting out of bed at night for her poor youngest son with his hesitant manner and scarred hand. From everything that her family had told us, it would appeal to her sense of importance – the

162

feeling that she alone could solve her little boy's dilemma. However, my thoughts kept returning to her broken pocket watch. If the killer had wanted to pretend that the murder occurred at midnight, did this help Stanislas because he believed that a member of his family would have seen him in the Great Hall later in the morning? Or was this the first occasion in the history of crime when a stopped watch really did attest to the time of death?

As soon as we stepped outside, Delilah raced over in search of attention. Just like when she was a puppy, she jumped about to express her joy, and Grandfather took a moment to scratch her ears and stroke her flank. I didn't know where we were supposed to be heading, but wherever it was would have to wait. My mother appeared by the copse of conker trees and motioned for us to join her.

"It's Cassandra," she called as we walked closer. "She's been in a terrible state ever since she left the cottage. I tried to convince her to stay there, but she wouldn't listen. I took her over to the lake to calm her down."

"Thank you, Violet," father told daughter. "You always do know what's best for people." He spoke these words as though he wished he could say the same of himself. As my mother is by far the most admirable person I've ever met – and even gave her blessed father a run for his money in the capability stakes – it did not surprise me that he would feel this way.

She led us through a gap in the trees to an ornamental lake with two white swans swimming upon it. They looked as though they had been put there especially for the wedding and glanced over at us rather haughtily. An even more graceful creature was perched on a green wooden bench under the shade of an alder tree. Though still only half ready for the big event, Cassandra looked both distraught and beautiful beside the water – like the frog princess, waiting for her prince.

Delilah embarked on a full circle of the lake, and I took the time to admire it. Bullrushes grew in the marshy shallows, their seed pods ready to burst with cottony fluff. Every now and again, a ripple appeared on the surface of the water and, from where I was standing on the bank, I spotted water boatmen and sticklebacks among the lily leaves.

When she saw us, Cassie attempted to hide her tears, rubbing them dry with her silky sleeves, but it would do no good.

"Dear child," Grandfather began in his softest voice, "I know this day has been a trial for you, but there is more evidence by the hour of Albert's innocence, and the inspector in charge of the case no longer believes him the likely suspect."

This seemed to cheer her a touch and she let out a ragged breath as though she had been holding it in until she heard good news. "That is wonderful, Lord Edgington. Thank you so much for telling me. But Albert's situation is not my only sorrow."

"Of course it's not," my mother replied, sitting down on the bench beside her (hopefully still) future daughter-in-law to offer what comfort she could. "No woman would wish for such tribulations on her wedding day, but you mustn't allow the sadness to overwhelm you."

I looked forward to seeing what silver lining my brilliant mother might land upon, but instead she turned to me for help.

"That's right," I began, and now I was looking forward to seeing what silver lining *I* might land upon. "You know…" To be honest, it was no easy task to think of an answer. "If you do get married this afternoon, no one will ever forget your big day."

Mother's expression told me that this was not the sort of thing she'd had in mind. Admittedly, she didn't do a great deal better herself. "And, if you think about it, by coming through such adversity, your love for Albert will be even stronger."

This was when Cassandra could take it no more and broke down in sobs. "It's all gone wrong, and it's my fault."

"Now, now, of course it's not." Grandfather knelt in front of her as though he wished to ask for her hand in marriage. Thankfully, that was not his intention, and he found a few words of consolation for her. "This could have happened to anyone, and you certainly aren't at fault."

"But I didn't love her." Her chest heaved as she fought for her words. "Mother is dead, and I feel nothing."

My mother, grandfather and I exchanged glances, and I realised that they wanted me to take a turn spouting platitudes. "It's completely understandable. By all accounts, the Duchess was horrid to the whole lot of you. If she was my mother, I would feel just the same."

Perhaps unsurprisingly, my two companions looked horrified. Perhaps surprisingly, Cassandra seemed grateful for what I'd said. "That's just it. She was a tyrant, and I never loved her the way a daughter is supposed to love her mother, but I should still feel… something."

"Now, now…" Grandfather tried again, but Cassie hadn't finished.

"And if Damian hadn't fallen in love with me, Mother wouldn't have had to refuse the engagement, and he would never have come here for revenge on the night before my wedding to a much more suitable man."

"There, there, Cassandra," Grandfather tried again. "It no longer looks as though Lord Ruskin is to blame for your mother's death. Since we last saw you, someone poisoned him."

"My goodness!" This revelation was almost enough to freeze her emotions entirely, but then she blinked a few times to grasp the news. "Is he actually dead?"

"No, no, don't worry. I managed to administer some medicine just in time. The doctor should be with him by now, and it seems Ruskin will recover. I've heard cases of people taking a little too much strychnine by accident, and, when identified immediately, the effects can be controlled."

"What a relief." Cassandra spoke in the ghost of a whisper, and I couldn't tell how sad this really made her. "I might not have wanted him here today, but I'd hate for anything so awful to happen to him, especially if he isn't to blame for Mother's death."

Every time she mentioned the dead duchess, I sensed the conflicting thoughts that were storming through her mind. She was mourning a woman whom she didn't entirely love. It would evidently be hard to come to terms with the fact she was now motherless, but what that meant in such a peculiar family was hard to say.

"I'm sure he'll be fine," I replied without proof. "It was lucky that we were there when he drank the coffee."

She looked blank again, and so Grandfather explained. "That's how he was poisoned. Scientists believe that strychnine is the bitterest substance in the world. If the killer had put it in water, it would have been undrinkable. Even in his coffee, Lord Ruskin could taste it, but he had no reason to suspect anything more than a particularly strong blend."

"But how could the killer have got hold of poison?" Cassandra kept her eyes on the expert. "Surely there are laws to stop people from buying anything that could harm another person. You can't just go into a chemist and say, 'I'd like a jar of strychnine and perhaps a bottle or two of cyanide while I'm here.'"

"You're absolutely right. Here in Britain, there is something called the poison register. All sales of hazardous chemicals are recorded and require a good reason if you wish to obtain them. However, strychnine is still sold in low concentrations to be used as a mild stimulant. I believe it is widely available as a tonic, in fact. It is also a common ingredient in raticide."

"Mother!" She suddenly sat more upright on the bench. "She took a tonic every morning to set her right for the day ahead. Well, that's what she used to say, but I assumed it was some sort of placebo."

"It might also be notable for its absence," my mother added, as she is far cleverer than me.

We had gone at least a minute without Cassandra sobbing, and it was about time someone scared her again. That task fell to my grandfather. "You do realise that, if we rule out Lord Ruskin and Albert, that only leaves your brothers, father and Sibyl Podence."

"Oh, how terrible." She sniffed a little but held herself together for the moment.

"Do you have any reason to believe that Charles's sweetheart would have plotted against your mother?"

She was distant once more. Her exquisite green eyes took on a distant aspect, and I couldn't tell whether she'd have an answer for us. When it eventually arrived, it was dripping with uncertainty. "I believe she is an angry person, but then we all lose our temper sometimes. That wouldn't make her a killer on its own." She looked off across the lake to the large nest where one of the swans was now sitting. "Have you discovered anything that could connect Sibyl to the killing? Or the attack on Damian, perhaps?"

Grandfather sucked in his cheeks at this moment and thought for a short while. "It is too early to say. I will have to consider the possibility in more depth." He was strangely noncommittal, which normally meant that he had discovered something interesting and wasn't willing to share it.

"All you have to worry about is today, my dear." My mother put one arm around the distraught bride and pulled her closer. "There's no pressure to go ahead with the wedding, but the guests will be arriving at

166

the church before long, and you'll have to make the decision very soon."

I had no desire to take part in this discussion, and so I stayed silent. The same couldn't be said for the ever-opinionated Lord Edgington.

"In my mind, Albert clearly isn't to blame, and the fact that he hasn't been led away in handcuffs suggests that the police agree." This was the good news that Grandfather could offer, but he had more to say. "The only question you must now consider is whether it would be worse to get married just after your mother was murdered, or let this day go by without some happy event to reclaim it."

I think that, had I been the one forced to make such a choice – even if my mother wasn't the loveliest person in England – I would have told everyone to pack up and go home. I wouldn't have wanted my wedding day to be marred by blood and poison. But then, I hadn't been looking forward to that moment for months or, as her family had said of Cassandra over dinner, even planning it since I was a child.

She leaned forward to look at my grandfather and, with half a smile on her face, she admitted how she felt. "I would hate for this tragedy to be the reason that Albert and I failed to wed." She paused for a few seconds and just about every emotion imaginable rippled across her features. "So, yes. I would still like to get married today."

My mother instantly enveloped her in another hug. "Oh, my darling girl. That's wonderful news." Her jolly declaration called Delilah back to us from where she'd been playing in the water.

Cassie's growing smile was infectious, and I couldn't resist copying her. Even our soggy dog was moved by the scene and rolled about on the ground by my feet.

"Of course, there's no guarantee that we can catch the killer before the service begins." Trust Grandfather to temper the joyous moment with a little realism. He looked at his watch and said, "Time is short, but we will do all we can. Get ready for your wedding, young lady. If your father turns out to be the killer, I will walk you down the aisle."

Cassandra stopped moving again, and the far too jovial lord had to explain himself. "I am so sorry, my child. That was supposed to be a joke. I have no reason to think your father is the killer. He certainly couldn't have been the lithe figure whom Detective Inspector

Lovebrook saw interfering with the body a short while ago." When this failed to reassure the bride – who was blushing for the wrong reason – Grandfather spoke again. "Come along, Chrissy. We have a murderer to apprehend and a little over an hour and a half to do so."

CHAPTER TWENTY-SIX

Delilah accompanied us back to the house, and we all beamed with great confidence. I don't know what it was, but I had a real feeling that we would catch the killer, Albert and Cassie would walk down the aisle, and the dinner afterwards would be delicious. Of course, there was about as much likelihood that Cook had prepared something nice and simple for the banquet as there was that we would wrap up the case in record time.

And so, a few yards from the lake, as Mother and Cassandra trailed off towards the cottage, I began to doubt our chances again. "Grandfather?"

"Yes, Grandson."

"What is left for us to do at this stage? Haven't we talked to everyone and examined every possible angle of the case?"

"No, of course we haven't. For one thing, we are yet to interview Eric on his own. And the key question upon which we must now focus our efforts is why Lord Ruskin was poisoned. I believe that, if we can establish this one essential fact, the rest of the evidence should fall into place."

I was about to discuss my theory that there were two killers again, but he never liked such outcomes. He preferred to believe that each case was pure and perfect. A two-killer solution was a fudge by Grandfather's standards, and he would not put up with such things.

"So how do we go about identifying the poisoner's motives?"

We had reached the loose stone pathway that surrounded the house, and Grandfather stopped to raise one finger most authoritatively. "We are going to talk to Detective Inspector Lovebrook."

"Oh," I said, failing to hide my disappointment. "Is that all? I was hoping you would have some clever scientific knowledge that – through a process of chemical testing, the temperature of Ruskin's breath and the residue in his cup – would lead us to the culprit."

His moustache looked at me disapprovingly. Well, obviously his moustache didn't have eyes, but I'm sure you know what I mean. It became rather scrunched together as he pouted. "No, Christopher, that will not do any good at this stage. We know he was poisoned. It appears that the substance came from some medicine in the house, and I have already inspected the dregs of his coffee to ascertain that the strychnine was administered in his drink. What we need to do is speak to the detective whose investigation is running in parallel to our own."

"Wonderful," I replied, as I'd long since found it was best to pretend to be positive around my grandfather rather than showing any doubt in his abilities. "Off we go, then."

"Oh, and we must tell your brother to get ready, too." He looked down at his perfectly turned-out grey woollen morning suit. "I believe I am sufficiently well attired. We'll see if we have time to do anything about you once the killer is apprehended."

The grey suit I'd been wearing for most of the day was, for some reason, a little muddy in places. However, I doubted that my tailcoat, which was still folded in the travelling trunk in my room, would be much better. I should probably have hung it up somewhere, but who can find the time when people are forever being murdered around you?

As the body had finally been taken away for medical examination, the constable who'd previously been guarding the door had moved on to other duties. I doubted the coroner would discover much beyond the fact the Duchess was stabbed through the back (and the heart, by the look of the blood stains she left behind). The truth was that some members of the household would be more aggrieved by the stain on the nice stair carpet than they would by the woman's death.

We found Lovebrook in a small study opposite the Great Hall. It was lucky he'd left the door open, or we might never have spotted him. He was sitting at a pretty walnut desk with cabriole legs that reminded me of the bowed stance of a cowboy I'd recently seen in 'The Dark Frontier', an exciting Western I'd watched at the cinema with my brother. The desk was Queen Anne style, like the house itself, and the room was just the place to sit contemplating the mysteries of the universe, or the complexities of a murder investigation.

The inspector didn't notice us at first as he was scribbling in a notebook, so we knocked to get his attention.

"Lord Edgington." He stood up with his usual reverence for the legend who walked among us, as though Cyril Sinclair's heroic character in 'The Dark Frontier' had just entered the room. "What can I do for you?"

170

Grandfather needed no further invitation and took a chair in front of the inspector's requisitioned desk. "We'd like to compare notes," he explained, pointing at the literal notebook within which Lovebrook had literally just been noting his notes down. I think this made the point clearly enough.

"Of course, my lord. It would be a privilege." He waited until I had taken a seat, then sat down himself. "According to the doctor, Lord Ruskin will make a full recovery. He's resting now, and there should be no long-term damage."

"That's excellent news." Grandfather nodded sagely with his eyes closed and his hands resting on his amethyst-topped silver cane.

"As for the murderer, I'm afraid I'm no closer to solving this case than when I arrived this morning."

"Oh, I'm sure that can't be true." The born mentor couldn't resist the chance to take a young detective under his wing and made some appreciative noises to that end. "Tell us what you've discovered, and we'll see if we can add anything that might help you."

This seemed to unnerve him a little. It was one thing to compare notes, and quite another to make a presentation in front of Lord Edgington. Lovebrook took a deep breath and began. "The way I see it, we're more or less restricted to the three Fairfax brothers, Sibyl Podence and the Duke." He got this far and had to stop for breath. Tossing his floppy fringe from his forehead – only for it to fall straight back again – he found another dose of confidence. "I'm willing to accept that they all had a hand in it, though."

I thought perhaps that Grandfather would wait until the inspector had said his part and then offer a critique— I mean, some helpful advice. I was wrong. "That is one hypothesis, but I think a more likely solution would be that one of them is responsible for the initial murder and the others have rallied around to protect their own."

"How interesting, Lord Edgington." The handsome young officer was beginning to fawn. "It's fascinating you should say that, as I had a similar thought myself. But if true, they've done too good a job of it. I can't tell which one is to blame."

"The attack on Lord Ruskin confuses things further," I decided to add. "I don't see what anyone hoped to achieve by lacing his coffee with strychnine. He doesn't appear to have witnessed the Duchess's murder, so what good would killing him do?"

"That is something for which I might have a possible explanation." Lovebrook took a moment to breathe, still clearly nervous about presenting his findings before the expert. "As I understand it, Ruskin began to feel the effects of the poison just before the killer appeared on the stairs. From his speed and size, we know that wasn't the Duke. The staff were either busy with their duties or attending to the stricken lord, and so it could only be one of the three brothers. It's my thinking that Ruskin was poisoned in order to distract from what was going on with the Duchess's body. What I can't say is what the killer was hoping to find at that moment. After all, the police surgeon and we three detectives had already inspected the scene of the crime. It all seems a touch desperate to me."

He looked in my direction as he said the word "detectives", which, I don't mind telling you, won him some points in my book. In fact, I liked the chap more all the time. With his careful manners and respectful attitude – not to mention his chic black Burberry mackintosh – he was the kind of police officer I hope will investigate my death if I'm unfortunate enough to be murdered.

"That is excellent work, Lovebrook," Grandfather said, and this time I wasn't jealous in the least. "Ruskin's poisoning might well have been a distraction. The Duchess was murdered in the most open part of the house and any inspection of the scene was likely to be noticed by ourselves, a servant, or one of your officers. The killer must have known you were busy with Albert and waited until the strychnine had its desired effect."

He bit his lip as he considered a significant piece of evidence. "The fact is that I don't believe the poison Lord Ruskin consumed was a lethal dose. While I detected the signs incredibly early, I very much doubt we would have been able to prevent more serious convulsions with the medicine we had at hand. This tells me that the killer either didn't know what he was doing and gave too small a dose or had no intention of killing the man."

I could see how inspired Lovebrook felt to hear my grandfather's theories. I hadn't been so different when I'd worked on my first case with him. It made me feel quite grown up to realise what a cynical old soul I'd become. Lord Edgington still had the capacity to amaze me; I simply didn't show it with such wide-eyed wonder anymore.

"I think we can also rule out your grandson Albert, despite certain evidence linking him to the crime," the inspector admitted. "My men have taken impressions of all the suspects' fingerprints, and the one on the banisters is definitely his. He had the motive too; by all accounts it would have served him well to remove the mother before marrying the daughter. But he was with me just before the killer was on the stairs and, if Albert murdered her with the help of an accomplice, he was incredibly careless about the whole thing."

"To be honest, that does fit with what I know of my brother." I cursed myself once more for continually promoting the idea of Albert's guilt. "My apologies, please continue."

In his usual amiable style, Lovebrook did just that. "For one thing, why wouldn't he have washed his hands before going to bed? Yes, there's blood all over his sheets, which would normally implicate a suspect, but he would surely have made some attempt to hide his guilt."

"I concur." Grandfather closed his eyes again, as though summoning the words he required from some parallel realm. "My grandson Albert is one of the silliest young gentlemen I have known in my life. He is soft-hearted, easily frightened, and a hopeless romantic. None of this leads me to believe that he would solve the problem of his future mother-in-law's ultimatum by murdering her. Knowing him as I do, I think it much more likely that he would send the Duchess flowers and give in to her every whim in order to maintain a happy home.

"Albert may not have the brain and acumen of his brother." He turned to me and, to be perfectly honest, I failed to stifle a laugh. "But he is a good person, raised by considerate parents and, from the very beginning, I have found it impossible to believe that he was involved in the killing."

To summarise all this, Lovebrook returned to his previous point. "As I said, I think we can rule out Albert. The timing is all wrong, anyway. Why would he do it the night before the wedding with so many people around and no alibi? Why would he have got out of bed in the middle of the night to carry out a murder? And how would he have got the Duchess to the stairs? Not only are these questions difficult to answer, it would be a waste of our time to try."

"What about Sibyl Podence?" I asked to move things along.

"Yes," Grandfather injected a frisson of mystery into his voice. "What about Sibyl Podence?"

It was Lovebrook's turn to deliver his ideas again and, I must admit, he did a good job. "In the first instance, whatever rumours we might have read about her in the papers, it bears repeating that, in the eyes of the law, she is an innocent woman."

"Precisely!" Lord Edgington clearly approved of his colleague's appraisal.

"However, past innocence does not eliminate the possibility of future guilt. If that were the case, every man in the country who was cleared of a crime would be running about the place, robbing banks and stealing priceless valuables from the British Museum."

"Exactly!" the inspector's new fan proclaimed.

"No, Sibyl Podence must very much remain a suspect. Like her boyfriend and rest of his family, she has made no effort to hide her hatred for the Duchess. If anything, I would say she has been the most vocal of them all. Her class of anger is quite different from that of the Fairfaxes. It's appealing to think of her as the likely suspect, but there's no physical evidence to connect her to either of the crimes, and the manner in which our victim was murdered doesn't seem to fit with a practical stranger being the culprit."

"I agree most heartily." Grandfather even mimed a round of applause for the chap. "From what I can tell, Sibyl hadn't intended to come to Hinwick House until Lord Ruskin suggested it. If she is the killer, she must have fashioned a plan quite spontaneously. The only possibility that comes to mind is that she met Albert at the party in the Great Hall last night and saw an opportunity to shift the blame onto a useful sap." He paused for a moment and, from his expression, I would have guessed he had a little trapped air. As it turned out, he was merely uncomfortable with his own theory. "The problem I have with this is that there is nothing very spontaneous about the crime. I believe that someone took the time to plan it."

I thought of some evidence to support his point. "It also wouldn't resolve the issue of how the killer lured the Duchess from her room. She surely would not have come out in the middle of the night to meet Sibyl when she had already refused to make her acquaintance in more formal surrounds."

"So then we can rule her out," Lovebrook suggested, looking from one to the other of us.

"I think that is a little precipitous. But we can set her to one side for the moment." Grandfather sat peacefully waiting for the next issue to be raised.

"We're left with the problem we've had all along." This had been bothering me for some time, and it felt good to express it out loud. "We must work out which of the Fairfax men is the likely killer, but there's really very little to choose between them."

The three of us mused on this point for a short while before Lovebrook spoke. "My first conclusion was that Stanislas is not the violent type. He is less obviously hostile or conceited than his brothers, and yet he is the one with an interest in warfare and, I don't know if you noticed, but he has a collection of weapons on the walls of his room."

"Everything you have said is purely circumstantial," Grandfather was quick to reply. "For one thing, we know exactly where the sword which killed the Duchess was previously displayed. Furthermore, it is Indian in origin – a Khanjar or Jambiya dagger, if I'm not mistaken – and is encrusted with cabochon diamonds and rubies."

For a moment, it was hard to know why he would go into such detail on the murder weapon, except as an excuse to show off his knowledge. I looked at Lovebrook in case he could make sense of it before Lord Edgington finally explained his prattling.

"To me, that does not seem like the type of weapon that would interest Stanislas. From the paraphernalia on show in his room, he is evidently more concerned with the long, gruelling battles of nineteenth and twentieth century Europe than exotic items from the east."

"Touché!" I found myself declaring as I came to understand his reasoning.

"Thank you, my lord. Your observations are no doubt extremely helpful." Lovebrook really was the most wonderfully polite man. "Nothing I have uncovered on Stanislas can directly link him to the crime. In fact, he has professed more love for his mother than anyone else in the family. He seems to have a tenderness towards her that goes against the treatment he received at her hand."

"Did he tell you about what she did on Guy Fawkes Night?" I asked with something of a grimace as I remembered the tale.

Lovebrook answered my question with a nod. "I noticed the scars on his hand when I spoke to him and felt compelled to ask. Lady Hinwick's cruelty is something we must not overlook. It is the most likely motive for her murder."

"Are you so sure?" Grandfather responded, as what else would he do but insert the possibility for doubt at every turn? "I believe there was an even more significant factor which the talk of her sadism overlooks."

"Her fortune," I thought out loud, and it earned me a "Precisely!" of my own from Grandfather.

"The Duchess of Hinwick was incredibly wealthy and, in marrying the Duke, had managed to keep her riches in her own name. As a result, she held her husband and children in her iron grip. For all that they like to dwell on the unfeeling manner in which she controlled them, their biggest objections came down to money. Stanislas himself is no longer so upset about his burns, nor the possessions that his mother had put on the fire without his knowledge. No, what he still struggles to comprehend is why she wouldn't support his chosen career. I believe that he loved his mother despite the fact that she murdered this one dream. She wouldn't let any of her boys slip away from her, whether it be to the army, a life in academia or to marry. Cassandra's case was different; the Duchess considered it her daughter's job to find a suitable husband. But for the men of the family, the situation is clear."

Lovebrook led us on to the next suspect. "I would say that Charles is a more duplicitous character. He runs hot and cold. He can seem quite charming when he wants to be and then turn like a viper." It was interesting to hear that the inspector had formed the same conclusions as I had on the eldest Fairfax boy. "More than anyone, he tried to show us just how much he hated the Duchess. And my theory that the family are working together was inspired by Charles's underhand manner. It's almost as if he wishes to deflect all the guilt onto himself. When we spoke to him upstairs, he seemed proud to tell us of the devious methods he'd employed to live his life without his mother's knowledge. I have no doubt that he was trying to shock us, and I came away from the interview with the feeling that he was capable of worse than a few white lies."

Grandfather might have complained that the detective was relying too much on his general impressions of the suspects and not enough on the evidence that would incriminate them, but I asked a question before he could speak. "Then who do you believe the Fairfaxes are protecting?"

Lovebrook placed his hands together before putting forward his big idea. "I believe it must be Eric."

I suppose he was hoping for a word of support or at least a show of interest from the expert, but Grandfather remained quiet. The inspector would have to make do with silence in place of encouragement.

"Eric is the only one who refused to speak to me, and he's also the brother who has shown the most irritation at my presence here. I believe that he was the cloaked figure I saw on the stairs, and that he murdered his mother and poisoned Lord Ruskin."

"Why?" was all he would receive for his efforts.

"I…" Lovebrook's resolve weakened before my grandfather's diamond-strength glare. "It had to be one of the brothers. I'm not saying that their father isn't complicit in some respect, but I'm certain that one of the three wielded the knife."

"Yes, but why Eric?"

"A feeling… No, it's more than that. When I saw them all together in the morning room, I had a sense of the hierarchy that exists here. All four of the siblings are very different; it would be hard to imagine they were from the same family if you met them in any other context. But when I arrived here, in my role as an officer of the Northamptonshire Constabulary, I saw that they treated me differently to everyone else. You may be a detective, but they accepted you as one of their own. I'm the outsider, and I think it frightened them."

Like a rabbit listening for a fox, Grandfather was suddenly more alert. "What did you notice?"

"It was the way they stood together before we spoke to Charles. He and Stanislas stepped forward with Eric safely behind them. I don't know whether it was conscious or not, but I think they were protecting him."

"And that's why you believe he must be to blame." I leaned back in my seat, a little impressed by his observation. "How interesting."

"What did Eric tell you when you spoke to him alone?" Grandfather was just as curious as I was.

"That's the thing." Lovebrook leaned forward to close the notebook he'd been using. "When I knocked on his bedroom door and asked to speak to him, he told me to go to the dickens."

"That is odd."

"I thought the same thing." Lovebrook tapped the front of the pad with his pen. "Eric said that he wasn't interested in a lowly policeman and would only talk to Lord Edgington himself."

CHAPTER TWENTY-SEVEN

Once all the major hypotheses and details of the case had been summarised, we left Detective Inspector Lovebrook with instructions to check Stanislas's clothes from the previous night and then went our separate ways.

"There's something I don't understand, Grandfather," I had to confess once we were climbing the servants' staircase to Eric's room. "We listened to all the evidence that our new friend had collected, but you gave little away on the topics that we've discussed."

He tipped his head back as he walked, as though he needed this information to roll into the right place. "Well, Christopher, I'm sure you've sensed by now that I like the inspector a great deal and see the potential he has to become a fine detective."

"Yes, I did notice."

"I enjoyed hearing his perspective on the case and always believe that collaboration is an essential tool for furthering modern investigative techniques and creating a fairer and more efficient police force."

"However...?"

"However, I decided not to tell Lovebrook everything we know in case he picks the right killer before we can." He allowed himself a real chortle then, before continuing in a more sombre voice. "I'm joking, of course. Time is running out, and we must finish our work."

I wasn't confident which part of what he'd said was a joke and what was supposed to be true. Either way, he was right. There was important work to be done, and every time we passed the grandfather clock in the upstairs corridor, it seemed that another fifteen minutes had elapsed. If we had any hope of solving the murder in time for the wedding to take place, it might be necessary to stay in one spot.

"One thing we did not discuss downstairs is the time of death," Grandfather declared before I could say anything so unhelpful. "The broken watch in the Duchess's pocket said midnight. And from the state in which we found the body, it was clear she had been dead for some hours, but we haven't yet heard the official word from the coroner."

"Surely that is an essential fact? We can't say what part the broken watch played unless we know what time the Duchess died."

We had come to Eric's door, and I stopped to hear his response. "Yes, that information could still prove significant. In fact, I hope to find out very soon just what part it played." Before he'd finished speaking, he knocked on the door to Eric's room and we awaited a begrudging moan of admission.

"Ah, you came. I'm glad you're here." He was lying on his bed as we entered, already dressed for the wedding in a black and grey swallow-tail dress coat. There was a small sitting area with three bare wooden chairs around a coffee table, and he motioned us over to them.

His manner was quite different from at any other time that weekend. He seemed friendlier and more interested in our task, as opposed to smugly aloof.

"Why exactly do you wish to speak to us?" Grandfather asked as he sat down in a small pool of sunlight in the otherwise dim room. The curtains were largely drawn to keep out the heat of the afternoon, but we could hear the guests gathering in the garden before they made their way to the church. I rather wondered whether the news of the Duchess's demise had filtered out to them. While I could understand Cassie and Albert wishing to go ahead with the wedding, I was surprised that so many of the guests had decided to attend. I had no doubt that some of them had stuck around for the subsequent gossip they could impart, rather than to see a loving young couple wed.

Ooh, you should have seen her face as she stood at the altar, bold as brass, I imagined the tell-tale-tits proclaiming. *And to think her mother wasn't dead a day when she got married.* I didn't give a hoot for such people and looked forward to standing beside my brother in church to celebrate his nuptials.

As I was conjuring up these imaginary busybodies, Eric answered the question. "I've been thinking about it a lot, and I understand what happened here last night." There was an incredible energy about him, as though he'd taken some of the Duchess's tonic. It was in stark contrast to his previous snide, lethargic manner.

"Is that so?" Grandfather offered in way of a noncommittal reply.

"It is. You see, I thought at first that the killer had to be a member of my family, as we'll gain the most from mother not being around anymore. Not just because she was strict with us, but because she was despicably rich and as miserly as Mr Scrooge." I would give

180

him one point for the Dickens reference, but only one, as it was an extremely obvious simile. "Our life will be an absolute paradise now that she's gone."

His whole face squished together in a smile. Some people's smiles stretch out their faces as though a rolling pin has passed over them, but Eric's somehow did the opposite. His eyes, forehead and cheeks crinkled inwards as his thin lips curled.

"I am so pleased for you." My grandfather: the master of the dry rejoinder.

Eric raced on as though he hadn't heard. "To be perfectly honest, I was convinced that the inspector would arrest Charles. It's not that he's the most evil of the lot of us. Goodness me, no. The thing with Charles is that he's the most active and organised. Stanislas and I have spent our adult years moping around the estate here. Cassie has spent hers trying to get away from Hinwick entirely, but Charles really does things with his time. I felt certain that he'd finally got around to murdering her, but he assures me that's not the case, and so I thought about who else could have done it."

"There really aren't too many options," I said in the hope it might calm him down a fraction.

"But that's where you're wrong. There are thousands of them. The Duke of Mayberry, for one. Old Timmy Mayberry wanted to marry mother, and she rejected him. It was partly because he was old enough to be her father, but he's still going strong at eighty – despite recently trying to burn down his neighbour's garden."

The more the man said, the faster the words came flying out of him. "Who's to say that he didn't come to the house in the night and do the deed? I bet that, if you asked him, he'd admit he never got over his love for Begonia Aster. Think about it; he's never married, has he?"

Grandfather had adopted a slightly concerned expression and made sure that the man had finished chattering before answering this question. "No, I suppose he hasn't. However, unless you happened to spot him on the premises recently, I doubt there's much to connect him to the crime."

Eric's eyes flicked between us but would fall still whenever he spoke. "Very well then, I have more ideas." His fingers were in a constant state of twiddledum. "We had a gamekeeper here on the estate. Father caught him poaching our own birds and had to let him go. He knew his way about the place and could have come into the house without much problem. And don't forget the poison. Who would have found it easier to slip some raticide or what have you into Ruskin's drink than a gamekeeper? Surely we must consider his part in all of this?"

"And when did he work here?" I could have been more civil, but I could already tell that this theory would not prove relevant.

He considered my question. "Well, I was only a little lad, but it couldn't have been more than fifteen years ago. There's a good chance that Peter Radler is alive and, if he is, he will definitely still be sore at the way he was given the sack."

There was a breeze that ruffled the curtains then. It caught the scent of alcohol and carried it over to me. Eric was clearly blotto, and I doubted that we would get much of use from him, but Grandfather had more to say.

"Now, Eric, that is all very helpful, but I have some questions of my own to put to you."

Instead of revealing how he felt on the matter, Eric swayed in his seat as though he were aboard a boat.

"First, I'd like you to tell me a little bit about your life growing up here."

"It was awful," he said without hesitation, and I once again noted that the Fairfaxes really didn't mind providing us with evidence against themselves. "Living with Mother was like being a serf in ancient times. She was the great ruler, and we were her slaves."

"She made you work?" I asked, taking him too literally.

"No, not that. In fact, she would have considered it painful to imagine us ever getting our hands dirty. She didn't put us to work, but she still expected us to obey her. And, in return, she'd bestow favours upon us. I think that she hoped we would turn against one another. She would have greatly enjoyed seeing us scrap it out for her love and favour, but it never turned out that way. Cassie and I have always been the best of friends, and Charles and Stanislas would look out for one another, so our bond could not be broken."

"Did that make her resent you in some sense?"

This question made him pause for a moment before his nervous energy surged once more. "I suppose it did. I suppose that she wished to control us because we never gave her exactly what she wanted. We were not the servile, submissive creatures she thought that children should be, and Father was not the devoted juggins with eyes for her alone whom she must have imagined herself marrying. We were human, no matter what she tried, and that was her biggest disappointment."

Grandfather's moustache performed its careful dance. "You said that she rewarded you with favours. Did she also punish you when you failed to meet her expectations?"

Eric's eyes seemed to inflate at this moment. I think he was excited that Grandfather had raised the topic. "Did she! The woman was a demon. When she wasn't whipping me across the bottom with a belt, she was—" He stopped himself then and thought of something more interesting to say. "When we were little, she gave Cassie a sweet little angora rabbit one day when she was well behaved." I already feared how this story would end. "Let's just say that, the next time one of us misbehaved, we had rabbit stew for lunch. Which isn't quite as bad as what happened to Stanislas's horse."

"That's disgusting." I immediately remembered my pet rabbit, Betsy, and felt outraged on behalf of bunnies everywhere. "I mean, it's totally inhumane to treat one's own child so savagely."

"And yet, she was your mother, Eric," Grandfather stated, knowing that this word held a thousand meanings. "You must feel some loss – some absence – now that she has passed."

"No, I don't. Next question."

Though he claimed to be unmoved, I detected something that didn't sit right in his story. "You won't miss her, you're not upset by her passing, and yet you're sitting in the dark on a sunny afternoon, drinking yourself silly. Why is that?"

He laughed again, but I felt that it was at himself as much as me. "You've discovered my secret. It's the booze that fills the hole. I don't know if you've realised, but alcohol is rather good at that… until you find yourself sober in the middle of the night and see the world for what it is."

"Is that what happened to you after the party?" Lord Edgington's words were somehow heavier than normal. The accusation seemed to roll slowly across the floor, and it took a few moments before Eric showed any sign of having heard. "Did you wake up in the debris of drink and dancing in the Great Hall and realise that you were not happy with this world? Is that when you sought a solution?"

He really laughed this time, and his eyebrows seemed to wobble on his forehead at the hilarity. "You're a clever one, aren't you? I mean, I know we've all heard the stories of the wily Lord Edgington, and I must say I doubted just how brilliant you were when Cassie told us she was marrying your idiot grandson, but you really are rather special."

"You didn't answer my question."

Eric leaned back in his seat and stretched up to his full height as his feet beat a rhythm on the floor. "Oh, fine. You've got me. Call the inspector, send for a couple of doltish constables to cart me away, because I'm the killer." His cheerful expression remained throughout. "I did it; you can lock me up. I left the Great Hall whilst everyone was asleep. I tempted mother from her bedroom and then stabbed her in the back as she descended the staircase in front of me."

When his confession had concluded, he sat watching us, his eyes brightened by the liquor he'd been drinking.

Grandfather folded his arms and waited a few moments before responding. "I didn't expect you to confess. I was just curious to see your reaction."

"You're not listening to me." He stood up then and put his hands together in supplication. "I'm the killer. It was me!" He practically sang the words. "I always hated my mother. I hated her because she rankled and bedevilled us for the pleasure that our disappointment could give her. I hated her with every ounce of strength in my body. I hated her, and so I killed her, and we've finally exorcised the demon from this house."

He collapsed back into his chair, and his manic smile only grew.

I looked at my grandfather, uncertain what to say or even think of Eric's performance. One thing that my mentor still hadn't taught me was how to hide my emotions, but he was a real master. As he watched the aftermath of the young man's outburst, his face was inscrutable, and I couldn't tell whether he was about to shout for the police, as Eric had commanded, or sympathise with our suspect for the pain he clearly bore.

"Maybe you killed the Duchess. Maybe every word you just said is true. But you'll have to prove it." If anything, his tone hardened, and he began to fire off questions. "Where did you get the weapon?"

Visibly more nervous than before, Eric answered the question.

184

"There's a rack on the wall at the top of the main staircase."

"That was an easy one. There can't be many jewelled daggers in this house, and you've lived here all your life." Grandfather drummed his fingers on the arm of his chair, and I'm certain that the repeated rhythm was designed to unnerve Eric even more. "Now tell me how you got your mother to leave her bedroom without waking your father in the room opposite hers."

"I went out into the garden, just in front of the Great Hall where we'd been all night, and I called up to her." He paused then and, either he was the killer and knew exactly what had happened, or he sensed there was something missing and guessed what it must be. "That didn't wake her, and so I found a stone to throw. Of course, Father was asleep in the Great Hall, anyway, so this probably wasn't necessary."

I would have liked to ask how he'd convinced the Duchess to leave her room, but we weren't trying to fill in every last gap in the story at this point, and Grandfather would not release the pressure.

"How did Albert's fingerprint find its way into the blood on the newel post?"

"What's a newel post?" Eric managed to smile again and, by this stage, I really couldn't say what was happening.

"The wooden posts that stick up above the banisters."

"Oh, of course. Then in that case… I don't know how it got there. Your grandson must have wandered downstairs and touched it after I killed Mother. Is he known to somnambulate?"

"At what time did you kill her?"

"Midnight, or thereabouts." Eric was so confident in his answers that I was certain that a lesser detective than my grandfather would have taken every word he said at face value.

"Why did you return to the body after the police had inspected it?" Eric hesitated then, and so Grandfather immediately fired off another question. "And why do you want me to believe that you're a murderer when you're obviously not?"

I think that, more than solving crimes and righting wrongs, the things Grandfather loved most about our investigations were the moments when he stunned a suspect into silence. He'd already tied Charles's brain up in knots that morning, and now Eric wore a matching startled expression.

"Come along, Christopher." The real sleuth had heard enough and pushed his seat back to leave. "We should stop wasting time with someone who clearly knows nothing about what happened last night."

Eric was frantic again. His eyes darted about from one wall to the other as he searched for something to make his case. The problem was that he evidently wasn't the killer, and nothing he could say would change that.

CHAPTER TWENTY-EIGHT

The door slammed shut behind us, and I was certain that Grandfather had noticed something significant that I had evidently ignored.

"What did you extract from our encounter with the last of the Fairfax boys?" he asked with a self-satisfied grin.

I hesitated, as I really hadn't a clue. "That excessive drinking can lead to emotional instability and irrational behaviour?"

I knew this wasn't what he wanted to hear, and his amused expression confirmed it. "No, Christopher. Although the ability to enjoy such pleasures in moderation is a useful one, I was thinking of something Eric said… or rather, what he didn't say."

This was just the kind of riddle that he loved putting to me. In response, I loved to look blank and scratch my head. "Was it that he didn't mention the wedding?"

"Well done, Christopher!"

"Was I correct?" I could hardly believe it.

"No, but you did notice that he didn't mention the wedding directly."

"And how does that help us?"

He thought for a moment as we drifted towards the scene of the first crime and our suite of rooms beyond it. "It doesn't, but you showed keen signs of observation, which I applaud."

He was really very chirpy just then, so I made no attempt to bring us back to the topic of what I hadn't noticed. When we got to the landing, however, he spotted the empty space halfway up on the wall of swords and shook his head mournfully. For a man who had experienced so much loss and destruction in his life, he was never one to trivialise death.

"Eric is clearly, in his own haphazard way, trying to protect someone, and there was a particular name he did not mention in our interview." There was a pregnant pause, as though he expected me to guess to whom he was referring. He soon got the message that this would not be happening. "Lord Ruskin, Christopher. Eric didn't mention Damian Ruskin the whole time we were talking to him."

"So he was protecting Ruskin?" I replied, without seeing how this made sense.

"Perhaps... Alternatively, he may not have wanted to discuss the poisoning, as it didn't fit with the story he presented to us."

I tried to piece this together with everything else we'd discovered. I couldn't.

"We must make haste." He moved off across the landing to the narrow corridor which led to our rooms. "We are almost at the finale. Wouldn't you say? The crescendo of this peculiar symphony."

"Undoubtedly." I don't know if I've mentioned this before, but I am a liar. I hadn't the first idea who the killer was or why Lord Ruskin had been poisoned. For all I knew, the big surprise that grandfather would present in his grand summation was that my brother was really to blame for everything and had been stalking about the house without anyone seeing him. For all I knew, the house contained...

"Grandfather! Does Hinwick House have a series of hidden tunnels between rooms?" I should have thought a little more before blurting out such a question.

He looked at me as though I'd recently suffered a knock to the head. "Just because one house we visited had secret passageways, Christopher, that does not mean that they all do." He sighed and pushed open the door to his bedroom.

Albert was lying on his back on the floor and bore a self-pitying frown. Though he had no face paint, and his clothes were all the right size, he looked rather like a clown I'd once seen at Bertram Mills International Circus at Olympia.

"I've been so lonely," he moaned in typical Albert fashion as he launched himself up to standing. "Tell me, Grandfather, are you here to arrest me? You don't have to soften the blow; I'm stronger than I look."

I'm certain that our grandfather would have enjoyed nothing more than a tut and a roll of the eyes at my brother's overly emotive behaviour, but he resisted the temptation and delivered some good news. "Not at all, boy. We've come to tell you that Cassandra is now getting ready for the wedding, and we must be at the church at five o'clock just as we informed the guests and the priest that we would be."

"Oh, thank goodness." He fell to his knees, the emotion rushing through him. And, just to prove his previous point, he burst into tears.

"This really is the happiest day of my life. My fiancée still loves me, and I'm not going to hang for murder."

"Ahh, the words that so many grooms have uttered on their wedding days," Grandfather whispered so that Albert couldn't hear. "The traditional declaration of innocence that every man surely makes before he says his vows."

I had something more practical to impart. "Albert, the police don't believe that you did it. The killer must have come into your room and placed the tip of your thumb in the blood. If you weren't such a deep sleeper, he'd never have got away with it."

He looked up at the ceiling and wailed. "Curse my singular ability to sleep through hurricanes and lightning storms." This was not hyperbole; it was almost impossible to disturb my dear brother's slumber. I once drew a moustache on his face with coal dust and he didn't know anything about it until he came down to breakfast and the footmen started laughing at him.

"There's no time for that." Grandfather walked over to pull him up to standing. He should probably have given my brother a bracing slap about the face, but apparently there was no time for that either. "I'll collect your wedding suit from your room. You must get dressed as soon as possible."

"It's not even four o'clock yet. There's plenty of time," he said, unaware of what was still ahead of us.

Grandfather had already gone in search of Albert's clothes, and so I was left to answer him. "We still haven't caught the killer, and you know how much Grandfather likes to make a show of these things. He'll have to gather all the suspects, then reveal the evidence against each of them before finally identifying the culprit in a dramatic and, let's be honest, rather overblown manner. That will take at least twenty minutes and, by the time you're clean and dressed, it will be almost five o'clock. It's lucky the church is so close."

This depressed him a little, but Grandfather reappeared with the necessary items, and we left Albert to deal with his forever shifting range of emotions.

"I sometimes wonder how the pair of you can be brothers," Grandfather told me once we'd closed the door to his bedroom and could no longer be heard.

"And I sometimes wonder why you think we're so different. I may not mope and moan like Albert, but I'm just as prone to talking nonsense."

He finally had his chance to tut. "Really, Christopher, you do talk nonsense."

"Precisely!"

"Very well, but the nonsense you talk is poles apart from your brother's. You're forever putting yourself down when you should be confident in your abilities. Though I see potential in Detective Inspector Lovebrook, and I'm sure his men are competent officers, you are by far the second-best detective here today."

This may have sounded a little big-headed on his part, but I took it as a real compliment. In addition to "Britain's finest detective," as Charles had described him, there were five policemen and my mother at Hinwick at that moment. I really couldn't sniff at second place.

"That's all well and good," I began, "but what of the investigation? How are we going to sew everything together before the service at St Mary's?"

"Simple, my boy." The old lord was already walking away. "Change your clothes, collect your brother, and I'll meet you both in the drawing room when you're ready."

"That didn't answer my question!" I called after him, but either he didn't care, he didn't hear me, or both.

CHAPTER TWENTY-NINE

I dived into my travelling trunk and came out with the black tailcoat for the wedding. It wasn't as smart as my other suit and, as with most clothes my mother bought me, it was a size or two too large. I ended up looking like a little boy trying on my father's clothes, but it would have to do. The accessories that Albert had chosen for the day helped with the overall effect, and I particularly admired the amethyst tie pin and cufflinks that would match my grandfather's glittering cane.

I emerged from my room a little crumpled, perhaps, but ready for a wedding. With my top hat in place and my dandified brother at my side, I felt just the part. I couldn't say for certain what our wise leader had been up to as we got dressed, but he'd evidently been carrying out some final investigations.

"Ahh, you're both ready. That's wonderful." Grandfather had a smile on his face to rival The Merry Fiddler's. "Come this way."

He led us to the drawing room where I'd last seen Lord Ruskin still suffering the effects of the strychnine. The scene inside was a great deal calmer than before. Ruskin was sitting up on the sofa and, though still drowsy, looked a thousand times healthier.

A doctor was taking his blood pressure as we entered, and I sent a question into the room ahead of us. "What's the prognosis?"

The little man with the large ears and incredibly sharp chin looked stern as he went about his work but became quite cheerful and replied in a lilting Scottish voice. "All's well that ends well, don't they say?" He tittered and his strangely shaped head wobbled on his shoulders as he removed the cuff from his patient's arm. "And it seems that Lord Ruskin here was very lucky indeed."

"I can't thank you enough, Doctor Marnoch." Ruskin smiled as he did up his shirt sleeve. "Or you, Lord Edgington. You saved my life."

The doctor turned serious again. "The fact is that, with a big enough dose of strychnine, there would have been little we could do for you. Bromide of potassium might have eased your convulsions, but if someone had put a couple of teaspoons of the poison in your coffee instead of just a pinch, you would have expired in the most unimaginable agony in the space of an hour or two." He was very blunt on the matter. "I've heard that there is no end quite so dramatic nor painful as death by strychnine."

"I'm unfortunate enough to have seen one or two cases during my days on the metropolitan police," Grandfather reminded us. "The bent and broken corpses I saw looked quite inhuman, and I'm very glad we didn't have such a case on our hands today."

"That's all that matters." Dr Marnoch finished attending to his patient and returned his equipment to the black leather bag that sat open on the coffee table like the jaws of a carnivorous plant. "I've offered Lord Ruskin a sedative, and he has refused. And so, gentlemen, as the physician to this family for over thirty years, I have a wedding to attend. I hope to see you all there." He winked at Ruskin, who limply extended his hand for the doctor to shake.

And then we were alone with the witness, and there were some questions that needed asking. Albert had taken a seat beside the far window. He clearly believed it was down to the two detectives to deal with the interview, which I can't say I minded one bit.

"Lord Ruskin, we still do not understand how your poisoning connects to the murder. Can you explain it at all?" Perhaps this was too optimistic an approach on my part.

The war hero turned dissolute drunk looked down at his hands as though he required a moment's pause before moving on to the problem before us. "I can't say that I have given it much thought until now. I've been too busy counting my blessings."

"You must think, man," Grandfather admonished him as he sat down on the neighbouring sofa. "While the police have concluded that you were poisoned as a distraction in order for the killer to return to the scene of the crime undetected, I do not believe that to be likely. For one thing, we are very close to where the Duchess's body was found, and so it would have been better to draw the police to the other end of the house. An explosion in the Great Hall or a sickly butler in the kitchen would have been a smarter ploy than the attempt to poison you."

"I see," Ruskin replied. "Yes, it is all a bit strange, isn't it? Unless the killer got a taste for the thing after stabbing the Duchess. Perhaps some people treat murder as a hobby."

"That's a common assumption in cases such as this one, but I can assure you that the majority of killers I have known took their actions very seriously. What's more, as the doctor mentioned, if the murderer had access to strychnine, it took more effort to ensure only the smallest dose was administered than it would have been to fill your cup with the stuff."

My brain had apparently been working without my noticing, and I had something relevant to say. "I might have an explanation for that particular point." The three men turned to look at me, and I tried not to be nervous as I presented my idea. "Grandfather, you told me that strychnine is the bitterest substance in the world. Perhaps the killer was afraid that Lord Ruskin would be able to detect it in his coffee and stop drinking it. In that case, it would make sense to administer a smaller amount of poison."

Ruskin laughed at this. "It's a shame I love strong coffee so much. I barely noticed the difference to how I normally take it."

"That is a possibility, Christopher." Grandfather was sitting down and couldn't pace about to consider my point, so his eyes wandered the room in his stead. "Yes, that may explain it, but we still don't know why Lord Ruskin was targeted." He turned back to our suspect-turned-victim. "Have you considered that you might know something the killer would prefer to keep secret?"

"I suppose that could explain it, but I can't think what that might be." He looked quite bemused. "I believe I've told you everything I've done since I arrived at Hinwick House last night. I came with Sibyl. We all drank our socks off in the Great Hall and, though I don't remember why or when, at some point I walked outside and fell asleep in a flowerbed. I can only assume your darling dog found me there and kept an eye out to make sure I was all right."

It was the perfect moment for Grandfather to reflect on Delilah's magnificence. Well, it wasn't, but he did it anyway. "Yes, she really is an extraordinary beast. I've kept dogs all my life, you know, and never known another like her."

I was standing near the window out of Ruskin's direct view and pointed to my imaginary watch to remind Grandfather to hurry things along. He did not understand the gesture.

"I doubt that the watch we found on the Duchess's body is relevant to the poisoning, Christopher. If anything, I'm inclined to believe it was left at the scene as a red herring." I didn't reply, and he turned back to our witness. "As I was saying, I believe the killer must think you know something that could lead to his identification."

"No, I'm sorry." Ruskin was adamant. "I've racked my brain and come up blank."

I was engaged in a similar endeavour but managed to muster an answer. "What if the killer saw him outside last night? We know that whoever was responsible for the murder must have gone into the garden to get the Duchess's attention through her window. What if he noticed Lord Ruskin asleep beside the…" I tried to remember the name of the plant that Grandfather had mentioned. "…flowers?"

This idea bounced around the heads of those present. Even my brother looked interested, but our grandfather would inevitably find a flaw in my suggestion. "Don't forget that the outside of the house has no illumination. It would have been quite dark, and Damian here was rolled up in a ball out of sight. It seems unlikely he would have been spotted and, as long as he was asleep, he was of no concern to the killer."

I realised then that he was quite right. The only reason I'd noticed Lord Ruskin in his makeshift bed was because our dear dog had been guarding him. If Delilah hadn't barked to get my attention, Ruskin might have stayed hidden all day.

"What about a simple grudge?" Albert asked to make his first contribution to the discussion. "Isn't it possible that someone here at the house wished Ruskin harm?"

The very idea seemed to offend the gadfly lord. "I jolly well hope that no one could so dislike me that they'd poison my coffee. I always make a point of being utterly charming." He emitted a poorly timed laugh, and Grandfather was quick to respond.

"The circumstances here at Hinwick House are hardly typical. I'm sure that you're the focus of every party you attend and are beloved by London's fashionable set, but the Fairfaxes are a peculiar bunch. Even if you hadn't tried to marry the only daughter, you might have upset one of them. Charles is proud, Stanislas is broken somehow and, based on our interview just now, Eric seems to have cracked entirely."

No longer so intimidated by the discussion, Lord Ruskin spoke fondly of our hosts. "Oh, they're all fine people once you get to know them. The boys are good sorts, really. And Samuel, or His Grace, the Duke, as he prefers to be called, is an old softy when you get to know him."

194

"So you had a good relationship with each of them," I tentatively began, "except for the Duchess."

"No, I even got on well with Begonia for a long time. It was only when I asked for Cassandra's hand in marriage that she turned against me."

Grandfather had been quiet for a few moments but cleared his throat to speak. "What reason did she give for her refusal?"

It felt as though we'd spent the day not finding out the real answer to this question, and I was eager to hear what the man had to say.

"She didn't," Ruskin replied. "Or, at least, she said nothing to me. All I knew was from Samuel. He told me that Begonia didn't want me in the house anymore, and I was to have no communication with Cassandra."

Albert suddenly looked uncomfortable, and I had to assume this was not because of the hard wooden chair in which he sat. It was only the night before that Lord Ruskin had been professing his hate for the groom and his love for the bride. Eighteen hours, a murder and a poisoning later, and we were sitting around together like old friends. It was hardly the most relaxing situation I could imagine.

"When was that?" Grandfather asked.

"Last year, before Cassie left for Oxford. I'm not the sort of person to kick up a fuss and tried to stay away as much as possible. As she was at university most weeks, however, I didn't see that it made much difference whether I popped by from time to time once the Duchess had retired for the night. I'm good friends with all the men in the house and, as far as I'm concerned, friends should be treasured like diamonds."

The frustration was too much for Grandfather, and he at last got to his feet to pace across the room. I can't say I blamed him for looking so disappointed. We couldn't say when the crime had taken place, or whether the broken watch in the Duchess's pocket told us what we needed to know. It was hard to pick a definitive motive, despite the fact that no one actually liked the first victim. And we still hadn't even detected a good reason for Lord Ruskin's poisoning.

Grandfather's solution to this was to have a bit of a think as he walked about the drawing room. "There must be something we're missing," he muttered to himself.

Back in my more naïve days, I would have done all I could to fill these gaps, to the extent of chattering away with no real idea of what I was saying. Fortunately, my grandfather had trained me well, and so it fell to my brother to spout whatever gibberish occurred to him.

"Perhaps Cassie's brothers aren't so keen on the old dog who tried to marry their sister after all. Perhaps whichever one of them murdered their mother thought they should make the most of the opportunity to kill another hated figure in the family." He cast his gaze towards his rival as he spoke. "It was evidently a wedding present! The controlling mother was dispatched before the killer decided to get the spurned suitor out of the way, too. Someone in the family was just looking after Cassie."

"I'll look after you if you're not careful," Ruskin bellowed, and I'm certain that he would have shot across the room with his fists leading the way if he hadn't been so weak. "Would you like to know what I really think of you, Prentiss?"

Albert no longer looked so brave. "Oh... Ummm... not particularly. Maybe if you—"

Grandfather put him out of his misery. Grinding to a sudden halt in front of our witness, he raised his voice to match Ruskin's. "We're not going to get anywhere by bickering." His words shook the plates on a Welsh dresser in the far corner of the room. "There has to be some connection we're overlooking. Some reason why the killer wanted to poison you. On the surface, you're an outsider here. Your only relevance comes from your friendship with the Duke and your subsequent wooing of Cassandra. But if we accept that the Duchess was murdered for the cruel way in which she controlled her family, why were you next on the list?"

Lord Ruskin had managed to calm himself by now, but he still wore a grimace as he considered Grandfather's question. "I agree that there must be a significant reason to explain why I was targeted. But I simply don't know what it is." He fell quiet and shook his head at the very idea of anyone not adoring him. "Except for your ill-mannered grandson, I can think of no one in the house who would wish me harm."

I saw the moment that everything came together for my grandfather. Indeed, as the pieces of the puzzle fell into place, I could almost hear it. With his eyes still fixed on Ruskin, the muscles in his face became stuck as though someone had glued them in place.

"I've been such a fool."

Before he could reveal his mistake, there was a knock on the door and the inspector led two uniformed officers into the room. "Lord Edgington? I'm sorry to disturb you, but my men found something we thought you'd like to see."

The first constable was holding a formal white shirt with a removable collar, white gold cufflinks and several bloodstains dotted across the front.

"Where did you find it?" I asked, unable to believe that the case could revolve around such a straightforward discovery.

"Stuffed under a loose floorboard in a cupboard in one of the upstairs bedrooms." Lovebrook took a deep breath and answered the only question that really mattered. "Stanislas Fairfax's clothes weren't in the laundry as he claimed, so we searched the first floor. We've arrested him for the murder of Lady Hinwick."

CHAPTER THIRTY

The police left to deal with their prisoner. Albert was no doubt wondering whether he could wait to tell Cassie that her brother had murdered her mother until after they were married, and Lord Ruskin seemed to have fallen asleep.

"Isn't it possible…" I was searching for some way to explain the evidence against Stanislas. It was not that I had any reason to protect the man. It simply did not feel right that, of all the dubious characters we had encountered, he would be the killer. "Isn't it possible that the real killer took the shirt and dipped it in the Duchess's blood, just as he did with the ball from the newel post?"

I think that the revelation had shaken my grandfather a little, as he replied in a harsh tone. "No, Chrissy, that's not the solution."

The idea was developing in my head, even as he dismissed it. "Wait, just one moment. I think I understand now. That's why our culprit distracted us with the strychnine and was there on the stairs. He needed access to the corpse to throw suspicion on Stanislas. The poor man is taking the blame for someone else's misdeeds."

Grandfather's response came quickly. "Don't be foolish, Chrissy. The man on the stairs was evidently Stanislas. Lovebrook didn't say anything about the cloaked figure having a shirt in his hand. Don't you see how it fits together now? Don't you understand what went on here?"

The answer to both of these questions was, obviously, no. I wasn't in the mood for him to insult my intelligence, – that was my job – and so I remained silent as he issued new orders.

"Albert, there's enough time to get to the wedding, but I have to finish this first. If you'd like to help, you can round up the Fairfax family."

"Even Cassie?" he asked with some hesitation in his voice.

Grandfather considered the possibility but finally shook his head. "No, no. Don't worry her with this just yet. We can tell her the details after the wedding is over. Giving her the peace she needs to get ready is the smallest kindness we can do for her." Albert was at the door and about to leave when the old wizard spoke again. "Tell Lovebrook and the constables to bring Stanislas to the canopy on the lawn if you see them. The guests will have left for the church by now, so we should have it to ourselves."

My brother was always more focused when he had a task to complete. He was a great follower of orders, and I could see the determination on his face as he disappeared from the room.

"I know it must be a strain for you, Lord Ruskin…" Grandfather was in something of a hurry and rushed through his words. "…but I'll send one of my staff to help you outside. I wouldn't have been able to identify the killer without your help, and I'd like you to tell the police exactly what you just told me."

Ruskin barely opened his eyes but raised his hand in acknowledgment.

"What should I do?" I asked as Grandfather moved to leave.

He consulted the clock on the mantelpiece. "We must be at the church in three quarters of an hour. Talk to Todd and make certain that the cars are ready for us to depart as soon as we've finished. Oh, and tell him to take Cassandra on the longest route possible in case of delays. I'll see you in the garden."

I nodded, and he hurried from the room. When I got outside, I found that a number of Grandfather's luxurious cars had been lined up in preparation for the wedding. The Silver Ghost at the front of the convoy even had a white ribbon tied around the flying lady. The gardeners from Cranley Hall were dressed in their smartest Sunday suits and waved to me as I passed. I wasn't entirely clear why we would need so many vehicles to transport two families, but I could worry about that later.

I ran around the house to the cottages on the other side of the property. My father was there, busy polishing his blue Bentley in preparation for the journey to his elder son's wedding. It was a fine automobile, and he loved it with all his heart, but I must admit that it looked rather normal next to my grandfather's new Daimler limousine. That singularly regal car was like a house on wheels and had a matching ribbon to the one in which Albert would be travelling.

Unsurprisingly, Todd was ready to lead the bridal procession. He stood ever so smartly by the largest of the three cars, dressed immaculately in his dark green livery. Though his position within the Cranley Hall household had risen somewhat, there was no way he

200

would let anyone else drive Cassandra that day.

"Is all well, Master Christopher?"

"Except for the mother of the bride being murdered, one of the suspects getting poisoned and the groom nearly ending up in handcuffs, I'd say things were going swimmingly."

Todd pulled on the chain in his waistcoat pocket to check the time, and I was reminded of the mystery watch that had been found on the Duchess after she died.

"I imagine that Lord Edgington has identified the culprit by now and is due to explain the whole affair before rushing to the church?"

"Well done, Todd," I replied, ever impressed by the fellow. "You're almost as accomplished at reading minds as your master."

He bowed his head a fraction. "It is in every good chauffeur's interest to be able to predict the timetable for the day. I suppose you'd like me to take Lady Cassandra on a circuitous route to the church in case Albert is late arriving?"

"That's just what I came to tell you. Obviously don't go too far. Around Northampton and back should do the trick, but I'll let you be the judge of that. I want to make sure that her future husband is standing at the altar when she arrives."

"Of course, Master Christopher. Once I see your grandfather's Rolls Royce there, I'll know you're ready for us."

"And if you don't?"

He smiled. He was a handsome chap at the worst of times but had the smile of a film star. "I'll explain that there's a momentary problem with the engine, and that I feel it would be in everyone's best interests if we went around the village once more."

"Excellent! Have a safe trip."

I was about to run back to the main lawn in front of the house when my mother came out of the cottage looking worried. "Christopher, is everything all right?"

I don't suppose it's typical for the mother of the groom to have so many responsibilities with the bridal party, but then it's also fairly rare for the mother of the bride to be murdered just before the wedding.

"Yes, Chrissy," Father stopped his polishing to add, "you must tell us if your brother's been locked up in the local police station. That happened to me once, and it was no fun at all."

"Don't worry. Albert will be fine, and we'll see you at the church at… approximately five o'clock." Mother still regarded me through doubting eyes, and so I added an explanation. "I just have one more thing to do with Grandfather, and then we'll be right with you."

She was elegantly attired in a long blue floral dress and oversized hat, so at least she wouldn't burn in the blazing sun. From her tone at that moment, I doubt it was the weather that concerned her. "I know what sort of last-minute tasks tend to occupy my father. You can tell him two things from me."

"Yes, Mother?"

She sighed and gave me my instructions. "First, tell him to keep the theatricality to a minimum; if the wedding is delayed, I'll blame him. And second, you can inform your grandfather that, if the grand denouement to the case turns out to be that Albert is the killer, I won't talk to him for a year."

I didn't reply, but gulped and ran away. Hearing my mother speak so sternly was more frightening than coming face to face with most of the murderers I had known.

CHAPTER THIRTY-ONE

By the time I got to the elegant white canopy under which the wedding banquet would eventually be enjoyed, several of the key players had already arrived. The two Fairfax brothers who were not wearing handcuffs had somewhat presumptuously taken their places at the top table. Eric had even found a bread roll from somewhere and was devouring it like a man who'd been lost at sea for several days. The Duke stood behind them, ever the peripheral figure in the family: the middle ground between his despotic wife and their wayward children. Oh, and Delilah was there, too. She was asleep beside the top table and looked as though she'd seen enough of her master's speeches to last a lifetime.

Albert arrived just after me, with Detective Inspector Lovebrook and his men leading Stanislas a little way behind. The youngest Fairfax boy showed no emotion as he was made to sit down at one of the round tables in the shade. The floral centrepiece and neat white tablecloths were quite at odds with the sight of the prisoner, with his tousled hair and blue-uniformed entourage. Sibyl arrived next and, once more in the purple dress she'd worn the night before, clearly had the forethought (or perhaps effrontery) to change for the wedding. In fact, Stanislas was the only one there who was not ready for the big event, and perhaps he wouldn't need to attend anyway.

Our footman Halfpenny soon brought Lord Ruskin to the impromptu congregation. This was quite amusing as he was almost twice the age of the man he had to help, and the pair of them took rather a long time to cross the lawn. Ruskin was so sleepy from whatever the doctor had given him that, now seated at the closest table, he could barely keep his eyes open until his assistant brought him a glass of water. I noticed that he began with an exceedingly small sip, presumably to make sure that the killer hadn't repeated his previous trick.

Once we were all assembled, Grandfather joined us. I was certain that, like an actor waiting in the wings for his cue, he'd been observing the stage and only made an appearance once everyone was in place.

"My lords, ladies and gentlemen," he began, as if embarking on the speech he would have delivered at approximately that time, had we followed the original schedule for the day, "I have gathered you here not to celebrate the union of two beloveds, but as a testament to the evil of man." That was a nice, jolly introduction to kick off the proceedings. I had to wonder what he would talk about at my wedding, should the event ever come to pass.

"A woman has been murdered, and almost every person in the vicinity of Hinwick House appears to have wanted her dead. Lady Hinwick was despised by her family for her authoritarian habits and, at some point in the middle of the night—"

"I heard from the coroner," Lovebrook interrupted from his post beside one of the poles that held the canopy in place. "The findings were inconclusive, I'm afraid, and a post-mortem will have to be conducted. All he could say was that the death occurred between midnight and four in the morning."

"How very helpful," Grandfather shook his head disbelievingly. It was simply one of those cases. The evidence we had uncovered was of a shifting, unstable nature. Each fact was merely a theory, each theory open to interpretation, and this was just one more detail that could not be ascertained with any certainty. "Well, whatever time it occurred, the Duchess was stabbed through the back and fell down the main staircase, banging her head against the banister as she collapsed. Thanks to the particularly vicious dagger with its watered steel blade, it is fair to assume that the initial blow was enough to snuff her life out in one go."

He paused then and looked around at our suspects. Eric had finished his appetiser and sat looking grim. The extreme reaction that we had witnessed in his room appeared to have subsided, but this had done little to improve his mood. Charles sat beside him with a studious expression, as though he wished to note down the inconsistencies in my grandfather's account, just as an opposing barrister would at a trial.

Sibyl Podence was sitting alone at a nearby table. It was the first time I'd seen her without her boyfriend, and she looked more than a little vulnerable. She kept touching the high neck of her lace cardigan as though afraid she had failed to dress appropriately.

Our footman Halfpenny, meanwhile, had obviously been charged with ensuring that Ruskin didn't fall asleep again. He stood behind the stricken lord's chair throughout and would poke him when necessary.

"In some investigations, it is hard to land upon even the suggestion

204

of a motive. I have encountered murder victims who were loved by all, and the challenge I faced was to discern who might conceivably be responsible for the crime. Today, I have the opposite problem. There was one obvious suspect who the police came close to arresting, another who is currently in handcuffs, and each of you has expressed your distaste for the Duchess without fear of how it might implicate you in the crime. It was not difficult for my assistant, Christopher, and me to consider the possibility that the whole lot of you were working together to befog our view of the evidence and the intentions of those involved."

This deserved a pause, and he made the most of it to cast his gaze from Fairfax to Fairfax. "However, I do not believe this is the solution we require." He walked between the occupied tables then, like a bobby treading his beat. "What cannot be ignored is that each of you had a major grievance with the Duchess, and one of them must explain why she was killed."

They were all frightened, that much was clear. Even Ruskin seemed to take Grandfather's words as a stimulating tonic, much as Lady Hinwick had been prescribed a measure of diluted strychnine.

"My grandson Albert had his reasons for wanting to murder his future mother-in-law."

"No, I didn't!" he said in something of a squeal.

"Yes, you did!" Eric and Charles replied as one, and I was worried for a moment that we would descend into the realm of pantomime.

Luckily, Grandfather was there to have the final word. "Yes, Albert, you did. And there was certainly plenty of evidence to point to your involvement." He put his hand on my brother's shoulder and Albert trembled. "Last night, having welcomed us to her home most warmly, she took you aside and explained exactly what your role in the family would be. She told you that, by marrying into the Fairfax clan, you would be under her control, and she would use your influence to keep her daughter in line."

Albert let out a doubtful huff. "I don't believe she was quite as threatening as you make her sound. She really only—"

"I was listening outside the door to the library when she spoke to you."

He had to grimace then. "Ah, I see…"

Grandfather did not concern himself with the groom's nerves at

205

this moment and continued to lay out the evidence that his grandson was a brutal murderer. "She gave you an ultimatum, which I cannot imagine being the sort of present for which a young man hopes on the eve of his wedding. Killing the Duchess would have been the perfect way out of her trap. She said that you could fall in line or call off the engagement and walk away. I heard the pleasure she took in tormenting you. She wanted you to break her daughter's heart or, failing that, become yet another of her puppets."

I looked at the three brothers as he spoke, and I could see just how painful it was for them to hear their position in the family summarised in so cold and succinct a manner. I realised at that moment that Charles was sitting just where Lady Hinwick would have been had she lived to see the wedding. He had taken one of the forks and now brought it down onto the table like Poseidon with his trident.

Albert made no further attempt to refute our grandfather's account, and so the story continued.

"One of the first things I noticed when we discovered the body was an extremely well-defined fingerprint in a splash of blood on the banisters. It was almost too perfectly positioned – pointing out at just the right angle for everyone to see. As a student of dermatoglyphics…" Our blank expressions told him that no one there knew what this word meant. "Dermatoglyphics is the study of fingerprints. And as a student of this burgeoning new field of science, I immediately noticed a rare characteristic in the print, which is common in my family. The chances of anyone here but my two grandsons and myself having a tented arch on the thumb were remarkably low, and so I worked on the hypothesis that this linked the groom to the crime."

I noticed that he avoided saying outright that this made Albert the likely killer. He was always particular in his choice of words, and I hoped this meant that my brother really was innocent. I knew in my heart that there was more chance of my grandfather himself being to blame.

"When he was first alerted to his mother's demise, Charles Fairfax decided that Cassandra's fiancé was the obvious killer. He led us to my grandson's room, where we discovered blood on the bedsheets and Albert's right hand. I was confident that Albert was no killer and so became suspicious of Charles's behaviour. I had to wonder whether he already knew that the blood would be there in Albert's bedroom."

"Of course I didn't." The eldest Fairfax boy brought his fork down on the tablecloth once more. "I told you at the time, I didn't believe that anyone in my family was capable of casting off mother's yoke in such a violent fashion, and so I could only assume that the newcomer was to blame."

"As opposed to your girlfriend, who had previously been on trial for murder?" Grandfather volleyed the question straight back at him. "Or the man whom your mother had prevented from marrying your sister?"

"I didn't say it was the obvious conclusion," Charles prattled. "It was merely the one that came to mind. I know Sibyl and Damian very well, but I only met Albert for the first time last night. Who would you be more likely to suspect?"

Lord Ruskin raised his glass of water at the mention of his name, and this gave Charles the idea to help himself to a bottle of ginger wine from a rack beside the top table.

Grandfather did not respond to Charles's point but returned to his account of the case. "Much of the evidence pointed to Albert, and yet the scene of the crime raised plenty of questions that we could not immediately answer. For one thing, the blood on the newel post was too high up to have resulted from the stabbing. Furthermore, it was not merely a bloody fingerprint, but a bloodstain with a fingerprint in the centre. To me, that suggested the killer had found a way to place Albert's finger on the blood. It was only later, as I considered the direction that the ball at the top of the post was facing, that I realised it could be easily removed."

There was a frisson of excitement from the uniformed constables as he revealed this. Though silent and patient as their job demanded, the four moustachioed, middle-aged coppers were no doubt excited to hear Lord Edgington's tale.

"If the blood could be taken to Albert as he slept, there was no longer anything to link him to the scene of the crime. We had already noticed signs that the Duchess's nightgown had been disturbed after her murder – the bloodstains on her clothes ruled out any other possibility – but now we understood why."

"Which means I'm not the killer!" Albert declared triumphantly, only to receive a disapproving shake of the head from our grandfather.

"No, Albert is not to blame for the violence here this weekend.

207

Among other things, he would have been unable to poison Lord Ruskin as he was upstairs, talking to Detective Inspector Lovebrook at the time that his rival's coffee was dosed with strychnine."

This brought a brief shiver from Ruskin, just as Grandfather glanced around the room in search of his next victim.

"Since the beginning of this investigation, I have struggled to understand the relationships within this unique family. We have already established that Lady Hinwick was a cruel and domineering presence, particularly over her three sons, but what struck me most was the fact a man like His Grace, the Duke of Hinwick, would have married such a person in the first place."

The Duke had been happy to remain silent and unnoticed until now, much like the Grecian statue that stood on a plinth in the middle of the lawn. I realised then that the same could have been said of him for much of the day. In one rush of cogitation, I noted all the relevant evidence that would suggest he was the man we'd spent the day hunting. It didn't get me very far, and so it was lucky that Grandfather was there to stitch everything together.

"Our interview with Lord Hinwick this morning was a microcosm of the arguments we have heard all day long. He was only too happy to tell us the reasons his sons might have wanted to murder their mother. But when I put it to him that Charles, as the oldest and most enterprising of the three, was the likely culprit, he refused point blank to listen to the suggestion and accused me of talking rot."

Grandfather crossed the large space as a warm breeze blew the elaborately fanned napkins. He arrived at the head of the celebration, where the white canopy hung down to the floor to close off the dining area to the lawn beyond. He did not look at the Duke as he spoke but addressed his comments to the wider audience.

"This was a perfect example of the Fairfax family's general attitude. They have been open to the possibility that one of them killed the Duchess but unwilling to consider the likelihood that any specific person could be to blame. I assumed this was a diversionary tactic and, as he rarely showed his face except when his presence was demanded by one of the investigators, I had to conclude that it was the Duke himself they were protecting."

Normally we would have expected some surprised chatter at this point, but it wasn't that sort of crowd. The suspects were too spaced out under the canopy. Even Charles and Eric, though seated at the same table, were a few yards apart. Sibyl was the only one who showed much of a reaction. She crossed and then uncrossed her legs beneath her long, silken skirt.

"Lord Samuel Hinwick married Begonia Aster for her fortune. Her distant ancestors had made their money in textiles, and then publishing. The Asters were not the sort of people with whom families like the Fairfaxes normally mixed. But even old-moneyed dynasties must make sacrifices when their wealth diminishes."

Grandfather had an amiable manner when he unwound his tales of murder and deception. He would have made a good Punch and Judy man, entertaining children at a summer fete – though, evidently, he would have had to learn some new stories.

He looked at the Duke with that same cheerful expression on his face. "I can only imagine how great a shock it was to discover that the woman you had so generously married would not be the milch cow you had expected her to be. The Duchess controlled the strings, and every other part of the family purse, so you had no influence over her whatsoever."

The Duke's ursine face remained dour and unmoved as Grandfather piled up the allegations against him. "The truth is that you, more than any other person, wished to be free from the shackles the Duchess placed upon you. Not only did she make your life unbearable, she tortured your four children and took pleasure in your reaction. She was a sadist of the highest order, and that is why you finally snapped."

He walked a few steps closer to direct his ire more precisely. "When we spoke to you this morning, you told us that you were a light sleeper and would have heard the killer if your wife had been attacked in her bedroom. My grandson suggested this as evidence of your innocence as, surely, you could have killed her where she lay. But, if that were true, I asked myself why you wouldn't have heard the stone that was thrown against the Duchess's window to get her attention."

"We've already discussed this." The Duke was irritated, though unflustered. "I wasn't in my bedroom. I was in the Great Hall when the murder took place."

Grandfather placed his hand on his forehead as though he were quite the spring fool. "Oh, how silly I am. Please don't think poorly of me, but this is a complicated case, and it went quite out of my mind. You see, I was keen to believe you'd killed the Duchess in order to end your children's mistreatment. If you were guilty, they would surely have done all they could to protect their father. I had to assume that the four of you were working together to make my job harder."

He wandered back to a spot in front of the long, rectangular table where Eric and Charles were sitting. "After all the despicable cases I've investigated, maybe I have grown cynical. I thought too poorly of the remaining members of the Fairfax family. None more so than—"

Before he could finish this sentence, Eric shot to standing and hurled his empty wine glass on the grass beneath his feet. "That's enough. It's time you left everyone else alone. I've already told you that I was the one who killed her."

CHAPTER THIRTY-TWO

Grandfather walked over to Eric and regarded our self-professed culprit without saying anything. When his words finally came, they emerged with stentorian depth. "I know you mean well, but sit back down until I finish the story. I'd appreciate it if you could keep interruptions to a minimum."

Eric's outburst had changed the atmosphere again. I caught Detective Inspector Lovebrook's eye and got the sense that he was re-evaluating all that he thought he knew about the case. If he was anything like me, he was wondering whether Grandfather would lead us through this labyrinth just to reveal that the man in handcuffs was the killer all along.

I tried to reconcile what I'd learnt in the drawing room with the idea that Stanislas was innocent. Grandfather had said that the youngest Fairfax boy was the figure that Lovebrook had seen on the stairs, but that didn't necessarily mean he was the killer.

Grandfather moved on to the next suspect. "Charles is the eldest son of Samuel and Begonia, I can only assume that he will inherit this impressive estate one day, and I considered whether his mother's killing was spurred by the simplest motivation dating back to the dawn of man." He paused then, as though offering the chance to guess his meaning. "By greed – by a hunger for power and wealth. I even considered the possibility that the poison that was put into Lord Ruskin's coffee was actually intended for Charles's father as part of a grand plan to seize the Dukedom."

Charles looked as though he would have liked to say something at this moment. He evidently recalled how the previous interruptions had gone for our suspects and changed his mind.

Grandfather's voice rose once more as he confessed to his mistake. "This particular consideration was wide of the mark. So, you must forgive me, Charles. You welcomed me and my grandsons to your house yesterday in a generous and open-hearted manner. The transformation you underwent after dinner – when you told Albert exactly what you thought of his marriage to your sister – left me believing you were a two-faced schemer, but I accept now that I was mistaken."

He paused to allow us to consider the very idea he'd just discarded. My grandfather was a wily old scrapper, and this really knocked the wind out of his opponent.

"There were certainly plenty of reasons to suspect Charles Fairfax, though all four of the Fairfax siblings have stories to tell of their mother's cruelty. Eric spoke of his childhood torment. Stanislas could not fulfil his lifelong desire to join the army, and Cassandra's plans were frustrated when the Duchess denied the first suitor who asked for her hand in marriage. Charles, however, had suffered two major injustices."

In a perfect world, I believe that the eccentric detective would have conducted the summary of each case as an extended dance routine. He could have sashayed between suspects, tangoed towards the revelation and finished off the whole thing with a swooping bow. Luckily, he was not entirely mad and restricted himself to pacing and the odd quick step.

"First, his mother denied him the opportunity to attend university. This was even more painful when she allowed Cassandra – in whom she generally showed the least interest of all her children – to go to Oxford to study…" It occurred to him then that he hadn't the faintest idea what his future granddaughter-in-law was reading at university. Several voices called, "Medicine!" so that he could continue. "Yes, of course. She left to study medicine while her brothers remained at home.

"The indignities did not end there as when, more recently, Charles fell in love, his mother would not even meet his girlfriend. Sibyl Podence has experienced any number of trying moments in her young life, and Charles's mother's unqualified rejection of her added insult to grave injury.

"Despite this, Charles continued the relationship with Sibyl, who would come to Hinwick House on occasion whilst his mother slept. In fact, she was here last night when the killing took place. Even more curiously, she was still here this morning when we all woke. As the Duchess would never have tolerated this act, it made me think that Charles knew his mother was already dead and could no longer object. What I couldn't say was whether this was evidence that Charles had been the one to kill her, or proof that he knew the real killer's identity."

For every doubt he presented, my head spun more. As his speech unfolded, the one thing of which I was certain was that I really wasn't certain of anything.

"Finally though, I do not believe that Charles is the killer. In our interview, he made the point that, if he had been planning to kill the Duchess, he would have done so in a way that was quite undetectable. For his part, he had neither an alibi nor anything to distance him from the crime. On the face of it, in fact, the whole thing was quite haphazard."

He'd been dancing about for a while now, but with every subtle *Pasodoble* step he completed, he moved a little closer to the round table in the centre of the canopy where Sibyl Podence was sitting.

"I came to a similar conclusion about poor Sibyl here." He peered down at her with compassion plain on his face. She had looked the most nervous throughout, and I had no doubt that Grandfather's dramatic delivery and grandiloquence brought back memories of the barristers at her trial. "Though she told my grandsons just how much she despised her nemesis and relented little when I spoke to her this afternoon, it would have been far too risky for her to come here and kill the Duchess, considering the past suspicions that had fallen upon her. I genuinely believe that a woman who had lived through the indignity of a heavily publicised trial would not kill again without knowing that she could get away with the crime."

Sibyl cleared her throat cautiously and, her voice shaking, said, "Thank you, Lord Edgington. I appreciate your understanding."

He had more to say. I knew he had more to say. He was never so generous with our suspects and, even if she wasn't a killer, Sibyl Podence was no saint. Unfortunately for his sense of the theatrical, he could no longer be so unkind as to stack the evidence against her.

"Even the fact that a woman who'd been accused of poisoning her husband was later present when a man truly was poisoned with strychnine did not dissuade me from my conviction that Mrs Podence had nothing to do with the Duchess's murder. I'm glad to tell everyone here that Sibyl Podence is innocent, just as she was in court."

"So who is left on our list of potential killers?" He stared around the group one last time. Albert swallowed noisily. Stanislas had no life in him and stared at his handcuffs, and I noticed that Lord Ruskin wasn't quite as drowsy as before. Perhaps this question had brought him back to his senses.

I must admit that I was eager to hear the final part of the tale, and so it came as something of a surprise when Grandfather responded to his own question by saying, "My Grandson Christopher is going to tell you."

I felt like an actor who'd been called at the last moment to perform the main part in some obscure piece of Renaissance Theatre. The only problem was that I didn't know my lines, hadn't the first idea about the plot and the play would be performed in a language I didn't speak. I looked to our dear hound for support, but she still had her eyes closed, and I knew that I would have to face this challenge alone.

Grandfather stretched one hand out to point me to the imaginary stage. I was tempted to steal Lord Ruskin's glass of water but resisted the temptation and forced myself up to standing.

"The remaining suspects…" My voice came out as dry as a rock in the desert, and yet it was squeaky at the same time. "The remaining suspects are… Well, I don't think it takes a genius to see that they are Eric, Stanislas and Lord Ruskin, the…" I had planned to give him his full title, but I didn't know what it was. From what I'd heard, he couldn't be much more than a baron, but that hardly helped me. "… the man over there."

I clapped my hands together as though everything was going just brilliantly. "Which only leaves us with three suspects. Actually…" Realising how short on time we were after Grandfather's extended performance, I pointed across the room to Lord Ruskin. "…he's guilty." I swivelled to look at Eric and Stanislas. "They're not."

CHAPTER THIRTY-THREE

This was the noisiest the audience had been. Perhaps understandably, Ruskin was not happy with the accusation. "How dare you, boy?" The arrogant voice he had used the night before had returned, and he looked at me as though he wished I would die on the spot.

I was more interested in Stanislas's reaction. He didn't smile, but a little light entered his gaze, and he looked up at me as though he hadn't expected to see me there. To be perfectly honest, I hadn't expected to see me there.

"Thank you, everyone," I continued as the exclamations of surprise died down. "We must leave here in the next fifteen minutes if we're to make it to the wedding, so please let me speak, and I'll explain what really happened. You see, Eric confessed to being the killer, but he didn't know the details of how the murder was committed. This suggested that he was trying to protect another member of his family – the person with the most evidence against them – his brother Stanislas."

"Exactly! Stan over there is the one in irons. He's the killer." Ruskin wouldn't give up so easily and managed to rise to his feet. "I'm the victim here. Someone tried to kill me!" He gesticulated wildly and this in itself was enough to make me think I was on the right trail; all the other suspects had remained quite calm as Grandfather detailed their supposed crimes.

I did not let his interruptions distract me, and dear old Halfpenny put a bony hand on the man's shoulder to make him sit back down.

"Stanislas may be the one that Detective Inspector Lovebrook saw fit to arrest, but he is not guilty of any crime." I looked across at our colleague from the Northamptonshire Constabulary and was happy to see that he did not seem too miffed by my statement. "The evidence against him appears damning, but the same could be said of Albert after we found his bloody fingerprint at the scene of the crime."

This helped quieten the restless audience and, taking a deep breath, I continued. "My grandfather said that Charles had the strongest reason to hate his mother, but that wasn't true. Stanislas wasn't just mentally and emotionally abused by the Duchess, as everyone in the Fairfax family can attest, he was physically scarred by her."

Grandfather's encouraging smile was much appreciated. His warm expression certainly stood in contrast to Lord Ruskin's, whose teeth I could hear grinding from ten yards away.

"Begonia Fairfax didn't merely require the obedience of her children; she wished to change their very way of thinking. To that end, whenever one of them disobeyed her, she would find a new way to punish them. She destroyed Stanislas's dream of joining the army, as it would have removed her authority over him. Even when he was forced to stay at home, that wasn't enough, and so the cruel woman set fire to his possessions, leading poor Stanislas to disfigure his hand in the flames as he attempted to extract them.

"She beat him because she knew she couldn't change him, and that galled her more than anything. For all that Lady Hinwick tormented her family, in the end, she achieved nothing. She couldn't shape them in her image. She couldn't indoctrinate them or make them as devoted to her as she wished. I imagine that she justified her attempts to destroy her children's dreams, as that is what they had done to her."

Since the beginning of the case, I'd struggled to understand the impact that the Duchess's actions had made on the family, but I felt it now. I felt every bit of their suffering. "She dreamed of a family of loyal followers but ended up with a group of individuals with minds of their own."

I hadn't intended to speak so passionately on the topic, but the emotion flooded out of me. "If one of her children *had* murdered her, they would have still deserved our sympathy, but that isn't the case. Stanislas couldn't have killed her because, more than any of them, he still loved her." I waited for a reaction from him, and though that distant expression still occupied his face, a tear descended either cheek. "He was the only suspect we interviewed who could still find something good to say about his mother. I considered that this was a way to hide the part he had played in her death, but that wasn't it."

I felt like a clown in a circus ring and had to keep turning about to see the various spectators. "When we spoke to Charles, he told us that the only people remaining in the Great Hall when he and Sibyl woke up this morning were Eric and their father. Stanislas said that his brother was mistaken, and that he had been there asleep. They couldn't both be telling the truth, but that didn't mean that one of them was culpable of the crime. And if Stanislas was the killer, why wouldn't he have returned to the Great Hall to hide the fact he'd left in the middle of the night to commit the crime?"

I was becoming too abstract in my thinking and tried to concentrate once more on the facts. "It was thanks to Stanislas's love of history that I was able to piece things together. I found an old coin of his in the Great Hall this morning and, when I returned it to him, he looked incredibly relieved. Try as I might, I couldn't understand what had so moved him until a moment ago, when Lord Edgington ruled out various other possibilities."

I threaded my way between the tables as I told my tale. "Detective Inspector Lovebrook spotted Stanislas on the stairs with his mother's body. The suspect had disguised himself in a black opera cloak that we later found tossed from a window, but it was a risky endeavour, nonetheless. It didn't make sense that the killer would want to gain access to the Duchess's body after it had already been inspected by the police surgeon."

I allowed a few moments for this mystery to puzzle my audience. "It was that point in particular that bamboozled us, but desperate people will do desperate things, and I should have known as soon as I returned the coin to Stanislas what had happened. Nothing that Lord Edgington said to him in our interview drew any great emotional response, and yet the coin did just that."

"He thought he'd left it on the body," Lovebrook exclaimed.

"That's right." I was over that way, so I stopped to look at the inspector and his charge. "Stanislas must only have noticed it was missing this afternoon, hours after the investigation had begun. Aided by Lord Ruskin's convulsions in the drawing room, he waited until there was no one around, and went to look for the coin that would link him to his mother's murder. It wasn't there, of course. In fact, it was in my suit pocket the whole time, but he wasn't to know that. If they'd found the coin and the bloody clothes in his bedroom, the police would have immediately picked him as the killer, and so he went back to the body assuming no one had found his coin yet."

"Hang on one second." Ruskin was still indignant. "That doesn't explain how he got blood on the clothes that no one has seen him wearing since last night."

"That's true," I began, felling less confident once more. "But I've already told you; Stanislas forgave his mother for burning his possessions, preventing him from joining the army and even the way she abused him in everyday life. I cannot say exactly how it happened but, from the lie he told, it seems logical that he was the first person this morning to wake up. The only thing I can think is that he found his mother on the stairs and sat with her. He cradled her lifeless body because he couldn't believe she was really dead."

"Is that what happened?" Lovebrook asked the still chained suspect, who gave a fraction of a nod in reply.

"How can you believe that?" Ruskin shouted. "Of course he'd say he loved his mummy. That doesn't make it true."

I needed to prove him wrong. "Fine. Then why did he poison you?"

Ruskin peered at my grandfather of all people as though he might come to the rescue. The ever-upstanding Lord Edgington offered nothing in response but a smile.

"This is insane." The real culprit got up to stalk across the space. It was amazing how he'd recovered from the effects of the strychnine so rapidly. "I refuse to believe that a man with blood all over his clothes, who has been shown to have interfered with vital evidence, can be cleared of murder simply because some child playing policeman thinks that the suspect loved his mother."

"You didn't answer my question," I told him, and it's more than possible that Grandfather's smile had found its way onto my face. "If Stanislas is the killer, why would he have poisoned you?"

"I've already explained that to your grandfather. I don't know why anyone wanted to harm me. As far as I can say, there is no good reason whatsoever."

"Thank you," I said, as he'd rather proved my point before I'd even made it.

He was wild by now, his gaze darting about the pretty space as the constables were called to attention. The four of them fanned out and, though too weak to run away, Lord Ruskin wasn't giving up just yet.

"Oh, come on, now. This doesn't make any sense. All the evidence goes against Stanislas. You can't prove that he's innocent."

"You're right, I can't prove that he didn't kill his mother, but I can prove that you did it." I didn't wait for his reaction but pressed straight on as the police closed in on him. "It was only when my grandfather made me stand up here that I saw the solution, but he'd given us all the clues. Even when we were talking to you in the drawing room just now, I should have seen that he suspected you. You said that there was no reason for anyone to poison you, and just a few moments later, he revealed that the time had come to confront the murderer."

I was so happy I could have laughed. "That was the moment when you gave yourself away. Because if there was no reason for anyone to poison you, then it was hard to see how it could have benefitted the killer, unless you were the killer yourself." Oh, I can't tell you how much I loved saying this next sentence. "You put the strychnine in your own coffee."

It was not just the Cranleys who were jolly by this point. The Fairfaxes were quite ecstatic too. Stanislas smiled at Charles, and the expression travelled around the family. Even Sibyl couldn't resist. They'd all been acting so guiltily because they believed that one of them had to be responsible for the murder. Now that the real killer had been identified, that weight was whipped from their shoulders.

The four plump bluebottles had wide grins on their faces as they approached their target, and Ruskin looked almost as sick as he had in the drawing room.

Just to make him feel a bit worse about things, I decided to tie everything together a little more tightly. "You thought that the supposed attack upon you would be enough to throw off suspicion, when, in fact, it only confused matters. You'd gone to a lot of trouble implicating Albert in the murder, but there was no way he could have poisoned you too, and so you muddied the pot."

"This is all wrong," Lord Ruskin complained, but his heart wasn't in it and the words emerged in a feeble moan.

"Just as you told us when we first met, you hated the Duchess for coming between you and her daughter. You loved Cassandra, but that didn't make you suitable for her. You're too old, you've made nothing of your life since the war, and you failed to win her family around to the idea. It's no wonder her mother objected."

"This doesn't prove anything, and you know it."

"You're right." I walked over to the two closest officers and stood between them as Lovebrook unfastened Stanislas's cuffs. "A lot of what I said is circumstantial, and it would take an excellent barrister to prove it in court, but I haven't told you the best part yet. My grandfather gave us the key to the whole case, but it wasn't the strychnine. It was the way you went about killing the Duchess. You threw a stone at her window, rather than going up to her room to kill her because you thought that her family would hear."

This was the moment when he knew his cause was hopeless. His whole being seemed to fold in on itself, and I was certain he wanted to melt into the ground rather than hear anything more.

"You were the only suspect who didn't know where everyone else was sleeping, and the only one who would have been so desperate as to kill your enemy on the eve of Cassandra's wedding. I genuinely believe that you were—"

"All right, that's enough," he finally declared, his voice devoid of emotion. "Arrest me, I did it, but spare me the misery of your lecture. I brought the strychnine with me to kill the Duchess, but I had no way to give it to her, and so I grabbed a knife from the house and, when I thought everyone else would be asleep, I got her attention through the window and told her to meet me in the drawing room." He stared at the floor as he recited the details of the crime. "She didn't want to come, of course, but I convinced her and then waited on the stairs. When the job was done, the dawn was near, and so I went to sleep outside, knowing you'd take me for the drunk I normally am."

Perhaps it wasn't surprising, but there was no sense of regret in his voice. As he made his confession, it was as if he was explaining some noble deed. "I hated Begonia for what she did to me and Cassandra. Even if we can't be together now, I made the world a better place by killing her."

Damian Ruskin did not possess the face of evil that newspapers often describe in such cases. He was an aging dandy who had done both good and bad in his life. Like most killers I had encountered, he had his reasons, and he believed they outweighed whatever right to exist his victim could claim. But when all was said and done and the inspector closed the vacated handcuffs around Lord Ruskin's wrists, he was tired and defeated. I'm certain he was questioning whether his wicked deeds were really worth the effort.

"I'm sorry to rush you, Chrissy," my brother said when I'd had my glorious moment in the spotlight and the various innocent suspects had shaken my hands in thanks. "But do you mind if I pop off to get married now?"

CHAPTER THIRTY-FOUR

"Come along, Christopher," Grandfather bellowed as we raced after him across the lawn. "Keep up, Albert. There's no time to spare."

As Delilah sprang alongside me and we rounded the main house, I could see that the cars were full to bursting with the staff from Cranley Hall. The Duke and his three sons weren't far behind us, and Sibyl was taking up the rear, her pretty dress swishing about as she moved – I must say that I, for one, wouldn't have liked to run in such an outfit, but then I also doubt that purple is the colour for me.

We piled into the remaining spaces in the cars. The groom and our grandfather had reserved the back seat of the Daimler, and there was just enough room in one of the Rolls for Delilah and me. It felt like a true celebration as we rolled off the Hinwick estate towards the village of Podington, a half mile down the road. I was in a car with Dorie, our enormous maid, and Timothy, our tiny page boy, who sang a raucous version of Vesta Victoria's 'Wedding Bells'.

"Wedding bells, wedding bells, How I love your melody.
You ring your bells for other gals, but never ring for me.
On the shelf, by myself, I've been lying all my life.
I wonder if I ever shall be somebody's darling wife."

I would have joined in if I'd known the words, but they had much better voices than me anyway. The jovial atmosphere was only dampened when we noticed Todd driving past us in the opposite direction. I had to doubt that his explanation of a mechanical malfunction would suffice, especially if Cassie had spotted us.

Whatever pitfalls and dilemmas we'd faced that day, we'd made it to the church, and we were more or less on time.

"I don't know why we're botherin'," Cook complained as the staff climbed out of the happy convoy. "We'll have to leave halfway through the service to get the food ready. We won't even get to see the vows."

"I love a wedding." Our footman Halfpenny ignored his colleague's complaints as he held out his arm for her.

I rushed past them to check on my brother, who looked paler than ever. "You'll be fine, Albert. It's not as though you have to stand in front of everyone and make a speech."

"No, that comes during the meal," one of the gardeners shouted over, as he made his way towards the church.

I was expecting my grandfather to say something encouraging, but he looked just as nervous as my brother and hadn't yet climbed out of the immense limousine. Luckily, Mother appeared from the church at that moment and skipped along the path to us.

"Come along, Albert. Todd's already driven past once. They can't start without you." She pulled him away, and I tried to bring our dear sleuth back to life with some inane chatter.

"Even though I revealed the killer, there are still plenty of things I don't understand, like why the Duchess was carrying a watch in her dressing gown pocket in the middle of the night. Was it really just a red herring? Also, why did it show midnight when—"

He lurched out of the car and, with the sun beating down, placed his grey top hat upon his head. "There'll be plenty of time for that later, Christopher. For now, I'd like to get a good seat."

He still looked a bit peaky, but then I remembered him telling me how panicked he'd been at his own wedding, and so I didn't bother him anymore. We were (almost) the last to enter the church, where all the staff were lurking in the space behind the back rows as we walked down the aisle to see Albert. It really was a picturesque little chapel. Round brick columns supported three pointed arches on either side of the aisle, and our path through the nave led us towards an elegant sixfoil window.

Our father was giving a few words of advice to my trembling brother, so Grandfather and I found our seats on the front pew. A few moments after we'd entered, the organist started playing and everyone rose to standing. I took my spot beside my brother and gave him a punch on the arm for good luck. He was so anxious that he didn't look back along the aisle to see his bride, but I did.

Cassie was breathtaking. Her long red hair was arranged like a fountain on top of her head, with curling strands springing down towards her shoulders. Her white and pearl dress couldn't have been prettier and, in saying all this, I realise that I do not know a lot about ladies' fashions. What I can say is that I wasn't the only person in that church who couldn't take my eyes off her and, as the Duke brought her to the altar, my brother finally turned to look at his bride.

They could never have imagined when they woke up that morning just how long a journey it would be to get there, but they'd finally made it. I can't say that Albert looked any less nervous now that those challenges were behind him. For her part, Cassie was crying with the emotion of the day – so perhaps getting married a few hours after her mother had been murdered was not the best idea after all.

The vicar gave everyone permission to sit down, and then the ceremony finally began. Conducting a wedding as a priest must be like a great musician performing at the Royal Albert Hall. It's the big one, isn't it? The time when they can really flex their holy muscles and talk of love, life, happiness and all those pretty things. If I'd had to stand up there to lead the service, I'd have been a complete disaster. Let's be honest, I'd probably have ended up marrying the wrong people or saying everything backwards, but Reverend Walls was a professional and did an excellent job.

My mother was in tears, which set my father blubbering, and I must admit I felt a small tickle in my throat. Grandfather was so moved by the whole thing that he was practically motionless, as though he couldn't let out a breath until he was certain that everything had gone to plan. He really could be as soppy as my brother sometimes.

When the time came for the readings, the Duke was in charge of the first one, and then my only responsibility finally arrived. I felt rather fortunate to get one of my favourite Bible passages. Colossians 3 is up there with the best of them, and I tried not to stumble over the words. What the bride and groom didn't realise was that I'd prepared a surprise for them. I had another piece to read by George Elliot.

> **"What greater thing is there for two human souls,**
> **than to feel that they are joined for life,**
> **to strengthen each other in all labour,**
> **to rest on each other in all sorrow,**
> **to minister to each other in all pain,**
> **to share with each other in all gladness,**
> **to be one with each other in the silent unspoken**
> **memories…?"**

Admittedly, I had to cut off the last few words of the poem to avoid having to talk about death, but it really made the congregation well up. Fine! I was a little teary myself, but Cassie's eleven-year-old head bridesmaid didn't seem to mind. She even made a gesture to me as I stepped down from the lectern as if to say, *when this is all over, we're going to have that dance.* I believe that I turned quite red.

Before we knew it, the vows were being read, and when the priest told my brother to repeat the words, "I, Albert Doris Prentiss, take thee, Cassandra Unity Fairfax, to be my wedded Wife," Albert replied, "I'm sorry, I can't. She's a murderer."

CHAPTER THIRTY-FIVE

"What are you saying, Albert?" The bride was crying for a different reason now. "Don't do this."

The church had fallen silent, and the fear that Albert had displayed ever since he'd got out of the car suddenly made more sense.

"You were afraid that I was getting cold feet, so you travelled halfway across the country to murder your mother. At the speed you drive, you could have got here in two and a half hours, done the deed and driven back to Cranley before the morning. No one even noticed you were missing."

"That was Damian." The elegant young lady in white pleaded with him to listen, but he wouldn't even look at her. He stared straight ahead as she attempted to explain. "My father told me before we came into the church that Damian Ruskin killed my mother. He was obviously obsessed with me, but I never imagined he'd do this."

For the first time I could remember, my brother's words were free of excess emotion, and he would not relent. "You made it look like I was the killer. You were the only suspect who knew that I could sleep through anything. You put my fingerprint in the blood to incriminate me."

A momentary rasp entered his voice, but he found the strength to keep going. "Chrissy noticed how odd it was that your mother should carry a pocket watch in her night clothes. It didn't seem to provide any of the suspects with an alibi, though. But it was you. You placed the broken watch on her body to suggest the murder had happened much earlier than it did. There's no way you could be blamed if she'd died just after we spoke on the telephone, rather than hours later when it really happened."

She looked at her father, but there was nothing he could do to help her. That was when I realised who the Duke and his sons had really been protecting. They must have known from the start that little Cassie was the only one capable of murder.

"I bet this was your plan all along. Ever since the day we met, you've been plotting how to use me." Considering the ridiculous story of their first encounter, this did seem possible. "I was dressed as a pig, singing 'When Father Papered the Parlour' on a table in an Oxford bar, and you thought, *here's the dupe I've been looking for all this time*. Grandfather told me in the car before we got here. He'd only just worked out that it had to be you. You didn't know where everyone was sleeping last night, whereas the man the police arrested would at least have peeked through the window of the Great Hall to check on his friends. He took the blame because he's never stopped loving you. And I can only guess you never stopped loving him."

"He's got everything wrong, Daddy." The truth ripped through her, and Cassandra's voice undulated between high and low notes in the same sentence. "Tell him he's wrong and that he has to marry me." There was something a little frightening about the way she said this. Something not quite nice enough for the girl who had charmed us over the last six months.

Albert continued as though he hadn't heard her. "There was something I didn't mention when we spoke on the telephone after the party. Lord Ruskin called by last night, which rather undid your plans. My grandfather worked so hard to understand the reason why Ruskin was poisoned, but nothing made sense, as his death wouldn't have benefitted any of the other suspects."

He paused then, perhaps hoping that she would confess the truth and tell the story herself. "But it benefitted you. You had to do something to suggest your lover's innocence and, if he was the potential second victim, he couldn't possibly be the killer. You timed your appearance in the house perfectly. You even asked him what he was doing there in front of everyone. The real meaning of your words didn't become apparent until my grandfather realised the part you had played."

While the great Lord Edgington had once looked nervous, he was now resolute. He was ready to step in if his grandson needed help, but the sheer force of pain and disappointment that Albert was experiencing pushed him onwards.

"I could have called off the wedding before either of us stepped foot in this church, but I wanted to see how far you would go. I needed to be certain of exactly who you are." There were tears in his eyes again, but he stood up straighter as he delivered his closing rebuke. "You're the kind of person who would sacrifice others for the sake of your happiness. You are your mother's daughter."

That was when the bomb exploded... Not literally, you'll be glad

228

to hear. But it was almost as destructive.

"How dare you say such a thing? I am nothing like her." The sweet and generous woman transformed before our eyes into a raging devil, and there was no going back. "Mother cared for no one but herself. No one. She destroyed each member of my family in a unique and personalised manner. She broke my heart, burst Charles's dreams and burnt Stanislas's hand. She turned my father into a ghost of the man he once was and my beloved brother Eric into a joyless cynic, but at least she loved them in her own way. I was a disappointment to her for no other reason than my sex. She had as much interest in me as the swans on the lake. The one time she even tried to be a parent was when she stopped me from marrying the man I love."

She could have kept listing her grievances for some time, but I couldn't stand to see Albert suffer, and so I spoke over her. "Lord Ruskin must love you dearly to have confessed to a crime he didn't commit. But then, he wouldn't have been the first. Eric attempted to convince us that he was the one who murdered the Duchess, all to save your black soul."

"Stay out of this, you little brat." Cassandra glared at me then, so I smiled back innocently, and she turned to my brother once more. "Damian Ruskin is a hero. He's worth twenty of you. I knew he was at the ball last night and never imagined him turning up here. He didn't know anything about my plan. I couldn't risk him getting arrested for it, so I kept it to myself."

When Albert wouldn't respond, my grandfather stepped forward to have his say. "There's one thing I still don't understand. What would you have done after the wedding? You say that you loved Lord Ruskin, but would you have let him hang for the crime you committed? Would you have married Albert, lived off his income and forgotten about the man who died for you?"

She looked quite wild now and ran to her family in the hope they could protect her. I truly don't believe she'd considered any further than the wedding, and her answer, when it came, did little to explain her intentions. "I would have found a way to fix it. That's what I've done my whole life. Whenever my mother stood in my path, I found a way around her, which is why she had to die now."

I was so wrapped up in the exchange that I'd hardly paid attention to Reverend Walls, who was lingering behind her with a Book of Common Prayer in his hands. He'd obviously got the message that

229

his services were no longer required that day, but there was not much more that he could do than stand with his mouth open. The wedding guests largely did the same and made very little sound as they strained to hear the demon bride's lament.

"You were supposed to be the solution to my problems, Albi." Her voice had changed again, and she'd become oddly coquettish. "The only way for Damian and me to marry was for my mother to disappear. And the only way I could kill her was if there was someone to take the blame. You couldn't even get that right."

I could see just how horrified my grandfather was by her casual tone. He wanted to pass sentence already – to hold up a mirror to the darkness that had infected her. "I don't think I've come across another killer who was quite so dedicated to her task. This was more than a murder for you. You have played a part for months – ever since you met Albert."

He stepped closer to impress his point upon her. "You realised that, if everything went to plan, you would have to play the heartbroken young woman whose fiancé was set to hang. That's why you tried so hard to ingratiate yourself with our family. You knew that Albert would be blamed for your mother's death and then you would be free to marry Lord Ruskin. But you needed everyone to believe you were truly innocent."

"Oh, please." She rolled her eyes just as Grandfather did when unimpressed by lesser mortals. "You should have seen your face at the lake today. You swallowed every word I said. You were all just desperate to be kind and sympathetic when I told you I felt nothing after my mother's death. Of course I felt nothing; I was the one who killed her." Her lips stretched wide across her face as she thought of the violent act. "And I enjoyed it so much. I loved the sensation of that blade going through her, and the exquisite calm I felt as I watched her die. But the truth is that even her murder couldn't make up for all that she did."

I don't know what had brought him there, whether it was simple curiosity, or because he loved a good wedding, but Detective Inspector Lovebrook appeared at the back of the church just then and instantly knew that something was wrong. He walked down the aisle towards us in his usual relaxed manner but stopped halfway in order to listen.

Cassie was clinging to the Duke's arm and had an apology to make. "I'm sorry I got caught, Father. I hope you're proud of me."

He looked down at her, perhaps struggling to reconcile the homicidal creature in front of him with the little girl he had raised. "Why would I be proud? I don't agree with this. I know what your mother was like, but killing her wasn't the solution. How could you ever think such a thing?"

She turned to her brothers next, but she was beyond their help. Stanislas was as distant as ever. Eric couldn't look at her and Charles hugged Sibyl to his chest as if he wanted to keep her safe from his own little sister.

"No." Her voice rose once more. "No, this is all wrong. You're my family, you're supposed to understand. You're supposed to care."

"We do, darling." The Duke stepped forward, but that just drove her closer to the inspector. "I do."

"We understand," Stanislas promised, but this was a long way from sanctioning what she'd done.

"No, this isn't fair. This wasn't supposed to happen."

Lovebrook saw his opportunity and rushed along the aisle to apprehend her. She was past fighting by now, and with one last cry, the bride took on a ghostly mien, and the handcuffs closed on her slender wrists.

CHAPTER THIRTY-SIX

Our possessions were still at Hinwick House, not to mention a number of our employees, and so we made our way back there once the church had emptied and the police had taken our statements.

In fact, with the Fairfax family busy at the police station, and vast amounts of food going to waste, we sat down at the tables under the canopy. My family and all the staff who weren't busy preparing the meal joined us to enjoy Cook's banquet.

Albert was sitting across the long table from me, still in a daze from the new disappointment he had lived. He ate with a blank expression on his face, which wasn't so different from how he'd looked when he first fell in love.

"Before we go any further," I told my grandfather once Halfpenny had served a delicious first course of melon soup with chunks of cured Spanish ham, "I have approximately seventeen thousand questions for you."

"Oh dear, we may need more wine." Before he'd even finished speaking, Peterson appeared with a new bottle of Bordeaux.

I would not be dissuaded and began my interrogation of the great detective. "I assumed at first that Cassandra changed her plan after Albert called home last night. She heard how badly things had gone and was worried he would call off their engagement. But if that was the case, did she originally intend to marry him and then kill her mother after the wedding?"

Grandfather couldn't answer immediately, so he sipped his wine and thought. "I've been pondering the same question, and I think you may be right. You do realise that she not only wished to marry your brother in order to have a scapegoat for her mother's murder. She chose Albert because he comes from an exceedingly wealthy family. Her mother would have accepted nothing less, and Cassandra had her eye on a chunk of our fortune."

This still didn't make sense to me. "But if she'd married again, she wouldn't have been part of our family anymore."

He leaned back in his seat to regard me. "Think of it like this, Christopher. If we'd had no idea of her guilt and poor Albert had been sentenced to death for the crime, do you really think that I would have thrown the girl he loved out onto the street?"

"No, of course not. She'd have lived at Trevelyan Place just as you'd intended." That was when something so simple and so obvious hit me. "Oh, my goodness! When we took her there last week, she was terribly grateful to see the estate where she would live. She told us how happy she would be there. She didn't say *we'll* be happy. She said, 'I'll'. How could I not have suspected her at the time?"

"Because it seemed a natural enough thing to say, and you are not the sort of person to suspect everyone you meet of having morbid intentions."

I didn't know how to respond to this without sounding rude. "But you are! After the career you've had, you must imagine that you're surrounded by murderers at all times."

"No, Christopher." He laughed and so I felt a little silly. "I do not spend my life imagining that every cheerful person I meet is a secret killer. We had no reason to believe that Cassandra Fairfax was any less lovely than she seemed. The only thing I regret is that I hadn't investigated her family to find out what loons they were. We might have been able to prevent a murder (and spare Albert any amount of heartache.)" He implied these last seven words with a sympathetic look across the table so that my brother didn't have to hear.

"She was taking a big risk, though, don't you think?" I persevered. "By killing her mother before the wedding, I mean."

He dropped his voice a fraction. "You told me how distraught your brother was on the telephone last night. Cassandra faced two possibilities; either Albert called off the wedding out of fear of her monstrous family, or she could murder her mother before they were married and face the possibility that we wouldn't support her after Albert hanged. At least in that second scenario, she would have been free to marry her beloved. What she didn't realise was that Lord Ruskin was already here at Hinwick, and so he was a more likely suspect than the fiancé she'd incriminated."

It was hard to put myself in the mind of a killer, but I suppose this made sense. Either way, I still had more questions for him. "What will happen to Ruskin now? And the Fairfaxes, for that matter? Have any of them committed a crime?"

Grandfather had finished his soup and sat awaiting the second course. "I don't believe they have. After you put the evidence of Damian Ruskin's involvement to him, he realised that, as he hadn't murdered the Duchess, the only other likely culprit who would not have known that the family were asleep in the Great Hall was his beloved Cassandra. We'd already spoken of the Duchess's broken watch in his presence, and he realised that someone had been trying to make it look as though the murder happened earlier than it really did. We'd considered that possibility, of course, but as far as we knew, changing the time didn't provide any of our suspects with an alibi.

"Somewhat ironically, time could have saved Cassandra, but it also proved that Ruskin had been lying. He said that he'd killed Lady Hinwick at dawn this morning though I knew by the temperature and colour of her skin that she'd been dead for longer. It was only after we got into the car that I recognised the discrepancy. I had just enough time to explain to your brother what had happened."

Mother and Father were sitting on either side of Albert, listening intently.

"How impressive." My father was the most taken aback by the whole thing. He was normally too busy at his job in the City to see my brilliant grandfather at work.

"You certainly saved us from a monster, Father," my mother added, and I was rather sorry she hadn't had the chance to assist with the investigation. She could have solved the murder faster than we had and saved us from missing lunch.

I wouldn't allow us to be diverted from the issue at hand. "But what about Cassandra's family? Do you think that any of them knew for sure that she was the killer?"

"That is a very good question."

I waited for the genius to say more and, when he didn't, I said, "Oh… thank you."

"I still assume that Charles kept Sibyl here because he knew his mother was dead, but I cannot say for certain. I also wonder whether Stanislas had heard his sister kill the Duchess, and that was how he came across the body. After all, the main staircase was far away from his bedroom, and he had no reason to be in that part of the house at that time of night. The family's behaviour today could have been motivated by other reasons. Perhaps they all suspected a different member of the family and not just Cassandra."

"Eric did," I said with some conviction. "That was why he confessed to the crime. He told us that he had always been closest to his sister and, by the time we spoke to him upstairs, he'd worked out what we'd failed to see. He had the advantage of being able to ask his father and siblings for the truth. He knew they hadn't done it and realised that she was the most likely culprit. After the upbringing to which their mother had subjected her, Cassandra was not a normal person. Eric knew that better than anyone."

I still had more points to raise but, before I could, Detective Inspector Lovebrook arrived.

"I don't wish to interrupt," he said, waving to everyone at the table. "We've a lot of work on our hands at the station, but I wanted to thank you for your help. An innocent man would have been behind bars tonight if it hadn't been for you, Lord Edgington."

"That's nonsense," Grandfather replied with unwarranted modesty. "I'm sure you would have seen the holes in Ruskin's story before long and realised who he was protecting. I should have been quicker about it myself." He stood up to talk to the officer. "In fact, I was very impressed with your efficiency throughout. Have you considered applying to work at Scotland Yard? There's a man there by the name of Chief Inspector James Darrington whom I think you ought to meet."

"My goodness, Lord Edgington. I don't know what to say." The pair walked off together, with the inspector smiling proudly as they talked.

"I have a question," a small voice eventually spoke up to fill the void my grandfather had left behind. "Why did she love him so?"

"I'm sorry?" I asked Albert, as I'd barely caught the words he'd spoken.

"Cassandra. Why did she love Ruskin so much that she would do all this?"

I was several years younger than my brother and had an even worse record in love than his, so I did not consider myself the obvious person to answer this question.

Luckily, our inspirational mother was on hand for such moments. "It wasn't love, Albert. Cassandra's character was shaped by her mother's cruelty and indifference. The only time that the Duchess showed any interest in her daughter was when she stopped her from marrying an unsuitable man. It became her obsession, not because she cared so much about Ruskin, or because he was so wonderful, but because she wanted to defy the woman she hated, even if she sent an innocent young man to the gallows to achieve her goals."

He sighed a deep and deeply troubled sigh, and I worried that he would never recover from the pain of that day. It shows how much I know as, a few seconds later, he was shaking his head and laughing.

"I can't believe how lucky I am." His laughter grew and the others along the table turned to look at him. "To think I could have been married to that terrible woman – or, worse still, hanged for her crime!" The body-shaking giggles threatened to overtake him. "If I'm totally honest, she'd always terrified me. She was the one who told me exactly when and where I had to propose to her – right in front of her mother, as it happens. She ordered me about like a donkey, but she was so pretty and seemed to like me, which was a big improvement on the previous girls I'd courted."

Mother frowned then, and her love for her son was unmistakable. "Don't worry, darling. I'm sure the next woman you meet will be just perfect."

He released another burst of laughter. "Gosh, no. I've learnt from my mistakes. I'm swearing off women from this day forth. Who knows, I might become a monk."

I don't think anyone there believed a word he was saying. It wouldn't have surprised me if he'd fallen in love again by the time we got back to Cranley Hall. And yet, I was relieved to witness his recovery. My unlucky-in-love brother was – at the very least – lucky in life. As I sat with my family enjoying that fine meal, I felt rather wonderful. We dined on roast lamb and stuffed capon. There were profiteroles for Albert, and the remaining staff joined us as Cook brought out the monumental cake.

It looked more like the stonework of an elegant fountain than a pudding. All around the bottom tier, white sugar angels stood with their wings aloft. Tiny flowers bordered each level and there were filigree panels all over. It was beautiful, but it was hard to know how much of it was actually edible.

No longer quite as vacant as he'd previously been – and with a smile across his face that wouldn't diminish for weeks – Albert jumped up to cut the cake. I'd rarely seen him so happy; he kept shaking his head as though reflecting on the close escape he'd enjoyed.

When everyone had a piece of cake and the champagne had been served. Grandfather returned to lead us in a toast.

"To my grandson, Albert." He raised his glass and looked around his family ever so fondly. "The luckiest young man I know."

We cheered and clapped and emptied our glasses to celebrate this truly wondrous occasion. It almost felt like a wedding.

The End (For Now...)

Get another

LORD EDGINGTON ADVENTURE

absolutely **free**…

Download your free novella at
www.benedictbrown.net

"LORD EDGINGTON INVESTIGATES..."

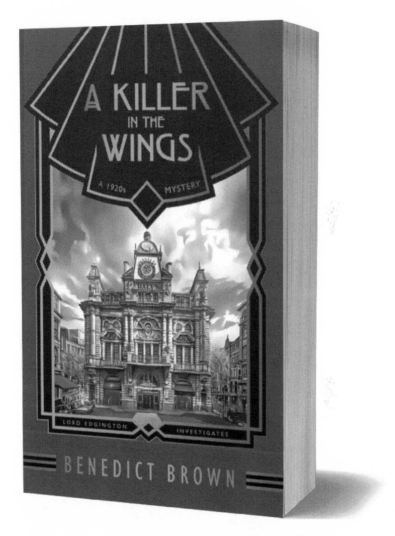

The eleventh full-length mystery will be
available in **Autumn 2023** at amazon.

Sign up on my website to the readers' club to know when it goes on sale.

ABOUT THIS BOOK

If you go back to the very beginning of the series, in **"Murder at the Spring Ball"**, Chrissy's brother Albert is the first character we get a real sense of after we've met the imperious Lord Edgington. Right from his first lines of dialogue, when he complains about being unlucky and no girl loving him, I knew who he was. I am terrible at planning characters or plots in advance, and they tend to come to me as I write, so everything that has happened to poor, soppy Albert since then was dictated by those opening lines.

There have certainly been times in the books when the elder Prentiss brother is a bit of a pain, and that has made him a perfect victim for misfortune and, in the case of this book, a rather torrid ordeal. However, it's also given him the chance to grow and learn from his mistakes. I like recuperating seemingly unlikeable characters in this way, and I think Albert still has some way to go.

As I am the youngest of three brothers, I think it's fair for me to say that Chrissy and Albert have undergone something of a role reversal. Albert is very much the whiny, hard-done-by character, and we've seen Christopher develop to become more confident and capable. Perhaps what's changed the most, though, is not the people that they are, but the way they see themselves. People – and especially Lord Edgington – have always told Chrissy that he can achieve a lot, and he's finally coming to believe it. I hope that Albert's travails in love will also make him more confident. In my experience, it's the obstacles we put in our own path that are often the hardest to overcome, so it's nice to think that things are getting easier for the two brothers.

Speaking of brothers, some of my early readers have asked questions about the Fairfax siblings and especially their names. Stanislas is not a common name in Britain, nor is it very common in France, but it does exist there. In fact, my wife's cousins are Charles, Albéric and Stanislas and, as we already had an Albert, I changed Albéric to Eric. I should probably point out that I really like my wife's cousins and they are nothing like the weirdos in this book! As for Albert's middle name,

Doris, to my surprise it was previously used for men and women and I wanted another chance to laugh at him, so that's what he's called now.

Spoiler alert! Skip this paragraph if you haven't read the book yet! I don't do myself any favours by writing mysteries set at weddings that do not guarantee the happy endings that many readers look for. The problem is that I love to surprise and find ways to do things with my mystery plots that people won't expect. As a writer, I want readers to feel satisfied at the end of the book, whilst still creating something that challenges all of us. Striking that balance is a difficult thing to do, and I hope you've all enjoyed it.

The title of this novel comes from a passing comment in a P.G. Wodehouse book. In the short story "Strychnine in the Soup", in the collection "Mulliner Nights", wimpish interior decorator Cyril Mulliner falls in love with a girl who is equally obsessed with murder mysteries as he is, and they discuss their favourites. I originally came across the name in a discussion on a murder mystery forum. Someone said something along the lines of "I'd read a book called 'Blood on the Banisters', and I thought, *All right then, I'll write a book called 'Blood on the Banisters'*. And now it's done!

As for the setting of the book, I've been lucky once more to have permission to use a real house both on the cover and in the story. Hinwick House is an incredible Queen Anne style manor, which is about sixty miles north of London near the city of Northampton. I found it not because I was looking for a house for my book, but because it is my Mum's eightieth birthday this year, and I have reserved the house for a weekend in July for a surprise party. As of writing, it's still a few weeks off, and she knows nothing about it except that we're going away for a couple of days. My plan is to give her this book to read on the way there, only to reveal when we arrive that she's staying in the real Hinwick House along with forty members of our family. So, please don't say anything. I'm trusting you, dear readers, with my secret!

The house was built in 1710 for Richard Orlebar and his wife, the early cookery book writer Diana Astry. Its design was based on Buckingham House – or The Queen's House as it was also known – which was the building that was eventually expanded and remodelled into Buckingham

Palace. So Hinwick House really is as close as most people can get to spending the weekend in a royal residence. The cost to build this incredible house in the early eighteenth century was £3848, which, somewhat comically, is almost exactly half what it will cost us to stay there for two days next month! If you would like to follow in the footsteps of prime ministers, aristocrats and the great Laraine Brown, who have all walked its halls, you can find Hinwick House on Airbnb.

By this stage in my career as a historical novelist (and the son of a history teacher), I have visited a lot of stately homes, but what makes Hinwick really special is that you can not only stay there, but it has been restored with a lot of period furniture (including some from Princess Diana's nearby childhood home) and lots of original features that belonged to the estate. There are even rooms devoted to Queen Victoria and Winston Churchill, complete with letters, paintings and important documents.

Almost everything I describe in the book is true to the house today, including the various impressive salons, the Great Hall and the stunning façade. One thing I didn't have time to mention is the "Diana Frieze" on the outside of the building. It was commissioned by the original owner as a tribute to his wife. What I didn't realise when writing the book was that he was apparently only able to build Hinwick House because of the dowry he received in marriage – which bears a rather nice similarity to the Duke and Duchess's relationship in this book.

Like many other grand houses (and the fictional Downton Abbey) Hinwick was used as a hospital for soldiers returning from the Great War. It also features its own deer park, two lakes, a dovecot, a clock tower and an extremely grand staircase. I can't wait to explore it with my family very soon.

If you loved the story and have the time, please write a review at Amazon. Most books get one review per thousand readers so I would be infinitely appreciative if you could help me out.

THE MOST INTERESTING THINGS I DISCOVERED WHEN RESEARCHING THIS BOOK...

Let the information-fest commence! Hmmm... where should I start? How about fingerprints?

Unrelated to anything else I'm going to mention, but fascinating nonetheless, ridges start to form on our skin from just ten weeks of gestation in the womb. Those patterns remain the same throughout our lives and only the size changes as we grow. Amazing!

We all know that fingerprints are unique, but certain features within them run in families. The nine main elements, e.g. loops, whorls, arches, etc., were identified in 1823 by a Czech anatomist. Though several people took an interest in them over the subsequent decades – the Metropolitan Police twice dismissed their usefulness – it would be almost seventy years before the first murder was solved thanks to a fingerprint. In Argentina in 1892, a mother killed her sons and pretended she'd been attacked, but her bloody fingerprint at the scene of the crime gave her away. Ha! Serves you right, horrible person! The scientific study of fingerprints, as we all now know, is called... hang on... urmmm... dermatoglyphics! It's called dermatoglyphics, which is a term that, appropriately enough, was invented in the 1920s.

What I found particularly interesting when learning about the patterns that exist in fingerprints is that some features – such as the tented arches in the Cranley family – are very rare and especially when located on certain fingers. I'm no expert on this, and I certainly don't have time to go into it in great detail with a baby in the house and four more books to write this year, but I believe the science is correct in the statements that Lord Edgington makes, and an experienced chap like our detective would have been able to identify Albert's print from sight.

Jumping a million miles away, let's turn to circuses (obviously). There is a fascinating article on the website of the Victoria and Albert Museum all about the history of British circuses, which were extremely popular

247

around the turn of the twentieth century. A particularly impressive figure in the field was Bertram Mills who, without any experience, built a circus empire on the back of a bet that he could set up a successful company in the space of a year. He went on to become synonymous with Christmas shows and would bring together acts from all over the world to his annual spectaculars at Olympia that ran from 1920 to 1966. He was a savvy businessman and decided to charge more money and attract a higher class of clientele than was typical for circuses. To do this, he would invite all sorts of bigwigs and luminaries to the opening of each show, including lords, politicians and lordly politicians like, that man again, Sir Winston Churchill.

Bertram Mills was responsible for reviving the popularity of circuses in Great Britain, but even more importantly, he sounds like a decent chap. Before the toffs were allowed to see it, he would have a dress rehearsal of each show in which poor children from around London could come and marvel at his incredible acts that included Japanese gymnasts, dancing elephants and Swedish trick-cyclists. The big top must have been absolutely massive, as up to ten thousand children saw each show. Since becoming a father, I have been to the circus a lot more than when I was a kid – my parents evidently deprived me. My daughter Amelie has already seen a fin de siècle circus, Cirque de Soleil on ice, and several travelling circuses. Sadly, the tradition has died out quite a bit in Britain, but I have developed a real love for the superhuman feats that we've seen each year.

Enough clowning around, what about food!? Okay, here are some fast facts to get us started...

In 1775, an Italian doctor called Filippo Baldini – which, let's be honest, sounds a bit like a clown's name – argued that chocolate ice cream could be used as medicine to combat conditions such as gout and scurvy. I would happily be a test patient for such a medical trial.

Lord Edgington dismissed the concept of a choux pastry dessert at a wedding on the grounds that every Frenchman has one. In my experience of French weddings, at least, this is true, and the pièce montée, which looks like a giant pyramid of profiteroles covered in caramel sauce, is ubiquitous, just as a tiered cake is in most English-speaking countries.

The term *pièce montée* literally means an assembled piece or structure and originally referred to non-edible centrepieces that were constructed in outlandish shapes by pastry chefs. The choux pastry version, also known as *croquembouche* – or crunch in the mouth – is thought to have been invented by Marie Antoinette's architecturally trained chef Antonin Carême, who apparently believed that "architecture is the most noble of the arts, and pastry the highest form of architecture".

Sticking with Frenchness, ortolans are a type of bird that is now illegal to hunt or eat but was a traditional dish in France. In fact, some people in southwest France, where my mother-in-law is from, consider them to be the highest of all cuisine. Cooked in Armagnac, then roasted for eight minutes, the diner traditionally places a napkin over his or her head before eating the bird whole and spitting out the bones. For some reason, that does not appeal to me. French President François Mitterrand took another view on the matter and not only served them at grand functions but ate them for his last meal. In fact, he invited thirty people to his house to have an incredibly calorific feast which was crowned by the songbird's consumption, complete with napkin over the head – which is used to heighten the senses or perhaps hide the diner's shame before God. He apparently did not eat another mouthful of food until he died eight days later. Madness!

A lot of the dishes mentioned in this book come from three key sources. Henrietta's initial suggestions for the wedding feast (including the ortolans) were taken from the menu of (Queen Victoria's daughter) Princess Beatrice's wedding in 1885. A mere twenty courses were served, and highlights of the meal included cream of rice soup, eight meat courses, three lobster dishes and eight desserts. The wedding cake is worth looking for online, as it is even more architectural than a *pièce montée* and is described to some extent in the final chapter of this book.

The suggestions for a truly traditional wedding that Lord Edgington puts forward are all from medieval times, and the British Museum has recently produced a medieval cookbook. Back then, like now, three was the standard number of courses to have, and the food sounds a lot simpler than a few hundred years later. Finally, the meal that Cranley Hall crew end up consuming is based on my own wedding in Spain for the simple reason that, by the end of the book, I really don't have the energy to do any more research. I think Izzy Palmer fans will find that Ramesh had a suspiciously similar menu at his wedding, too.

Enough blathering about food, what about drink? Well, you can learn about Todd's Duke of Norfolk Punch on the cocktail page, but I'm going to talk to you a little about tea and coffee. Though Lord Edgington makes a fuss about a nice cuppa being the only real drink for an Englishman, coffee has been consumed in Britain for centuries. The first coffeehouse was set up in England in 1650 and, within twenty-five years, there would be three thousand of them.

They were hugely important places for various reasons and became known as penny universities as, for the price of penny, you could have a drink, engage in a debate or listen to speakers lecturing on all sorts of topics. They attracted the greatest minds of the day, helped strengthen the major English political parties, and even gave birth to Lloyd's of London and The London Stock Exchange, both of which started life in coffee houses. In fact, the freedom of discourse that these meeting places gave men (and only men, I'm afraid) was so powerful that successive monarchs tried to shut them down and arrest their patrons with little success. So, in a way, one might say that there is nothing quite so English as a cup of coffee…Unless you're Lord Edgington, of course.

These coffee houses also increased the popularity of the humble cup of char. Tea was first sold to drinkers in 1657 in a coffee house in London, which even produced a pamphlet to explain what customers were about to experience. It was initially only drunk by the wealthy, but soon became popular due to its claimed medicinal properties. The famous diarist Samuel Pepys reported that it had been prescribed to his wife as it was "good for her colds and defluxions," whatever that might mean. It also offered a social function as the upper classes (both ladies and gentlemen, this time) adopted it and would call on one another's houses to take tea and show off their fancy tea sets.

The first tea house, which opened on The Strand in 1706, is still there today and this ushered in a century of popularity for the drink. Thanks to the strength of Britain's maritime and shipping links in the eighteenth century, the country controlled the tea trade and this in turn helped grow the empire's wealth and influence. With forests' worth of the stuff being imported every day, prices dropped, and the drink spread to the middle classes. Within two hundred years of its introduction, the working classes were also big drinkers, and it is believed to have offered nutrition to millions of people throughout the industrial revolution. Various factors led to its dominance over coffee and to becoming something that we consider terribly English, but the history of the two went hand in hand – to begin with at least.

I must admit, when I was a child, I don't think I knew anyone who drank coffee, and I remember the strange moment when I discovered that my cosmopolitan older cousin had asked for something other than tea. My family are tea junkies to this day, and I am the only one in the family who doesn't drink it. In fact, it makes me incredibly nervous, and I put this down to the gallons of the stuff that my mother no doubt drank when she was pregnant with me in the eighties. Oddly, although they all know I don't drink tea, when the kettle has boiled, my family will offer me a cup without fail. It's slightly annoying after at least three decades of saying no.

I think that Lord Ruskin's poisoning might be one of my favourite scenes that I've written. I had to read quite a lot to not just pick a poison that could be stopped in its tracks but learn about the effects it has on the body. There is an excellent book that I've used quite often called "A is for Arsenic" by Kathryn Harkup, which goes through Agatha Christie's use of poisons in her novels – Christie apparently killed more than thirty people with the stuff!

The Queen of Crime gained a lot of experience with medicines when she volunteered as a nurse in a hospital dispensary during the First and Second World Wars. In fact, her knowledge of poisons was so detailed that her 1961 book "The Pale Horse" both saved and killed people. A nurse in London was reading the book and recognised the symptoms of thallium poisoning when treating a nineteen-month-old girl who had been exposed to a chemical for killing cockroaches. The doctors were at a loss, but the nurse (and thus Christie) saved the little girl's life. Sadly for Dame Agatha, 'The Teacup Poisoner', Graham Young, also read that book and poisoned up to seventy people in the village where he lived, three of whom died.

Strychnine features in her first book, "The Mysterious Affair at Styles" from 1920, and she would go on to kill four more characters with this particular chemical. I think it's a particularly good choice for a mystery novelist as it provokes a truly eerie death – complete with rictus smile and arching back, as we have seen. However, the reason I chose it was simply because I found hard evidence of people managing to reverse its effects. In the nineteenth and early twentieth century, strychnine was used as a pick-me-up. A medical student in 1896 was preparing for some exams and took more strychnine than he should have and began to suffer just as Lord Ruskin did in my book. Luckily for the student, and this book, he realised the danger and self-administered bromide of potassium and chloral. He lived to write up the experience in the Lancet, though that is surely the most dangerous way imaginable to win the respect of your peers.

It also works well for this story, as the chemicals used to treat it would feasibly have existed in the medical cabinet of a large house. One thing that would have worked even better – but was not commonly used at the time – is activated charcoal. As it happens, my hippie family and I have sticks of activated charcoal to filter our water, and this simple form of carbon has the most staggering properties. It is incredibly microporous – and has millions of tiny holes – which makes it a phenomenally good filter and excellent at absorbing toxins. It is so effective that, in 1831, a pharmacist in France swallowed ten times the lethal dose of strychnine, then took some activated charcoal. He expected the famous symptoms to kick in, but they never did. Isn't science amazing? And aren't some scientists completely mad?

It's time to lighten the mood a little after all that, so I think I should tell you about dancing; well, formal dances to be precise. I read about a number of long-running society balls when choosing one for Ruskin and Sibyl to attend, but sadly none of them take place in the right month, so I made up my own. The Ghillies Ball is perhaps the most famous and exclusive that continues to this day. Initiated by Queen Victoria at her Scottish hunting estate in Balmoral, only royals, their neighbours from the local area, and castle staff are invited and it's surely one of the few places where normal people get the chance to dance with the British monarch.

I was more interested in the Chelsea Arts Ball, though. It grew out of the elaborate fancy dress parties that a group of artists held in their studios at the end of the nineteenth century. By 1910 the ball had become so big that it moved to The Royal Albert Hall (home of the Proms) where it continued to be celebrated until, in 1958, the party got out of hand and the ball was banned from the premises for thirty years. What is particularly cool about this event is that every year has a different theme from Noah's Ark to Earthly Delights. There are lots of photos online going back through the years of its celebration, and I really enjoyed looking at the ones from the twenties. The event became known as the most famous party in the world and was well known for pushing boundaries and scandalising polite society. It continues today in the clubhouse of The Chelsea Arts Club, and it looks like a lot of fun.

But you can't have dancing without music! I'm going to go out on a limb and say that there aren't many murder ballads played at such balls. Stanislas certainly doesn't know how to get a party started but, as gloomy, violent songs go, "The Unquiet Grave" or "Cold Blows the Wind" can at least be sung at a good clip – check out the Bellowhead version, if you don't believe me. It's a traditional English folk song from seventeenth or eighteenth century and it's about death, graves and heartbroken lovers, but it had the fastest tempo of any such songs I listened to, and I enjoyed the contrast.

Far more cheerful is the song made famous by the Music Hall mega star Vesta Victoria. She really was the Taylor Swift of her day and there is, quite incredibly, a video on YouTube of her singing "Waiting at the Church", another song about a wedding, way back in 1907. "Wedding Bells" was composed by Fred Murray and Fred W. Leigh and tells the oft-told story of a woman who is forever the bridesmaid but never the bride. Both men were prolific songwriters and, between them, wrote such Lord Edgington favourites as "I'm Henery the Eighth, I Am", "The Galloping Major" and, oh yes, "Waiting at the Church".

I even sneaked in two poems in this book. I really love the first by the romantic poet, John Clare. As Lord Edgington attests, Clare was something of a natural talent who had come from farming stock and wrote the most beautiful verses. I chose "I Love to See the Summer Beaming Forth" simply because it was a period-appropriate poem

253

about summer, but then I found out that its author was from very close to Hinwick House. I love such coincidences, but it's also a beautiful poem. As is the second that Chrissy reads at the wedding, by the always incredible George Elliot – or Mary Ann Evans as she was really called. I could tell you about her fascinating life, but there are whole biographies about her so go out and read one of those, or better still, read her magnum opus, Middlemarch, which is one of my favourite classic novels.

Right, I was going to tell you about the murdered soldiers who haunt Hinwick House, how incredible bullrushes are, and how bad 'The Layton Court Mystery' is but that will have to wait until another time.

ACKNOWLEDGEMENTS

With this book, I once again had an expert appear when I most needed one. My long-time reader James Woodworth rather handily turned out to be a trained pharmacist and gave me a page of feedback on my depiction of strychnine poisoning. So I hope the final text is close to accurate. Thank you so much, Jim! I hope this book made more sense than a Marvel movie.

A massive thank you, is also due, of course, to the owners and staff of Hinwick House. Galina has been very helpful not only with the cover of this book, but also planning my mum's party!

Thank you, too, to my crack team of experts – the Hoggs, the Martins, (**fiction**), Paul Bickley (**policing**), Karen Baugh Menuhin (**marketing**) and Mar Pérez (**forensic pathology**) for knowing lots of stuff when I don't. And to my fellow writers who are always there for me, especially Catherine, Suzanne and Lucy.

Thank you, many times over, to all the readers in my ARC team who have combed the book for errors. I wouldn't be able to produce this series so quickly or successfully without you…

Rebecca Brooks, Ferne Miller, Melinda Kimlinger, Emma James, Mindy Denkin, Namoi Lamont, Katharine Reibig, Linsey Neale, Karen Davis, Terri Roller, Margaret Liddle, Esther Lamin, Lori Willis, Anja Peerdeman, Kate Newnham, Marion Davis, Sarah Turner, Sandra Hoff, Karen M, Mary Nickell, Vanessa Rivington, Helena George, Anne Kavcic, Nancy Roberts, Pat Hathaway, Peggy Craddock, Cathleen Brickhouse, Susan Reddington, Sonya Elizabeth Richards, John Presler, Mary Harmon, Beth Weldon, Karen Quinn, Karen Alexander, Mindy Wygonik, Jacquie Erwin, Janet Rutherford, Anny Pritchard, M.P. Smith, Molly Bailey, Nancy Vieth, Ila Patlogan, Lisa Bjornstad, Randy Hartselle, Misty Walker, Carol Vani and Keryn De Maria.

READ MORE LORD EDGINGTON MYSTERIES TODAY.

- **Murder at the Spring Ball**
- **Death From High Places** (free e-novella available exclusively at benedictbrown.net. Paperback and audiobook are available at Amazon)
- **A Body at a Boarding School**
- **Death on a Summer's Day**
- **The Mystery of Mistletoe Hall**
- **The Tangled Treasure Trail**
- **The Curious Case of the Templeton-Swifts**
- **The Crimes of Clearwell Castle**
- **A Novel Way to Kill** (Free e-book only available at www.benedictbrown.net/twisty)
- **The Snows of Weston Moor**
- **What the Vicar Saw**
- **Blood on the Banister**
- **A Killer in the Wings** (Autumn 2023)

Check out the complete Lord Edgington Collection at Amazon

The first seven Lord Edgington audiobooks, narrated by the actor George Blagden, are available now on all major audiobook platforms. There will be more coming very soon.

THE "BLOOD ON THE BANISTERS" COCKTAIL

Duke of Norfolk punch appealed to me as I've heard a lot about the man it was named after over the last six months. Since 1672, the Dukes of Norfolk have held the position of Earl Marshal to the British sovereign. It has been their job for the last three hundred and fifty years to organise the funerals and coronations of our monarchs. The current fella, Edward Fitzalan-Howard, 18th Duke of Norfolk, had apparently been preparing for the Queen's funeral for the last twenty years. I bet poor Elizabeth II wasn't happy to hear that.

Why there's a punch named after him, I cannot say, but if you have the time (and a massive batch of ingredients) it sounds like a nice one to try. It dates back to at least 1745 when there was a recipe printed in "Scot's Magazine" and in the 1820s there was even a poem written about it. Most recipes I've found call for 30 lemons and oranges, but this is a nice simple one from Jerry Thomas's Bar Tender's Guide from 1877.

> **"2 quarts of brandy.**
> **1 quart of white wine.**
> **1 quart of milk.**
> **1¼ pound of sugar.**
> **6 lemons.**
> **3 oranges.**

Pare off the peel of the oranges and lemons very thin; put the peel and all the juice into a vessel with a close-fitting lid. Pour on the brandy, wine, and milk, and add the sugar after having dissolved it in sufficient water. Mix well and cover close for twenty-four hours. Strain until clear, and bottle."

WORDS AND REFERENCES YOU MIGHT NOT KNOW

Tom and Tib – similar to Tom, Dick and Harry. Used to refer to any ordinary couple of people.

Bacchanalian carousal – a boozy party inspired by Bacchus (Dionysus), the Roman God of wine-making, fertility ritual madness, religious ecstasy and… theatre.

Funeral of bachelorhood – a translation from the French "enterrement de vie de garçon" which is their term for a stag do or bachelor party.

Pilasters – pillars attached to a façade for decoration rather than function.

Puppet (verb) – to manipulate and control.

Lip-labour – that ever-tiring job of kissing.

In nuce – Latin term for "in a nutshell" i.e. when something has been summed up.

Dundreary – a character from a successful 1858 play who was the archetypal foppish toff with the clothes, hair and whiskers to match. Lord Dundreary's name was leant to many English phrases at the time.

Pot-valiant – brave when drunk! I wrote this word down a long time ago and finally had a chance to use it.

Milk-and-water – feeble, sentimental, mawkish and gooey.

Saccharinity – much as above. Overly sweet and whimsical.

To stand shilly-shally – to umm and ahh over an action – from the words *shill I, shall I?* when undecided.

Nulli secundus – Latin for "second to none".

Eighteen and a half – oddly, the age from which you could become a police officer.

Pocket-burner – slang for a coin.

Orchid bob and kiss curls – hairstyles common in the 20s. Look 'em up, they're pretty.

To nettle – to tease and irritate.

Corpus delicti – proof of a crime. Surprisingly, the term "smoking gun" is from 1974!

Monday head – a lovely euphemism for a hangover.

Opisthotonos – severe spasms that cause the back to curve uncontrollably, as with strychnine poisoning, rabies and tetanus. A horrible way to die!

Twiddledum – I thought I'd taken this word from somewhere, but perhaps I made it up. Twiddledum, if it does exist, would be the noun of twiddling.

Juggins – a sap, someone easily led.

Befog – a nice old-fashioned word for "to fog up".

Pantomime – in Britain, pantomime is a specific kind of popular entertainment that is often performed at Christmastime. It's hard to describe, but though aimed primarily at children, it can be very bawdy, features lots of stock jokes, audience participation and over-the-top characters.

Dermatoglyphics – the study of fingerprints.

Milch cow – a person from whom you can easily sponge money.

CHARACTER LIST

Hinwick House

Cassandra Fairfax – Albert's fiancé – the youngest child of the Fairfax family.

Duchess of Hinwick – Begonia Fairfax – the controlling matriarch of the family and Albert's future mother-in-law.

Duke of Hinwick – Samuel Fairfax – her quiet, unimposing husband. Both parents are in their fifties.

Charles Fairfax – their eldest son, friendly at first appearance, perhaps not so much later on.

Eric – the shortest but middle brother, smug, smarmy, in his early twenties.

Stanislas – the youngest brother. Detached, with a military tone, as though he's been through a war… which he hasn't.

Peterson – their butler.

Lord Damian Ruskin – the man who asked Albert's fiancée to marry him before the Duchess said no.

Sibyl Podence – Charles's scandalous secret girlfriend.

Dr Marnoch – the family doctor.

Detective Inspector Lovebrook – well-spoken inspector from the local police force.

Cranley Hall

Lord Edgington – master detective, occasional mind reader, and snappy dresser.

Christopher Prentiss – his grandson and assistant.

Albert Prentiss – his brother and the groom-to-be.

Violet Prentiss – their mother.

Todd – the Cranley Hall chauffeur and newly appointed head of household.

Cook (Henrietta) – the Cranley Hall cook with an unusual line in turnips.

Halfpenny – the Cranley Hal footman.

Delilah – Lord Edgington's golden retriever.

THE IZZY PALMER MYSTERIES

If you're looking for a modern murder mystery series with just as many off-the-wall characters, try **"The Izzy Palmer Mysteries"** for your next whodunit fix.

Check out the complete Izzy Palmer Collection in ebook, paperback and Kindle Unlimited at Amazon.

ABOUT ME

Writing has always been my passion. It was my favourite half-an-hour a week at primary school, and I started on my first, truly abysmal book as a teenager. So it wasn't a difficult decision to study literature at university which led to a master's in Creative Writing.

I'm a Welsh-Irish-Englishman originally from **South London** but now living with my French/Spanish wife and presumably quite confused infant daughter in **Burgos**, a beautiful mediaeval city in the north of Spain. I write overlooking the Castilian countryside, trying not to be distracted by the vultures, hawks and red kites that fly past my window each day.

When Covid-19 hit in 2020, the language school where I worked as an English teacher closed down and I became a full-time writer. I have two murder mystery series. There are already six books written in **"The Izzy Palmer Mysteries"** which is a more modern, zany take on the genre. I will continue to alternate releases between Izzy and Lord Edgington. I hope to release at least ten books in each series.

I previously spent years focussing on kids' books and wrote everything from fairy tales to environmental dystopian fantasies, right through to issue-based teen fiction. My book **"The Princess and The Peach"** was long-listed for the Chicken House prize in The Times and an American producer even talked about adapting it into a film. I'll be slowly publishing those books over the next year whenever we find the time.

"Blood on the Banisters" is the tenth novel in the "Lord Edgington Investigates…" series. The next book will be out in Autumn 2023 and there's a novella available free if you sign up to my readers' club. Should you wish to tell me what you think about Chrissy and his grandfather, my writing or the world at large, I'd love to hear from you, so feel free to get in touch via...

www.benedictbrown.net

Made in the USA
Middletown, DE
29 July 2023

35889217R00156

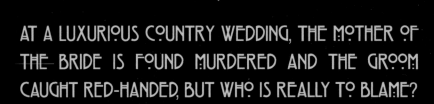

AT A LUXURIOUS COUNTRY WEDDING, THE MOTHER OF THE BRIDE IS FOUND MURDERED AND THE GROOM CAUGHT RED-HANDED, BUT WHO IS REALLY TO BLAME?

When the Duchess of Hinwick is found dead on her daughter's wedding day, renowned sleuth Lord Edgington must prove his grandson's innocence by discovering the real killer's plot.

As he unravels the mystery of the murdered aristocrat, it becomes clear that even her own family are happy to see the back of her. With the bride's ex-fiancé, a suspicious butler, and a plethora of plotting relatives among the suspects, how will the famous detective find the truth when just about everyone wanted the duplicitous woman dead?

A fast, funny and fabulous 1920s whodunnit filled with countless twists and surprises. "Blood on the Banisters" is an Agatha-Christie-style mystery with a cast of brilliant characters that will have you racing to the final chapter. Even if Lord Edgington can save the groom, will they get to the church on time or die trying?

ISBN 9788419162212

9 788419 162212

9000

Scraps
.MNANTS OF THE GIRL I LEFT BEHIND
emma Wasserman